BERGMANN'S FIRE

The Parable of the Hill and the Boulder

Praise for **Bergmann's Fire**

"I would recommend this story to family and friends, and already have as a matter of fact. I have told them that if they want a romance without the period confusion of Jane Austin or Nazi feminist depression of *The Yellow Wallpaper*, then they should read Bergman's Fire."

- Helen Chappelle
Author of *Wizards of the Fallen World*

"Dave Firestone breathed life into very real and delightful characters who provide us with a warm and tender story, mixed with a sense of history. The concept of destiny is cleverly woven into this captivating novel from the first time author."

- Steven Perry
High School English and History Teacher

"You need to read "Bergmann's Fire: The Parable of the Hill and the Boulder" by Dave Firestone."

- Genie Walker
Associated Content

"I feel a need in my heart to say "Thank you" for writing *Bergmann's Fire*. Reading this book - I had the feeling it was written for me and everybody else who has felt Bergmann's Fire in their hearts."

-Ina Straessler, Vienna

"Dave Firestone has masterfully crafted a portrait of our rebellion from destiny within an original and surprisingly romantic story. I truly enjoyed it and eagerly await his next piece."

- Stephen Blackmon
Author of *The Price of Paradise*

BERGMANN'S FIRE

The Parable of the Hill and the Boulder

DAVE FIRESTONE

www.consumingfireinc.com

HAMPTON, VIRGINIA

Published by Consuming Fire Incorporated.

Consuming Fire Fiction
Consuming Fire Publishing

Consuming Fire Publishing
206 W Taylor Ave, Hampton, VA 23663

Visit our websites at www.consumingfireinc.com
& www.kingdomrule.com.

Printed in the United States of America

First Consuming Fire Publishing Printing: August 2009
ISBN: 0980246075 and 9780980246070

Cover design by Stephen N. Blackmon.

I dedicate this work
    and the days to come
to Eva, my B'shert,
    my Jerusalem sunset
of oranges and apples
    of bread and honey
of butter and oil
    of Lamb and Olive
of mixed roots from distant soils
    of golden bands and silver strands
Growing
    Teaching
        Learning
Eating
    Sleeping
        Building
Together. With dedication.

    Along our path to the sunset

BERGMANN'S FIRE

The Parable of the Hill and the Boulder

Your absence has gone through me
Like thread through a needle.
Everything I do is stitched with its color.

W.S. Merwin

PROLOGUE

Dynamiting was never a special kind of event, but it's something worth seeing if you've got the time and a safe position to watch from. A thousand pounds of earth comes squirting out the side of the mountain like it's suddenly scared of something, but then the smoke ("It's *dust* Daddy," I once told my father, and he answered, "Smoke *is* dust darlin'. It's just dust that's caught up in the sudden windy breath-a-God"...yeah! He really said that. "Sudden windy breath-a God, and hangin' there for a tick before returnin' to the Earth...just like us. Just like so much I seen.")...the smoke holds itself above the blast point wondering if it ought to try going back in. But it never does. It always falls away. You can never get the smoke back in the hole.

How big the smoke plume'll be depends on what you're working on, how much explosive you're using, and how deep you're blasting. The engineers try not to make too big a plume if it can be helped; too much polluting, and it usually means you could've used the explosives more efficiently. But sometimes geology, geometry, physics and demands-ofmanagement can put even the best engineer in a corner.

That's when you come to having big plumes. That's when big stones can fly.

Now, some boulders come jutting up outta the ground, and you can look at how the Earth's split up and open by them and know that they've got roots running deep. Those boulders aren't boulders. They're the tips of mountains. But a big stone that falls from a big plume pulls the earth down around it. You can look at those boulders and see that they aren't running deep. They don't have any roots. They're heavy, sure, but they aren't attached to anything.

One of those big stones got planted within view of our house when I was just a small girl. It didn't actually hit there. First it struck the top of a nearby hill before rolling down the side towards our home. Daddy figured that if that hill hadn't been there, the boulder could've smashed our house to bits.

This gave a kind of celebrity to the hill within my family. But I felt a keener interest in the boulder. The hill's always been there, and I figure it always will be. But the boulder seemed to me charged with mystery and conflict. Its origins and purpose were always so unknowable. It flew even though it's made of rock. It moved with incredible speed, but ever after sat so still. Just a scrap from the mountain – and the mountain is a foothill, really – but it seemed complete in and of itself.

For a while, my little brother, Tommy, called the hill 'Boulder Hill,' but the name quickly wore down to just "The

Hill." I was glad in my secret thoughts when the name was simplified. Even at a tender age I knew that I couldn't call the boulder 'Boulder Boulder.'"

My daddy was always a religious man – a *spiritual* man, he would say – even before he went off to fight in The War (which was before he and my momma even met.) He's always seeing or looking for signs in whatever happens. As a girl I was both awed and tickled by how he saw God's plan in the simplest things. Everything suggested a challenge, test or message.

Too many accidents at the plant was a call for deeper and more sincere prayer. When anyone was pregnant, even if it was a girl out of wedlock, he would rejoice in the continued blessings of God. But if it *was* a young girl, then it was also the beginning of a great challenge for the girl and her family that would be filled with a host of tests. It could even be a test for our family. Tommy was a bit skeptical about those kinds of tests. "What kinda test for *us* is it that Maryan McCarthy's gone and got herself pregnant?" he once asked.

Daddy answered, "It's a test of love, Tommy. Just like every test. Are we gonna love our neighbor or are we gonna act like hateful gossips? What would we hope the McCarthys'd do if it was our little..."

"PSSSHHT!" Momma sputtered, "You wanna bring a curse on my baby girl? Shut your mouth!" Momma was religious in her own way too.

But, even though he saw a lesson on patience in every

burned tongue, The Boulder – big and bold as a new smell in a small room – seemed to have him stumped. He stared at it from our doorstep for a long time, not daring to get too close; like it was some kind of radioactive meteor or angel fallen from heaven.

"What do you figure it means Daddy?" I asked from his hip, "Is it a warnin'?"

"Could be." he answered softly.

"Somethin' bad commin'?"

"Could be, but I wouldn't worry about it being anything like that. What do you reckon happened there darlin'?" he asked, finally looking down into my eyes.

I looked at the big stone; fallen from the sky and skip-slid down the side of The Hill. The deep pits and trenches wouldn't be overtaken by rain, grass and time for a good couple of years, and at that time it seemed to my young eyes that The Hill was scarred like some of the boys who got hurt in accidents at the plant. "Looks to me like God chucked a big stone at us, and just barely missed." I said.

"Oh no, Sarah," Daddy said. He squatted down beside me, and looked at me like I was hurt or something. "No darlin'. If God chucked a big stone at us, we'd be havin' some other conversation up in Heaven right now. That's how it is when God calls you up. God don't never miss, darlin'. He wasn't trying to hit us with that stone. God already hit whatever He was aimin' for. God don't *never* miss."

Then he smiled his big toothy loving smile right at me.

Anyway, since Daddy said that The Boulder wasn't any kind of attempt on our lives, I wasn't really afraid of it. He isn't a prophet, but to a little girl a gentle and loving father is about as close to God, Himself, as she can imagine. I suppose it's true even if the girl's daddy isn't gentle too, but I'd be deathly afraid of God if my father hadn't been the way he is.

He says he had enough of beatings and blood back in The War to last himself and every child he'd raise for a lifetime. I heard him say that a long time ago, and I said that I was sure thankful to the Nazis that I didn't have to get any beatings like some of my cousins got from some of my uncles. Daddy just looked at me with his mouth hanging open.

Momma shooed me out of the room right then.

He wouldn't ever tell us anything more than that about his time in the war, but Tommy and I figured that he must've done something good or important because of the package he'd get every year. Some time around Easter, there would be a package waiting for him at the post office. Every year it was a bottle of wine, and he'd never say who'd sent it. Momma once told me it was from Europe when I asked, and there were two languages written on the bottle.

The first language looked like English, except the letters were all jumbled up. Some of the words were longer than any word I've ever seen, and some letters had some little dots above them. The other language was just a plain mess. It was all kinds of crazy swirls, squiggles and half-finished shapes, and most of the dots on this one were below the letters. For years I thought it was just decoration, but once – when Daddy was nearly finished with the wine (he'd always drink the bottle within a few weeks of recievin' it) – he said it was the "language of God." Only years later did I manage to convince myself that he wasn't just talking to himself through the wine.

At any rate, in the coal fields of Kentucky, a daddy who gets bottles of wine from Europe is as good as a prophet getting scrolls from Heaven – at least to his little girl – and when he said that the boulder wasn't an attempt on our lives I was satisfied. It became a safe and special place, sanctioned by the highest authority in my childish heart.

The Parable of the Hill and the Boulder

Summer, 1967

Eastern Coal Fields Region of Kentucky

PART I

The Guest, The Bottle & The Challenge

Tommy met me at the bus stop, and that was strange enough. I gave him the kind of hug that we reserve for long lost family, and he refused to explain why he had been waiting for me until I'd get into the cab of his truck.

I threw my bag onto the bed, slammed the door as I got in, and turned to him before he could turn the ignition. "Give." I said. Tommy smiled his best wicked smile and made the engine rumble.

"Dad's outdone hisself this time," he said, shaking his head.

"*Himself*, Tommy," I corrected before thinking.

"You told me that before, Sarah, and I told you that if you wanna correct me with your high Yoo-nee-ver-sit-tee English you can jus' call me Thomas."

I laughed, "Sorry Tommy. Or do you still want me to call you Thomas."

"Don't you dare," he said with a wink. Then he jammed the truck into gear, and began to carry me home.

"So are you gonna tell me, or what?" I cried out after a few minutes of *Still gettin' good grades*, and *Y'all like the weather up there in Lexington?* Tommy could've small talked all the way from the bus stop to the front door, and I wasn't having any of that.

"Tell you what?" he asked through smiling teeth.

"Tommy!"

Laughing, he said "All right! All right. I'll tell you. Don't get your panties in a bunch."

"Never mind my panties Tommy. We're both gettin' a little old for this. Are you gonna tell me what brought you and this sorry truck all the way down to the bus stop instead of Daddy or Momma, or aintcha?"

"Too old for teasin' but still young enough for 'Momma' and 'Daddy'? Now, don't go lookin' at me like that. Mom and Pop couldn't come down to meet you 'cause they're *entertainin'*, so I had to wind up my beautiful pickup tru..."

"Wait." I interrupted. Tommy did, but I sat silent next to him, allowing myself to be bounced and shaken as the road became rougher.

"Well?" He asked. I still sat staring out the windshield. "Well, okay, as I was saying, I had to break up my busy..."

"Entertainin?" I said, riding over him again. "Whadda you...Entertainin' who Tommy? If we got family visitin' why don't you just say so. It's Uncle Robert ain't it? You can just come on out and say it if it is, cause…"

"It *ain't* Uncle Robert. It shore ain't any family I ever heard of…but then I don't know…it's as good a guess as any, I suppose."

"Thomas Hanover what the heck are you talkin' about!? Who or what in this world could they be entertainin' instead of commin' to meet their only daughter?"

"Ooooh! You're gettin' warmer now! Who in this *world* is exactly right," he said nodding like a damned fool. I could almost say it wasn't my fault I slapped the back of his head; what, with him nodding like that. "HEY! Sarah! What the…"

"Tommy! I am sore, worn out, and plain ole' tired. I have run myself ragged waitressing, studying, and taking tests that weren't like nothin' we ever saw in school round here. I got on that bus expectin' to be greeted by - at *least* - my daddy and - with *luck* – my momma, but when I got off all I found was you and your jokes and your mysteries about '*entertainin'*' someone that *might* be family; and how do you *not* know if they're family?! NO! Don't answer me with another smilin' riddle. Tell me straight now. Who's with Momma and Daddy that's too important to let them come and get me? What is goin' on?"

Tommy drove, silent and serious, for a while; mastering his temper. It was one of the things Daddy had gone to a lot of trouble to teach us both. Tommy had always been better at it than me, and it's something I've always adored in him. Watching him hold together and keep us on the narrow back road gave me a taste of shame, but it was mostly drowned out by my curiosity. Why was this making him mad? Wasn't *I* the one who was being messed with? Normally, I'd have expected him to be placating me or else laughing even harder. But he seemed to be choking back his temper.

"Okay," he finally said, "Truth is, Sarah, I don't rightly know *who* it is, or why he's here. Pop says he won't tell us more than once, so we've all had to wait for you to come home so he can tell us *all*. Personal like and together." He said the last bit in a fake-sweet tone while bobbing his head from side to side.

"Well, at least I know now that it's a *he*." I said, grasping. "So, what's *he* like?"

Tommy's description of our visitor wasn't much help, but then he had never been one for crafting words or appreciating the features of other men. All he could tell me was that the guest was, in fact, a man, that this man had dark hair and that he was shorter than Tommy while being taller than me.

Unfortunately, Tommy has corn-blond hair and is as big as a bulldozer, while I'm shorter than most grown men. So, nearly everyone had dark hair by Tommy's standards, and most men stood between us in height. But Tommy was able to finally surrender some useful information when pressed.

"He talks funny." He said scrunching his face up as he said it.

"Talks funny how? Like he's got marbles in his mouth?"

"Naw naw!" Tommy cried waving me off.

"What?" I asked, laughing now. "He talks like Elmer Fudd?"

"Naw Sarah, cut it out, now." He said, easily warmed by my laughter. "We're nearly there, now, and I don't want Pop thinkin' I've been making fun of his special guest."

I looked out the windshield just in time to see the trunk of my over-the-road tree. She's an ancient among the ancient ones with thick arms reaching out in all directions, including a few low enough for little girls and boys to climb. One bushy arm stretches over the road (hence the name) where I used to dangle my feet, waiting for…well, anything of interest.

My over-the-road tree also served as a marker to indicate that we were, like Tommy had said, nearly there. So I stowed my jokes, and asked, "OK, Tommy, tell me. How's he talk funny? Can you do an imitation or somethin'?"

"I swear, he talks like somethin'...out of a movie, or somethin'."

I waited, but Tommy had grown quiet. Seeing that we were truly getting close to home, I prompted him in a serious tone, "What sorta movie? Like a western? Does he talk like John Wayne or Clint Eastwood?"

"Naw," he said softly

With a sharp right we pulled in. The house is a low roofed single story; once red, now brown with weather. It's smaller than most houses you'd see in town, but larger than most mountain cabins. From the driveway we saw the north-facing side of the house. There were two windows to be seen. On the left was a high tiny dark window to allow fresh air into the pantry. It was high enough to keep out most scavengers, and close enough to the overhanging roof to minimize sunlight most of the year. About three feet to the right was a lower, larger bedroom window; Tommy's room. The pantry window is too high for anyone to peek outside, and Tommy was in his truck with me. So, understandably, there were no faces to be found in either portal.

The front of the house, with its porch, faces east to catch late morning sunlight. The Hill, further east, obscures the earliest morning rays. The Boulder was nestled at its bottom along the side facing the house.

Tommy swerved the truck left then right to park in front of the house. When Momma didn't come running out of the house I realized that I'd been hoping for her to come. The guest kept her obliged to stay inside.

Tommy was almost whispering. Whatever he was trying to say it wasn't coming out easily, and that wasn't his way at all. He always found a way to get things across, even if it made gray hairs pop up on the heads of English teachers all over the world. "He don't talk like one'a the good guys."

"He's Mexican?" I asked astonished.

"Naw, Sarah! It ain't like in a western at all!"

"Well, you're just gonna have to spell it out 'cause they

don't teach Tommy-code in Freshman year."

"Like in a *war* movie, Sarah." He was glowering, and that *really* wasn't his way. I just stared blankly at him. "He talks. He talks like…well, damn…he talks just like one of those war movie Nazis."

My University of Kentucky roommate, Gloria, used the question "Are you mad?" as a rhetorical exclamation. I'd picked up the habit myself, and had used it occasionally in a playful way. "Are you mad?" would've been a good response to Tommy's statement, especially if delivered with Gloria's particular tone of incredulity.

Unfortunately, "Uh, Nazi, Tommy?" was the best I could come up with.

"C'mon," Tommy said, offering no further explanation. "No sense keeping 'em waiting. They'll've heard the truck pull in." The road in front of our house is gravel. The driveway (if you're willing to call it that) is a broad patch of the same stones spread wide all the way up to the northern face of the house and reaching around to the east side porch. Footsteps, bicycle wheels, cars and trucks can only snap, crackle and pop their way to our front door. Out in the foothills of Kentucky there's plenty of wildlife and windy trees, but there weren't enough on that afternoon to mask our crunchy arrival.

So we got out of the truck, and I embraced my pride – which I tried to disguise as self-respect – refusing to chase Tommy and beg for an explanation. All I had to do was march a couple of feet and go through the door to find out what kind of magician could crack wise about Nazis to a World War II veteran and get himself invited into that veteran's house.

The answer, of course, was bound to be no kind of magician and no kind of Nazi.

The guest had arrived in town one day before me, and was smuggled into our home. Just as the sun burns our necks red every year, delivered under the cover of cool mountain air, he – a stranger if *ever* there were a stranger in our remote parts – was sneaked into our home under my father's arm with a foreign accent and a foreign bottle of wine.

The bottle had two languages on it – one clumsy and one squiggly – and I knew that that meant I might get some answers to some very old questions. I just had no idea it'd mean so much trouble for me personally. The answers didn't come quickly, but the trouble rolled right up without hesitation.

He was handsome. Of course he was handsome. Where Tommy's sun bleached hair was thin, and his sun browned skin was tough this man was the opposite; Pale skin under dark hair. And straight teeth. He was almost like a creature from one of those "negative worlds" or "opposite worlds" in the trashy comic books Tommy likes to read, except that he wasn't tall or thickly muscled enough. He was obviously a few years older than Tommy or me, and his hair was nicer; thicker and well styled, unlike Tommy's bowl cut.

He wore a white cotton button down shirt as casually as my father wears blue denim, and made Tommy's "Reds!" T-shirt look silly. No jeans on the stranger, either. Dress trousers hinted nicely at the length of his legs, and I could only guess what the rear did for him as he bent to shake my hand and murmured his own name; too softly for me to understand.

That's not to say that I really fancied him overmuch those first seconds. I really only caught a glance before being swept up in my parents' enthusiasm. They looked older, each in different ways. The sliver stripe down Mamma's brown locks had thickened, and was accompanied by a few new spidery strands. Her face showed a few more creases, but it all served to make her long thin features look stronger and grander. She reached out to me, from her red and blue sun dress and tan sandals, with both hands spread wide, and tied me up like a wrestler with her muscled arms. She rocked me from side to side, and made high squeaky sounds that may have had words in them. A few more kisses on the face and she released me to my father.

It made my heart ache to look at Daddy. He'd been old,

just past thirty, when he married my mother. I never saw him age as I grew up, but now…I could hardly recognize him. He looked more like somebody's grandfather than a college girl's father. He'd always been wiry, but had crossed into the territory of rangy. His gray hair was thinner than memory told me it ought to be. The coffee colored eyes still glittered, and his cheeks were still round. But his square jaw was weakened by wrinkled skin beneath the chin. He seemed to sway slightly in tan corduroy pants and a red, black and white checked shirt as he watched Momma try to throw me around in her embrace, and I worried that a strong breeze might come by and blow him over.

But, when he saw his turn, he moved towards me, and I could see the cougar beneath his skin. He stalked towards his girl with the energy I'd always known. His strength was revealed as he squeezed the breath out of me; even harder than Momma had done. My eyes bugged and watered. It was sweet.

After his traditional bear hug my daddy introduced us all by first names only, like we were school children. "Sarah, this is Daniel. Daniel, this is my daughter, Sarah." The stranger reached out to shake my hand, and nearly fell over since he kept his feet planted to his spot on the floor. His eyes were wide open; huge, like a pair of moons falling at me from an alien sky. I might've been a little bit flattered, but I was mostly creeped-out by how close he leaned in.

"It iz zo nice to vinally meet you!" he declared. "Your

fahter and mutter haf told me very much about you since I haf come!"

I looked over to my father, wondering if he was going to punch this joker in the face, but Daddy just smiled. I looked back at the guest, and - as I realized that Daddy didn't want to punch him - I felt the strongest wish that he would. I would've settled for Tommy giving him a smack, and was debating taking a swing at this Daniel character myself.

Two minutes before he'd spoken I'd have told you that it wouldn't bother me. Tommy's warning hadn't even helped. I had never known an accent to effect me so strongly, and it probably wouldn't have bothered me in a play or from a friend making a joke. But for a stranger to stand in my father's home, sip water from my one of my mother's glasses, and make himself out to be…well, I couldn't guess what he was making himself out to be, but it created a knee-jerk reaction where I'd never known I had a knee to jerk. I was standing there, shocked at how offensive I already found this guy when I realized that everyone was silent; waiting for me to respond to what had actually been a friendly greeting.

"It's nice to meet you too, Daniel." I said through a smile that wouldn't let my upper teeth separate from the lowers. I turned to Daddy again. I wanted to ask who the hell this stranger was, what he was doing in our house, and – most important – why he was talking with the weirdest German accent I'd ever heard. It wasn't quite like you hear in the movies; softer, but still definitely German.

"Daddy?"

My father took a deep breath before saying, "Why don't we all sit down. Seems Daniel and I got some explaining to do. Don't worry. It'll all be clear in just a few."

"Lemon-iced-tea Sarah?" my mother offered, bending abruptly into my point of view.

Typically I've never paid much attention to the subtle cues given off by family or friends, but my parents' absence at the bus stop and Tommy's strange but (I had to face it) essentially true description of the situation had me keyed up. Plus – and this may not be easy for some people to understand as a motivation – some clown was standing in my daddy's house talking like the war had gone the other way! So, I was doing my best to watch everyone and catch everything, and from my mother's offer I was suddenly aware of a few things:

First, whatever my father was about to spill, she already knew. It isn't that Momma never offers her children a bite or a drink when they get home. But she has always had a sense of the rhythm of things, and her offer was off. We all – which is to say Tommy and I – wanted answers; not beverages. Daddy had invited us to sit, and Momma made a bump in the conversation to make sure there was a glass full of lemon-iced-tea in front of me. Momma was always a loving mother, but she only broke "protocol" (as Daddy called it) when she had reasons.

Second, Whatever my father was about to spill, it was

going be a doosey. I didn't even get a chance to give a nod or say "thank you" before she was pouring me a glass of her famous lemonade/iced-tea mixture. I remembered that she would always hold off giving Daddy bad news (like one of my middle-school report cards or the first and only fist fight Tommy ever had) until after dinner. She'd wait long enough to let everything settle in our stomachs. She wanted my strength up for this, whatever it was.

Third, decisions had already been made. The only reason I could figure my mother would give me sweet tea when her guest had chosen to drink just water was that she wanted me to have something sweet in my mouth when I got told how things were and how things were going to be. When decisions were up for grabs and Tommy and I could have a say in what we'd do Momma let it all happen on an even playing field. But when decisions had already been made Momma and Daddy were a "Unified Front," and, like the song says, "a spoon full of sugar helps the medicine go down."

German was his mother tongue, but Daniel was quick to say that he was no German. He wasn't a Nazi either, but – almost as bad – he was an Austrian trying to become a lawyer.

"But I do not yet…" he scrunched his face up. "… repeat law? No…practice!" He smiled with obvious pleasure. "I do not yet practice law. I haf been working…under? Yes?

Under a man who has worked as a lawyer many years."

"You've come pretty far afield if you're here looking for business for your boss, Daniel." I said. Tommy smiled slightly, but Momma made a real frown.

"Please? I know the words, but I do not…" he looked to my father for help.

"She's asking what brought you here, Daniel." Daddy said slowly. "She wants to understand," his eyes flicked to me for a second. "She wants to understand why a man like you - with an education in *the law* - is coming out to the hills of Kentucky."

"Ah," he looked between us, clearly aware that something was passing between the lines. If my father were a temple 'The Law' would be one of the biggest pillars supporting the roof. Pointing out that Daniel was educated in the law meant something. I didn't know what, exactly, but it was clear that Daniel meant something to Daddy. "Vell Sarah, I am here for *some* reasons. First, I came for curiosity. Your fahter has been at deh end off at least one of deh questions that has made me very curious for some time, and I sink dat he vill be able to answer some ozers."

"What question could my daddy possibly answer a lawyer from Vienna that a lawyer from Vienna can't answer for himself?" I asked as plainly as I could. I was balancing between curiosity about this man's story and my father's. "I mean, I'm assuming it's got somethin' to do with somethin' that happened during the war, but you've gotta have good enough information there. What could Daddy tell you that no one in Austria or Germany could tell you."

Daniel smiled. This one was warmer. Less eager than the first one he'd shown me. I liked this one better. "Vell," he said "deh first question Mr. Hanover has already answered. I wanted to know who this was. Who was I sending bottles of wine each year. I already had deh name, and I am alzo guessing that it is over something that happened in The War. But I wanted to know who he is, and that is something that can only be answered here."

"Wait. What?" I said only a second before Tommy spluttered more or less the same thing. "This is all coming pretty fast for me. I only just found out someone was here less than an hour ago, and now I've found out that it's a German…"

"Austrian," Daddy corrected.

"…Austrian someone here about five minutes ago. So, maybe I'm just not up to speed here with everyone else, but… well, I ain't no Math major, but Daddy's been getting those bottles from Europe since before I can remember and I don't reckon you're more than a few years older than me."

"I am sorry." Daniel replied looking pained, "I did not understant all that you haf said. It was very fast."

I took a deep breath, did my best to put the words together in my head using only simple words, and then spat them out like one of my professors in slow motion "Are you saying that you have been sending bottles to Kentucky since you were a small child, and you don't know who you were sending them too?"

His eyebrows pinched the top of his nose as he concentrated on my words. He took a few seconds piecing it all together as Daddy shook his head, eyes closed. "Ah! Aha! *Sie ist zynisch.*" Daniel cried out half-laughing "No! No no! Of course not! I haf only been sending bottles for the last *tree* years."

Daniel went on to explain that the lawyer who employed him had been the one sending the bottles of wine. It was a task of basic bookkeeping to keep track of when it was time to send the bottle, to actually go out, buy it, send it to the specified address and, finally, to bill the client who had left the standing orders for the task.

Daniel wouldn't even say who the client was, seeing as how he was acting as their lawyer. He said it wasn't his place to tell it, but that he figured Daddy could. Daddy just nodded his head, and said that he reckoned he could. Then he began to stare out the front window.

We waited.

Daddy smiled at whatever he saw framed there for a few million minutes before asking if anyone wanted more lemon-iced tea or water. Daniel looked down at his glass and seemed surprised to find it empty. Momma took his and Daddy's glasses into the kitchen, and began to pour. Tommy and I just sat, starring at Daddy like a pair of hungry dogs watching a can of food that just might open if stared at long enough.

He pretended not to notice, fooling no one.

This stalling, I figured, could be very good or very bad. Sometimes Daddy liked to stretch out a good yarn to really give it some punch. He could make us wait, and he could make the wait worthwhile. But sometimes that second glass of lemon-iced tea was the first stone of a first class stonewall.

In the end, all Daddy would tell us was, "God saw fit to involve me in the saving of certain lives in The War, including my own."

Of course, from Daddy "save someone's life" could've meant about a half dozen things. We knew it, and he knew we knew it. I could tell from the afternoon summer light in his eyes as he said it.

Anyway, he figured one person was saying "thanks" in his own way.

Daniel's eyebrows knitted at the summary, but, thanks to his damn fool impulsive mouth, I would never get around to asking him about it. And by the time I understood that look I'd already know more than I'd ever dreamed I wanted to know anyway.

Chapter 3

A good looking lawyer from Europe shows up with your daddy's permission, shows proper deference to your momma, likely has answers to questions you'd long given up on, keeps peeking over his dinner plate at you every chance he gets and looks at you like he can't believe you're there; well, that can have some appeal even if the European accent *is* from the bad guys in the war movies.

I was hoping he'd try testing out his English skills on me. Maybe I could figure out more of what he knew about Daddy's time in the war. If he happened to smile real friendly, and pass a flattering word or two at me I figured I'd only push him away a little. That's not what happened, though.

I know it's immodest of me to say that I slapped him real *real* good, but the perfect clap of my hand across Daniel's face was an explosion that echoed into Hanover legend. Tommy still laughs about how he thought someone had lit a firecracker outside the house or else fired a gun not far off.

If I felt – or feel – any guilt about The Slap Heard Across The Atlantic (as we have secretly called it over the years) it would be over the position I put Momma in when I stormed off to my room. Daddy and Tommy pushed their way through my door before I could properly slam it behind me. That left Momma to make sure our guest hadn't been rendered permanently deaf by the pop I'd delivered. As a child I learned to put my whole body into a strike, and I'd painted that red hand print on the side of Daniel's face with perfect follow through.

It's hard to feel too bad, though. I learned later that Momma couldn't help chuckling while checking the damage. I've heard that she told Daniel that he can't expect to deal with the salt of the earth without getting a little spice. I doubt that he had a clue of what that meant.

In my room Tommy stood with his arms crossed, and Daddy's fists made bulges in the pockets of his tan slacks. They stood and waited for my explanation.

"What are y'all doing in here!?" I bellowed.

"Sarah." My father said with expectation.

"What!? Why're y'all in here? Didn't you hear what he said to me?"

"No, Sarah." Daddy said, "And we'd be right grateful if you'd tell us."

"He…" I started, but I couldn't even think of the right words to call such presumption.

"He what, Sarah?" It was Tommy this time. He was tilting his head slightly; showing me his better ear but keeping his eyes wide and locked on me. Daddy was still and staring straight at me. They were both riding a fence, and I wanted to be sure they fell on my side.

"He. He. *Claimed* me!"

Naked confusion broke over their faces. I waited. Daddy was just a low ranking officer in the war, and he started working as a miner after that. Tommy had never seen anything more than twenty miles north of the Ohio river. But they were, neither of them, stupid.

"You mean...like claimed you to be his girl?"

"Wife, Tommy." I spoke over the end of his sentence. "He said I'm *gonna* be his wife!" I watched their mouths open and their eyes widen, and it wasn't satisfactory. I wanted to see outrage. "Yeah! Crazy man over there in the other room's decided that y'all can say bah-bye to Sarah."

"Why...How...How's he figure he's claiming you Sarah?" Daddy said in his soothing voice. This was Daddy-the-peace-maker. I wanted Daddy-the-avenger.

"He figures that he's crazy, and that makes me his. Maybe the rules say that when crazy man likes the look of you then you're his fiancée. Maybe that's how things work in crazy town...or maybe it's crazy*burg*." It got a snicker out of Tommy, but neither of them seemed in a hurry to get angry.

That just made me angrier.

"Daddy! He could be out there claiming Momma right now!" I said, pointing at the door. As if to weaken and strengthen my accusation at the same time, Momma could be heard chuckling in the other room. "See?" I creaked.

Tommy's eyebrows pulled together, but Daddy's face was the sea before the storm.

"Why's he gotta be crazy to want my Sarah for his bride?"

"But I..."

"You know, maybe it's just a language problem." Tommy cut in. "Or maybe that *is* how they do things in" he cleared his throat "Daniel's burg. Maybe 'We'll marry some day' is Vienna's version of askin' a girl for a stroll in the moonlight."

Daddy looked over at Tommy, and we all held silent until he closed his eyes and shook his head. "Enough of this nonsense. Our guest is in the other room wearing Sara's mark across his face..."

"Hey! That was a terrific smack, by the way, Sarah! Hoo! I bet you could feel the teeth under his check when you landed that wallop."

"Tommy." Daddy and I said in unison. He stopped talking but he kept shaking his head and chuckling to himself. The legend had begun.

"Sarah, I'm asking you straight, and I expect a straight answer: Why do you say Daniel is crazy?"

A few words passed through my mind that I would never allow to pass through my lips in front of Daddy. I could feel myself getting into a corner here, and I tried to put together an answer that would blow the winds in my direction. But Daddy saw my hesitation, and guessed my calculation.

"Naw, Sarah. You're taking too much care. Answer me

straight. I wasn't watchin' y'all when you slapped him. I nearly jumped out of my skin when it cracked behind me. What happened? Did he grab you?"

Shame rushed me as Daddy's fears began to leak through his face. "Naw, Daddy." I looked at my knees, and the quilt I was kneeling on. "He didn't try anything like that."

"Now, it *could* be a language thing like Tommy said. The handful of German I picked up in the war was slipping through my fingers before you were a twinkle, but maybe there's something there. But if I've invited a threat into our household I need to know it. So, what did he say *exactly*?"

I took a deep breath.

Early in my middle school years I lied about doing my homework every day for more than a month. My teachers gave me notes to be delivered to my parents after the first week and a half, but I never delivered them. I found myself covering my lies with more lies like dead leaves in Autumn, but I couldn't cover things forever. The report card had to come sooner or later, and it did. With a vengeance. I sat there in my room with Daddy and Tommy, remembering how things had kept getting worse and worse with those middle school lies. I didn't want to tell Daddy Daniel's exact words, because I knew that it would change everything. But, clearly, I couldn't get Daddy and Tommy properly riled up. I had to tell the whole truth before things spiraled too far out of control.

"He said that he was excited to finally meet me. I

thought it was kinda funny that he'd said 'finally,' so I asked him if he'd been corresponding with you, Daddy." I didn't tell them how I'd smiled at Daniel when I asked. "I asked if you'd said nice things about me. He said that you'd mentioned me, but that it wasn't your correspondence that had anything to do with it."

"What was it about?" Tommy asked, no longer examining me. He was a kid being told his bedtime story.

I clenched my jaw for a second. "He said," *uuunngggbh* "He said that, before he left for America, God told him that he'd meet his future bride in the U.S., and that he'd figured he'd travel around The States for a while after his time with us; you know, to find her. But, he said that when he saw me…" My mouth tightened, and I looked at my feet as I tried to make fists with my toes. That was about all I could bear to say aloud.

"*B'shert,*" said Daddy.

"What?"

"Nothin' Darlin'. Just a word I picked up during the war."

"Is it German or French?" Tommy asked. Daddy had spent time in both countries.

"Neither." You could re-shingle the roof with a tone that flat. "So, Daniel figures you're the one?"

I nodded.

"Decreed by 'The Holy One, Blessed Be He' and such?" his voice half ironic.

I looked at them both. "'The Lord of Hosts.' Yep." Daddy's face grew only a little bit calmer. But Tommy's face elongated as his eyebrows rose, and his jaw fell.

"Well…" said Tommy, "Oh."

In our father's house that changes things a bit.

If I believed there's such a thing as a normal family, I'd reckon the father of that family would've bodily removed Daniel from our home. Being humane, I wasn't hoping for Daniel to be stuck out in the hills. It can get cold out there at night, even in the early breaths of summer. Knowing Daddy's preference for the gentle hand I'd hoped Daniel would get a late night drop off at the bus station of a nearby town.

But they talked the two of them. They talked all night. When I rose the following morning Tommy's truck was cold and still in the driveway, untouched since our arrival.

Daddy was sitting in his favorite chair – the one facing the fireplace – with a mug in his hand; dawn glimmering, weak blue, through the window and darkening his face to a simple silhouette. Daniel was just standing up and stretching his back. "I must now sleep." He said.

"Alright," Daddy said. They had laid out a guest bed for Daniel in Daddy's workshop. "Go on and get some sleep." He glanced over at me, and Daniel was still clear headed enough to follow it. When he saw me, he had the decency to blush and watch the floor as he approached me. I watched Daddy watching Daniel as he came nearer.

Daniel looked at my face, and said, "I am sorry Sarah. Please excuse how I… spoke… yesterday. Vat I said, it vas…" he looked back at Daddy, "rash?" Daddy nodded, and Daniel turned back to point his nose at mine again. "It vas rash of me to say such dings to you when I haf known you only a little time. I should haf vaited."

"Alright Daniel," I said looking from Daniel to Daddy and back, "But a word of advice: I'd think two or three times before declaring God's word while you're here. Folks take God pretty seriously in these parts, and you should never be…rash (so long as that's the word of the day today) to say what you think He" I pointed at the ceiling with familiarity "has said. Maybe it's okay where you're from to put words in God's mouth, but around here...well, you'd better really've heard from God, Himself."

"Oh!" Daniel said, "But it *is* as I haf told you. I *haf* heard from Gott." He took a step backwards, still underestimating my smacking range.

"What?" I said, arms stiff at my sides. I looked (Daddy says I glared, but I don't remember it that way) at the two of them. "Just what have y'all been jawin' about all night? Did my father talk sense into you or not?"

"I am truly sorry, Sarah. I know you will haf more anger. Vat I said yesterday vas true, but it was wery wery false of me to say these things so fast. I was thoughtless, saying such a thing to you so early." My whole body was rigid now. I was fighting a loosing battle, trying not to go for a repeat performance of The Slap; maybe across the other side of his head.

"Daniel." My father said, standing at his chair. It wasn't a shout, but it carried that tone of command that always made my ears prickle. Daniel jerked around to face him. "Go on to bed now."

Daniel glanced at me for a moment, but he didn't need to be told twice. He was gone.

Daddy returned to his seat. I went to stand in front of him as he took a sip. I waited as he grimaced at the drink that had cooled or perhaps warmed against his preference.

Finally I said, "Well that Daniel must be one heck of a lawyer in *German* if he could sell you *that* in English."

He closed his eyes and took a deep breath before putting his glass on the side table with practiced care. "Sarah, It'd do you well to remember something: Your momma didn't raise no fools." He opened his eyes to me, gluing my feet to the floor. "And neither did mine." He waited a few beats before going on, "Now, are you hungry?"

"Naw Daddy, I ain't hungry." I didn't look away, and I wouldn't go away. He looked into the dregs of whatever lingered in the bottom of his mug.

"Not hungry? I guess I can understand that. You never did have much of an appetite when you were upset, and I can see how all this can be upsettin'." He looked me in the eye with the gentle face of the man who told us Bible stories – talking as if he was telling us about his favorite members of the family – while we sat by the fire. "But you've gotta eat somethin' darlin'."

"Naw Daddy," my voice started to shake, "I don't need to eat just now." I took a seat on the couch to the right of Daddy's chair. He waited. "I need you to tell me somethin'."

"What d'you mean? Y'want me to tell you a bedtime story at 6:30 in the mornin'?"

"I don't know what. Tell me what happened."

"'What happened'? I assume you don't want me to start back in Genesis and Exodus."

"Tell me what happened last night. Tell me what happened in the war. Tell me what happened that could move you to let that crazy man stay here and stay crazy. Tell me somethin' that'll help me understand."

He stared out the window, face flush into the sunlight that was finally pushing it's way through. It made his skin look hard and worn, but his eyes showed walnut and gold flecks. It was an old man's face with a boy staring through. He was drinking the light in. It was like he was praying. Maybe he *was* praying. Whatever the case, he found his answer in the shadow puppets played by the trees out front.

"I'll tell you three somethin's to suit you, but it may be that none of it suits you at all. First, it could be Daniel's crazy, but I ain't sure. Second, it could be he'll never be nothin' to you, but I ain't sure. Third, God always wins, and I am dead certain of that.

"What's that mean?"

"Mostly it means exactly what I've said, but I hope you'll start thinkin' about the third somethin'."

"Daddy, a chicken can't run through the kitchen without hearin' that God don't miss."

"Hearin' ain't learnin'."

"Come on Daddy. I ain't fully awake yet. I've got no head for riddles. Just tell me what I've missed."

He took my hand, still gentle. "I don't know that you've missed anything Sarah. I just know that God's involved in this now. No. Don't gimme that face. I ain't sayin' that God's on Daniel's side in all this, I've got no way of knowin' that. But Daniel *has* brought His name into all this, and that changes things."

"Maybe it changes things for you, but that kraut's crazy by my way of lookin' at things, and callin' God into things just makes him crazier still."

"It don't have to change Daniel for you, Sweets, but please sit with me a moment longer." I realized that I had been trying to stand up, but that Daddy was holding me down with his hand resting on mine, and his eyes on my face.

I sat back down.

"Puttin' God's name on somethin' never made anybody right if they were wrong to start with," Daddy continued. "But when folks call on God to take sides on somethin', it's best not to take any sides until you know where *He* sits.

Cause the side that God is sittin' on; that side's gonna win. Maybe not right away. Sooner. Or later." He winked. "But always."

"'Cause God always wins."

"That's right."

"So, after talkin' to Daniel, you think God's maybe on his side?"

"No. After talkin' with Daniel, I'm pretty sure that he doesn't believe God is a tool or a tactic for him to use to get what he wants. Someone who thinks like that, does God's work by accident; when he's very lucky or very unlucky. None of that puts God on his side or yours."

"So what do you think we should do?"

"I'm waitin' fer now. Plus the usual: Prayin' and hopin'."

"Okay, Daddy. So long as you and Tommy keep an eye on him, I guess I can stand to wait a little while." I squeezed Daddy's hand, and he squeezed back. "Just what are we waitin' for?"

"Waitin' to find out where God stands on all of this, and then we'll try our best to get our sorry butts on to that side of things. Y'know why?" He grinned deep and mischievous.

I rolled my eyes. "'Cause God always wins."

"That's right." He chuckled, and tapped my hand softly. "Now let's get us some chow, and then I'll need a nap."

Daddy had scheduled his holiday time to include the first few weeks of my visit, so it was doubly special to sit and eat with him in the uncharacteristically quiet kitchen. Momma rose not long after Daddy and I had begun our breakfast. She clicked her tongue at our cold cereal, and started frying up eggs without asking who wanted how many. Tommy was the last person to rise that morning. He chewed some toast sleepily with a cup of jo.

This was all a change from what I'd known most of my life. For nearly all my years, Momma would wake me and Tommy up while outside was a dim blue. We'd sneak sips from Momma's coffee while she busied about the kitchen, and now she was laying a mug in front of me and asking if I'd "Like any sugar, Sugar?"

Tommy nibbled and sipped to my right, and Daddy flanked my left as long as Momma was at her station. Finally, when he saw that Momma was done, he rubbed his eyes, asked for a lunch time wake up call and bobbed off to his room. Momma took his seat and dug into eggs that had been scrambled, salted and peppered with careless generosity.

I didn't say a thing while Momma ate and Tommy fingered the breadcrumbs on his plate. They were surrounding me. Buffering me, Daddy only leaving his shift at the table when Momma was ready to take over. It was unconscious, like an accidental family hug. The late morning was warming up, and it would have been perfect. It should have been perfect, but we all sat and bit our tongues. I tried my best not to think of the man dreaming in German in Daddy's workroom, its tools replaced by a spare bed. But I had to face that that *Elefant* was just too big. He was going to keep hovering over our breakfast table as long as we kept trying to dodge him and his crazy talk, but I just wasn't ready for him to inhabit our lips as we chewed the last of the morning sunlight with Momma's eggs and toast.

Finally, breakfast was too over to ignore. Momma's plate couldn't get any emptier, and we'd each taken turns tipping empty coffee mugs back and trying to suck that last imaginary drop of jo. We were trading glances, and it was clearly time to talk or stalk.

I chose a little bit of both.

"Hey Tommy, I'm gonna go and see if the trees are still hangin' like the use'd to. Wanna come?" I got up, and headed for the swinging door and the porch steps behind it.

"Sure," he said looking down at his crumb free plate. "but I can't be out too long. I gotta bring Daniel into town later this afternoon."

I nearly bolted for the front door at the sound of the name, like a dog near a gun shot. I pointed my fingertips out at my sides for that little bit of extra balance. "What? Why?"

"He asked me late last night if I'd bring him into town to visit a shop or two."

"And you said 'Yes'?"

"He's still a guest here, Sarah," Momma observed, "and we're gonna be hospitable as long as that stays the case." Hospitality was closer to godliness than cleanliness as far as Momma was concerned, and cleanliness stood pretty close. The warmth of the breakfast table in morning light was still on my skin, and I loved the both of them too much at the moment to snap at anyone.

I sagged, suddenly tired and sick of myself; sick of snapping. I'd come home to be a laughing girl again; the one who climbed trees even though she was too old for such play. I'd thought that I'd just left her like a favorite dress in a house shaped box in the foothills while I went off to be serious in the college world for a while. I was aching to put her on, and cartwheel down The Hill again. But the house had been burgled, and the defeated Austrians were holding her prisoner with marriage proposals instead of guns. I couldn't play with her until I dealt with them, but that wasn't going to happen that morning; Not in our kitchen. My belly was full, but a bitter taste began to pool on my tongue.

Enough talk I decided. I walked.

As I left the house, I heard the phone ring. I didn't stop to see who it was. Old high school friends would know I'd returned. Some might've just returned themselves, but I just couldn't stand the thought of lingering in the house and trying to smile into the phone.

I passed The Boulder and rounded The Hill. I headed into the woods, already regretting my choice. I was headed away from my intended destination. I found one of the lonely paths that aren't really paths - but a string of familiar trees, rocks, strips of clear ground and bushes. I hooked back around the house, and, finally, to my over-the-road tree.

"I've been sitting up here a full ten minutes," I said when I heard Tommy stomping to the tree along the same path I'd taken.

"I would've been here before you if you'd taken your own call," he said from below, and began to climb. "Or at least sooner if I'd known for sure that you were headed here." I leaned back on the trunk, like I'd fantasized doing five thousand customers ago. "Move," Tommy said when he reached me.

"No." I said with a smile.

"Fine," he grumbled, and continued to climb to a higher branch. Tommy had always been a sloth in the trees, even if he stomped like an elephant on the ground. I sat with my head tilted back to watch as he lumbered, near silent, above me. After a small eternity he hanged from above, and maneuvered to a further part of the same huge stalk I was sitting on.

"Dang, Tommy, why're you so slow?"

"I can catch three of you on the ground at the same time *little* sister," said my younger brother.

"Yeah, and I can catch a nap waiting for you to climb a tree after me." It was something I'd always known and accepted about Tommy when we were kids, but the distance of the months apart made me finally wonder. "Why *are* you so slow up in a tree Tommy?"

"'Cause I'm afraid of fallin'."

"Then why are you so quiet?"

"Same reason. If I don't hear any branches breakin' I probably ain't fallin'. And if I do hear a branch creak I might have a chance to do somethin' to keep from splittin' my skull on the road below."

"Jeeze Tommy, we ain't that high up."

"How high you reckon you've got to be before you start worrying about landin' your head on that gravel below? Or fallin' under a moving truck?" We both looked down the line of stones that lead to town. Not even a breeze was skipping down that road let alone a car or truck. "I may not scramble as high or fast as you do, Sarah, but I'll get where I need to go in due time. I ain't no dummy just because I ain't going to no…"

"I know," I interrupted, "I know you ain't no dummy.

Never said you were." I'd never seriously thought it either. "I was just saying that you ain't much of a climber, that's all."

"Nope. But my beer's just as cold as what they drink at college parties. I know that, 'cause I've had a few college-party beers. And I can put in a day's work at least as hard as any professor you learned from."

"I know it, Tommy. Relax, and tell me who called. Was it," I grinned, "one of my old boyfriends?"

"Naw," he chuckled, "but it *was* one of my old girlfriends."

I closed my eyes.

Tommy had taken three of my five closest friends out on at least one date each, and even seriously dated one of them for a few months. He knew all along how it got under my skin, so he referred to all three of them as old girlfriends.

We lived, not even within the city limits of a small town, and Momma had pulled me aside some time before Tommy had asked any of my friends on a date. She must have noticed a wandering eye I didn't even know to look for. In a town as small as ours, Momma warned me, girlfriends and boyfriends were bound to change hands. It didn't really bother me much since I'd learned from my roommate, Gloria, that that kind of stuff happens in bigger cities too.

But it gave Tommy a chuckle to needle me with it, so I just let my eyes slide shut and took in the cool summer mountain air that Lexington had failed to provide.

"Well?" Tommy called when he saw I wasn't going to

bite, “Doncha wanna know who called?”

“I asked didn’t I?” I said with my eyes still closed and my mouth still smiling. “I just figured you’d get around to it a bit slower than a normal person. We are in a tree, after all.” My smile broadened in Tommy’s disgusted silence.

After about an hour, Tommy did a hang-drop onto the terrifying highway below, and walked up the gravel road to our house. Almost an hour after he'd disappeared from sight, his truck appeared and passed under the perfect crotch of wood on which I sat. It was the only vehicle I saw on the road that day.

I scaled my way down to the soft earth next to the road, and walked deeper into the woods. The ground didn't stay even for long. Soon I was leaning back into the steep declines and forward into the inclines as I went in search of a stream I could hear but not remember. By the time I found the brook I was huffing, but not yet puffing. I thanked God that Tommy wasn't there to see me gulping air with my belly on a flat rock in the middle of the newfound stream; twenty tips – fingers and toes – dipping in the water. I cooled off with help from the shade of the thick canopy above and the cool surface of stone and water below. I sat up and folded my arms around my knees.

"Thank You God," I said out loud with a glad exhalation,

"that Dan…I mean Tommy…*dang*!" I shook my head and grimaced. All the lakes, rivers and brooks of our county were my sacred places. Church and my parents had always set the rhythmic days and events of our family's spiritual life, but the waterways were where I sang my own hymns. I didn't want to start a prayer over the soft-traveling waters and leave it unfinished, so I continued, "Thank You that neither of them can see me now. Thank You for bringing me to the waters safely, and to those who love me." I felt my chest knot up at the thought that Daniel might count himself as someone who loved me. I slapped my foot into the shocking cold water, and splashed out again with a grunt.

I pulled my shoes back on, and tried to stomp with energy back to the house. But the foothills were bound to get the better of me. I was worn out and settled down by the time I walked in the front door.

Tommy's truck, thankfully, wasn't there.

"Did Tommy tell you Theresa called, Sarah?" Momma asked when I arrived.

"Yeah," I answered without looking at her. "Think I'll have a bite before I call her back." I said, turning to give her my pretty-girl smile. "Got anything sweet to go with that Lemon-iced-tea?" I knew she did, and I knew she always would; or else she'd make something on the spot. Having a guest was no reason to forget to make some "tasties" for her daughter's return. If anything it was another reason to remember, and Momma's little Sarah always did like her "tasties."

Momma smiled me a sideways look, and headed to the pantry.

After the walk in the woods, Summer's blossoming temperatures and two slowly eaten slices of Momma's Grandma's-Southern-Rhubarb-Pie I drifted off to bed without a thought of returning phone calls or returning pickup trucks. Even the a tall glass of Lemon-iced-tea couldn't hold me up, but it must have kept me sleeping lightly because I heard the doors of Tommy's truck slamming shut. I even heard the double footsteps coming up the front porch, but still hadn't gathered their meaning.

Then the screen door creaked, flopping from side to side, in and out, open and shut. I heard another man laughing with Tommy, and I started to really come around. From the kitchen Momma's voice said, "You boys had a good time in town I guess?" My eyes popped open. I remembered everything.

I didn't know what to do. I don't know why I was in a panic, but the idea of dealing with the whole Daniel issue seemed suddenly too awkward to bear. I could see that I'd walk into the room, and Daniel would start gawking at me. We'd all know what was on his mind, and I'd turn three shades of red. Momma and Tommy would feel uncomfortable; maybe annoyed at all the fuss. Who wants to walk into that?

I tried squinting my eyes. I even threw the bed sheets over my head, but it only made me feel hot and sweaty. Besides, coming more and more awake, I realized that I couldn't just hide in bed night and day.

I threw the sheets off, and eased onto the cool floor. I scooped up my hairbrush, and sat in front of the small mirror mounted on the wall next to the door. Brushing my hair before leaving my bedroom was more of a habit than anything, but, staring at my reflection as she stroked her hair smooth and full, I had a shock. "What am I doing?" I asked aloud. I didn't want to end up looking all fresh and pretty to Daniel.

I slapped my brush on my thigh, and reached up – sinking fingers and thumbs into my hair. But I didn't mess it up. Momma simply wouldn't accept it, and Tommy would laugh his fool head off. I wouldn't normally come out of my room disheveled. "What in the world am I thinking?" *Getting ready to mess it up for* him*?*

I finished cleaning myself up; made my hair smooth

beyond any brother's reproach. I ducked round to the bathroom, and made my face clean enough that Momma would've been satisfied the first time on a Sunday morning. I checked myself one last time in the mirror before standing straight.

I grabbed the doorknob, and squeezed it furiously. "Foolishness!" I hissed, and stepped out the door.

My stomach had settled heavily with sleep, tea and rhubarb pie. So there was no temptation in the sight of Momma fixing sandwiches of salty meats and cheeses for the men – already seated and laughing – or the open wet bottles of beer. I glanced at the three of them in front of the black fireplace.

Wait. Three?

Daddy had risen while I had dozed.

Momma brought them the dark wooden platter holding sandwiches, a small jar I knew to be mustard, butter knives for spreading and some freshly cleaned napkins. She gave me a peck on the cheek, my second "Good mornin'" of the day and a wink before going back, smiling, to the kitchen to straighten up.

The men lounged to my right. The woman bustled to my left. I wanted to be neither. The food was salty and about to be eaten. Mine had been sweet, and was long gone to my belly. They were fresh and active and greeting me with the good cheer that usually comes with a fresh bottle. And I…

I had to get out of there.

I didn't reckon it was all that rude. I did raise my hand part way and said, "Hey, y'all" as I made my move for the door. I clomped down the three front steps, rag doll, and began to wander. I knew in the back of my mind that I was headed towards The Boulder. It was my second favorite place to go for peace.

In the front of my mind I couldn't escape the fact that I *did* want to sit down with Daddy; and even the boys. Why did I leave then? Well, I had already learned that I didn't like beer. I'd tried it a few times in Lexington. Most of the girls publicly cried their hatred for the stuff, but quite a few of them secretly confessed to enjoying a beer as much as anyone. I, on the other hand, quietly refuse it in public and privately hate the bitter taste. "It's an acquired taste," Gloria used to say. I never managed to acquire it, and I doubt I ever will. Also, if I was honest with myself, I had to admit that I didn't mind snubbing Daniel.

There was Momma in the kitchen, but I didn't want to sit there and be part of that scene: The little women in the kitchen while the men drink their beers and laugh by the fire. Even if the fire was unlit.

I heard the screen door and Tommy's thunking footsteps, so I stopped and turned to watch him coming. He moved his broad bulk up beside me. Seeing the sunlight shining off his blond-almost-white hair I wondered how this almost-man could be my brother. I stood four or five inches shorter with narrow everything – hips, shoulders, cheeks, nose…you name it – and dark brown hair; the only thing on me that runs longer than his.

"What?" he said flatly at the expression on my face.

"I was just thinkin' about how much you remind me of a giant fire plug."

"That's fine commin' from a squirrelly faced little girl like you."

"Squirrelly?" I laughed. "I thought you always said I was mousy."

"Yeah," he said, scratching his head, "but that was before you showed me your expert tree-climbin' skills. It was either squirrel or monkey, and I figured it was better to keep you in the rodent category."

"Respect your elders, boy. I'm still your big sister, now."

"Well, big sister, we need to talk." He walked past me, and leaned against The Boulder. Now the sun was in his eyes, but he didn't seem to care. "You've gotta make peace with Daniel. You can't go stormin' around like this the whole summer."

"I wasn't stormin'. I said 'Hi,' before I left. I just didn't wanna stay in the house is all." We stared at each other for a few seconds. Tommy sought his words, and I was determined not to say more.

"Well, I reckon that's a smart enough answer. And, being my big sister, and all, you probably already know what I'm gonna say next."

"No, Tommy, what?"

"That you're scared."

"Scared of what, exactly?" I kept my voice down, but I could feel my hair fighting to get up.

"Of Dad's new friend. 'Course we both know that any guy that looks at you with half a glimmer in his eye scares you outta your wits."

"What?!"

"Well, of course you're scared, little big-sister," he said grinning into the sun. "You and I know he must be crazy. Any guy that wants to date you...well he's *gotta* be nuts."

"Date me, Tommy? That man wants to marry me, and he doesn't even know me!"

"Aw, come on! I took him to town this morning, and he told me himself that he knows it was a mistake to say that. Trust me, once he gets to know you he'll forget all about marryin' you."

"Yeah, he told me too, but I was listening. He said he's sorry that he *said* it. He still believes it though."

"Psh! Who knows maybe *you'll* want to marry *him* before summer's out. Ha! That'd be funny. He'd actually wise up enough to know better than to want you at the same time that you'd find that he's actually good enough for you. 'Course, that'd be a first."

"Just what the H...!" I remembered our parents in the house over my shoulder. "Just what's that supposed to mean? What'd be a first?"

"Sarah, you know as well as I do that no man could ever be good enough for you. You're Daddy's precious little sweet."

And that's when I said, possibly, the dumbest thing I've ever said in my life. Even in the years that have followed, I haven't managed to say anything that has topped it. I've thought about it a lot since then. I know that I was half joking. Maybe I thought I'd turn things around by joining up with Tommy against myself. But, after years of reflecting on it, I honestly don't know how such a thing passed my lips.

"Sure he could be good enough. Man moves The Boulder you're leaning on there to the top of The Hill, and I'll marry him!" We both laughed for a moment before I heard Daniel's voice from behind me:

"I will do it."

He wouldn't be swayed. We tried explaining that it had only been a joke, but He didn't care. *"In every joke der is some troos."*

To be honest, we didn't try that hard. We only tried to talk him out of it until we reached the front steps of the house, not wanting to upset our parents. Daniel, for all his rashness, wasn't stupid. He'd have to see how ridiculous the idea was as soon as he stopped to think about it. At the door, Tommy put his hands on Daniel's shoulders and turned him to face The Boulder. "I've got just one word for you Daniel: How?"

The Boulder was just a bit larger than a VW Bug, so even if Tommy was willing to lend Daniel his truck (and he most certainly wasn't) even that beast wouldn't have had the horsepower to uproot that great chunk of mountain; not even close. And, drag it *up* a hill? No chance in this world. Daddy's truck, which had sat still, covered by a tarp under it's lean-to since before I'd arrived home, was almost twenty years old and struggled to get it's passengers and a few bags of "provisions" (groceries, really) to town and back. No one was going to rent any kind of heavy machinery to a stranger from another continent, especially not so he could drag it up to our place in the hills.

Recognition of the problem poured down Daniel's face, and color drained from it. Tommy and I walked into the house – our gripes temporarily forgotten – and I let him persuade me to give beer just one more try. "There's nothin' better for a hot day," he said with a wink; signaling, I believed, celebration of a victory over a mutual enemy.

Daniel remained, staring, from the porch for a while before coming in. He didn't look happy, but he didn't look hopeless either. Looking back now I can see that it was a look of mulish determination.

He didn't say much in the late afternoon. He seemed to take an unusually long time washing up for dinner, but he was smiling and cordial at the table, and I took it as a sign. I hoped that, in the impossibility of the Boulder, he had seen a reflection of the impossibility of pursuing me.

Such an idea was a relief, though it may be hard to imagine considering the appeal he had had before blurting his prophesies. Sure, I found him handsome, and he showed an interest that I'd have likely returned in a normal situation. But the situation was far from normal. It's one thing to have caught a man's eye, but it is something else to be proposed to within a handful of hours of meeting. Even that could be gotten over, given enough space and time. But Daniel was living in our house; my mother and father's house. I was going to have to look at and live with this man and his proposal day and night. I was going to have to face him and it over every meal. In fact, his status as a guest afforded him a limited diplomatic immunity, which meant that he would be more than constant. He would have to be tolerated and endured far more than a stranger on the street. As long as he was here this was going to stay weird, and the only way for the weirdness to pass was if he would quit the silly idea before too long. Daniel's good spirits at the table that evening allowed me to entertain the possibility that he was doing just that.

Who knows, I speculated over roasted potatoes, *maybe we can get back on proper footing before too long.* The idea and what it implied made me smile.

Tommy was almost giddy. Seeing that my stormy mood had passed and that Daniel appeared resolved about me tipped him to a similar idea that we'd all get along. Momma and Daddy presided over the dinner with greater pride and pleasure than the previous meal. What a bounty God had graced them with that evening: Good food, happy family and a welcome guest.

The bottle Daniel had brought sat on the counter. It had gone unopened the previous night thanks to Daniel's loose lips and my fast hands, and I noticed that we hadn't pulled the cork for this evening's dinner either. I asked why we didn't open it to better enjoy the "bounty."

Daddy looked back over his shoulder at the bottle for a full 30 seconds. Momma's hands stopped moving. I couldn't see his face, but his stillness chilled me. He shook off whatever those squiggly letters told him, and turned back to us with a smile.

"It's a good night tonight. But not the right night for that." The table held its breath for a moment, but Daddy wouldn't let the mood fall. Grinning, he turned to Daniel. "So, our little town can't compare to Vienna, eh Daniel?"

"It is not zo different from some of the villages outside of Vienna," he replied. "But, you are right zat Vienna is different to American cities." Daniel then turned to Tommy and said "I very much enjoyed the tourism of the town you showed me today, Tommy. Do you sink you could take me again tomorrow? I would like to buy some sings."

Tommy agreed readily, rolling with the spirit of the meal.

It was so pleasant, in fact, that I actually went to bed with a smile that night. It was my second night home; the first of peaceful slumber.

Waking and breakfast were easy. Daddy and I shot each other private raspberries over our coffee cups while

Momma kept herself busy doing God-knows-what between sink, stove and pantry. I wondered at her. Didn't she realize that there were movements burning across the country to free women from being stuck behind a stove? How could she take so much pride in housework? And then I saw the meal, our men (I was even willing to include Daniel in that description,) the orderly kitchen and my own plate. How could she not take some measure of pride in what she'd done? But could this possibly be enough? Was there more I couldn't see? I didn't know what to think or how to feel about Momma, and – not for the first time – I wondered how she thought and felt about me.

Daniel kept a pleasant tone. He ate the eggs, bacon, toast and butter with curiosity and zest, but repeatedly lapsed into his own thoughts. *Who knows*, I wondered, *what crazy people say to themselves over sunny-side-ups and coffee?*

Tommy ate a horse's share, which surprised no one. Smiling, he checked that Daniel still wanted to take another spin through the town. Daniel looked around the table. I guessed that he was looking for meaning. But he seemed to catch on, and he agreed before anyone could interpret for him.

I'd guessed wrong. He'd understood from the first, and was searching us for something else: To see if anyone suspected.

✦ ✦ ✦

Momma's face lit up when I offered to help her clear the table without having to be asked or told. The boys (as Momma now called Tommy and Daniel) went off to Tommy's truck and our small town below. Daddy retired to the woods. Since the first days of his vacation from the plant, Momma said, he liked to stroll among the trees each day for a while. It seemed that yesterday I had taken his shift while he slept.

I wanted to sit and talk with my mother in that rare private time. I wanted to ask her about the strange thoughts I'd been having at the table; about housework, women's liberation, pride, the choices she'd made and my own choices still to come. I wanted to ask her about being a woman in the face of this world and being a girl in a University that had mostly men.

Daddy had always been the one I'd talk with about ideas and the world. He was the one who'd *seen* the world, and thought beyond the practicalities. But he wouldn't have any way of talking about being a woman.

Momma had watched me closely as I grew. She was there to prepare me for my first period and the attention some boys wanted to give to a mousy girl like me. But her advice had always been practical: What to do when such-and-such happens. How could she advise me about facing a world she'd never seen; university life, for example, when she'd never set foot on a campus? What could she say about the new ideas I'd been learning about in far off Lexington?

Instead of finding out I scrubbed and dried, and, as I

reached for the last plate, I noticed something missing.

"Did y'all hide the wine?" I asked.

"What?"

"The bottle Daniel brought. It was right here on the counter last night. Did you and Daddy hide it after the rest of us went to bed?"

Momma laughed. "No, Sarah. It's in the pantry, where anyone who cares to go in there can see it. I do say, you like a good mystery wherever you can find it; even if there ain't none to be found." She said it with so much love and warmth that I couldn't help smiling. "I guess that's what makes you so good for the university. You spot a missing bottle, and you've gotta see what it's all about."

There it was; an opening as clear as daylight. But instead of talking about Lexington and ideas, I pressed on about the bottle. "Why'd you put it away?" I asked, studying the plate I was drying.

"I told your daddy last night that you were right about the bottle, and that we should either open it up or put it away. It just ain't right to leave spirits out on display like that."

The idea of Momma telling Daddy that I had been right about something surprised me. It wasn't the kind of thing I imagined them talking about in private. Also, a bottle of wine hardly seemed like "spirits" to me, but I knew better than to argue something like that with my mother in her own kitchen. I wanted so badly to bring up deeper questions, but the deepest one I could manage to ask was, "Do you know the story behind those bottles, Momma?"

She put her plate away, and stared at the counter top. "Yes." She paused for a beat. "Of course I know it, darlin'. I wouldn't tolerate my husband getting such gifts from some far off place without a proper explanation, and your daddy's an honest man." She then turned to me with a smile that didn't match her eyes. "But it ain't my story to tell, and it wouldn't be right for me to try. I wish..." Her smile faded, and the pain in her eyes became wetter. Then her smile returned brighter than before. "Well, I don't rightly know what I'd wish if I were one to make wishes. But he's set to wait a bit longer, and you know there's nothin' to do but wait when your daddy sets his mind." She chuckled a bit. "stubborn ole' man."

Ever the daddy's girl, I asked myself silently if Momma was really the one being stubborn here. Then I surprised myself by wondering who among us wasn't.

I had put off returning my friend's call for about as long as I could.

"How are y'all doin' girl?" *Har'yall doin' girl?* "I been wonderin' what's been takin' you so long to get back to me."

"I'm okay, Theresa. How's your family doin'?" Each word came out slow and painful. I couldn't understand why

I was so reluctant to talk with her. Then the names of her kin began to roll out of the ear piece (Georgie, Abigail, Kat and Lilly) with stories of who got how sick; broke both legs ("the only injury in the plant for the last two and a half months,") scarlet fever ("Poor thing,") beat up ("Won't say who did it, but everyone already knows…") and chicken pox ("Better early than late!") She revealed who in her family thinks who else in her family is stupid (everyone) and who ("let's face it,") *is* stupid. Next came the names of the friends, and she spoke about them with the same warmth and venom.

"Listen Theresa, I'm glad as can be to finally hear your voice after so long, but I've got to get goin'. I just didn't want to wait any longer returning your call."

"Gotta go?" Her tone was one part disappointment, two parts curiosity. "Are you feelin' sick?"

I decided that that mill already had plenty of grist. Besides, Momma always said even though the truth won't suffice for some people, it usually will for most. So I just spat out the outsider's edition of the truth. "Naw, naw, I'm fine. But Daddy's got this house guest, so things are extra busy 'round here."

"Oh yeah! I heard about that from Lucy over at the dime store. Says he's good lookin', but he seemed kinda' outta sorts; from outta town."

"Yeah, Lucy always did have a good eye."

"So, when do I get to meet him? Bring him into town, and we'll *accidentally…*"

"I've really gotta' go, Theresa. Momma's fixin' to look at me cross-eyed if I don't get over and help her out." Momma was humming a happy tune out back, but couldn't be heard over the phone. The truth may suffice for most people, but for some it won't.

"Alright hon. You call me when you get a chance, okay?"

"Okay, Theresa. Talk to you real soon. Bye."

I sagged into a chair, and scratched at the back of my head. In high school I'd been one of the biggest gossips in town, and proud of it. I tried to season every meal with someone else's business, whether I was delivering it or receiving. But all of Theresa's "news" made me nauseous and exhausted. It was like having dirty little ants crawling in my ears.

Momma came into the kitchen still humming to herself, carrying a wax paper package of butter in her hands. But I knew that she was also carrying real "news," even if it was old news; it was thick and weighty, like the brown paper in her hands.

I watched her skate among the trappings of her kitchen, and I saw in her a dignity. The secrets she bore weren't gems that she would hoard or display. They were promises to be kept. I wondered who else, besides my father, she'd kept faith with, and how it made her who she was. I saw a woman who could talk to me about integrity. In fact, I realized, she *had* talked to me about integrity just a little while ago…and about who knows what else. Things that could even be useful in that wide world that was giving me the heebie-jeebies.

"Momma…?"

She turned at my call, and I saw for the first time in far too long how open and beautiful she really is.

"Yes, darlin'?"

I only managed to say, "Can I ask you somethin'?" before the phone rang.

Momma said, "Sure," between rings, and picked it up.

I felt my nerve slipping, and gritted my teeth against it as she took a message for Daddy. She was shaking her head and sighing as she joined me at the table. "That Dick Bouliard only ever calls when he knows perfectly well your daddy's out."

Further from deep talk, closer to gossip and yet still close enough to home to be worth talking about, I began to forget my fears. "Why's he do that?"

"Well he says it's the only way to hear my sweet voice since Daddy decided to use all that built up vacation time and I don't have any reason to call down there. But that's really just an excuse."

"Daddy must *love* that excuse," I smiled.

"*Safer for a man to flirt with another man's wife than to admit the truth? What kinda world we livin' in, makes a man think that way?*" Momma put just a hint too much gravel into her voice, but the imitation of Daddy was perfect otherwise. I laughed along with her despite my confusion.

"What truth?" I finally asked.

Momma chuckled worth half a breath more before saying, "That he can't be seen callin' your daddy. He can only afford to be seen *getting* calls *from* him."

I was not less confused.

"But he *does* call, doesn't he? I mean, he just did, right? Wasn't that just him on the phone?"

"It certainly was," she sat down and leaned back into her chair, and gazed at me with half-lidded eyes, "but you can be sure no one saw him do it. He shoos everyone outta the office at around 8:30 most mornings, but sometimes he tells at least one of them that he has to be back at 9:15 to do 'stuff around the office.' The poor man – usually Stanley Forrester, bless his soul – has to be back just to be held up there for all sorts of sorry excuses until the phone rings with Daddy's return call."

I'd met Mr. Forrester, my father's head clerk, at a company picnic a few summers earlier. He was a short, skinny balding man with a slightly bulbous nose. My father always said he was smart as a whip. He was kind to me, and I especially remembered that he didn't talk down to me, or try to get on my good side just because my father is his boss. He spoke to me like I was just another adult at the picnic. It won me over, and I wasn't the only one. It was never said aloud, but his tall, slim, auburn haired wife, Jean, was known as one of the most beautiful and kind hearted women in town.

He must have worked his magic double-fine on her, as she'd never had an eye for any other man but stumpy little Stanley Forrester.

I tried to imagine the charming little man trapped in the head office with the white haired Mr. Bouliard (tall with a thick chest and a thicker gut) being made to shift papers from one corner of the room to another and back.

"Naw!" I cried.

"Sure-ly! Once he's sure it's the call he's been waiting for, Dick rolls his eyes like he's doin' some terrible duty – humoring the ole' man. He just can't let go – and calls out, 'Hey there, Joe!' to your father over the phone before finally wavin' off poor Stanley (or whoever) to take the call."

"Why in blue blazes does he do all that?"

"I already told you, Sarah. He can't bear to let the other men know that he's calling your father for help. He said flat out that he knew he was 'loosing the men.' Psh! They never do let go of that military speak when they're talkin' to each other."

"But how do you know all this?" I asked salivating for details. In high school I'd learned that while gossip was good, confirmation could be even better. Why did this gossip feel okay where Theresa's had felt so wrong? My best guesses were that it involved my own family without casting any shadows over them, it was coming from my mother and it kept me warm enough to keep on talking with her. They were excuses, but they were excuses I could live with. I needed to continue if only to see how far Momma and I could reach together.

"Oh, I shouldn't tell you about that," she tittered. I couldn't believe my ears. My own mother was using a feint. Theresa and our group of friends had used it on each other and everyone else in town as easily as most people talk about the weather.

I just eyeballed her with raised brows, a forward tilt of the head and a slight frown. *You must be joking.* "Momma…" and left the rest to hang understood in silence.

"Oh, don't look at me like that, Sarah. I feel bad about sayin'. It was said in all earnestness at church, and I hate to feel like I'm laughing at such a sweet man as Stanley."

"Mr. Forrester? He told you all this?"

"Well, he didn't mean to. In fact, I'm pretty sure that he still doesn't know himself."

The hook was in my mouth, and I had no interest in letting it go until I'd gotten the whole worm. "How's that, Momma?"

She wrung her hands. She *actually* wrung her *hands* with *guilt*, and stared down and to the right at the floorboards. I never knew she could be such a performer! "Well, I guess it *is* kinda' funny. In a sweet way."

"Come on, Momma! You're killin' me!"

"Well, okay." The guilt smoothed to make way for her polished ivory smile. "He and Jean – Mrs. Forrester – came to us after the service last Sunday, and talked some niceties and such. And after things started to get a little quiet for somethin' to say, Stanley turned to your father and said that he hoped he'd be callin' the office to check up on things more. Well, naturally, we got real serious and asked why; what was wrong? He said it's nothin', really. It's just that sometimes Dick calls him into the office in the mornings, and he just can't seem to get away until someone calls to distract him. Most of the time, he mentioned, calls from Daddy did the trick best. 'Just a call now and then,' he suggested. 'There's no need to worry so much as you seem to be. There's no real need to be calling in on Dick to ask about the operation. But it'd be a help to me to get on with doin' my job in the mornings if you called in a friendly way. Give Dick a pep talk once in a while.'

"I thought your daddy was gonna blow his stack at the suggestion that he was calling Dick to check up on things. But he just looked at Stanley real serious, and nodded his head. 'I'll keep that in mind, Stanley,' he said. He thanked him for the suggestion, bid him a 'God bless,' and a 'take care,' and we went on our way."

"So, Mr. Bouliard is still getting away with it?" I slapped the table and leaned back into my chair. "I can't believe it. How'd he manage that?"

"Oh, Daddy feels real serious about it. In fact he felt real bad about last week, before we found out how Dick was 'maneuvering.' That's what Daddy calls it."

"Why? What happened the week before?"

"Daddy got so fed up with being disturbed during his

holidays that he stopped returning the calls!" I laughed hard, and Momma's giggles began to follow. "Poor Stanley," she said, causing the laughter to crescendo. "He must've spent hours digging up old papers," my laughter went up another notch, "and clearin' and coverin' desks..." tears began to blur my vision, "...before Dick finally gave up and let him go off to do his job." I was laughing so hard that I had to let myself down off the chair onto the kitchen floor to keep from falling off. Momma's laughter at watching my display pealed higher and louder. My stomach hurt, and it felt good as only a laughter-induced stomach ache can. On the floor, I curled into a giggling ball.

Once we were both in chairs and stable again, I returned to my inquiry: "But, if you know all this, then why does he still flirt with you or make any excuses at all?"

She put her earthen gray coffee mug down, mid-sip. "Oh! He can't admit it to me any more than the men working for him. Besides, it's none of my business in the first place."

"Does...Has...Did Daddy at least tell Mr. Bouliard that he knows?"

"If he has, it hasn't stopped the badly timed calls or the flirting." She continued her sip.

"I don't get it," I pressed, "Why does Daddy go along

with such tom-foolery?"

She paused her drinking again, her mouth hidden behind her mug, her eyes wide with entertainment. "Well look who thinks she knows what is or isn't tom-foolery. She watched her half-full mug as she placed it on the table, and did not look up. You'll have to ask your daddy if you want an explanation for his doings, but ask remembering this: He does have his reasons for his ways of dealing with the Dick Bouliards of the world."

"There's more than one?" I quipped, fetching her eyes back.

"Oh yes darlin'. You'll find there are plenty of Dicks out there."

Our eyes widened in unison as we realized what she had just said. Our cheeks crimsoned together. Our smiles stretched together, opened together and laughed harder than ever together. We rocked and hooted in concert, tears streaming our cheeks in that moment of sorority.

Amid the laughter, just before the front door opened, I considered that now was as good a time as any to start asking for some of that deeper and broader insight; the kind to bring into the scary wide-world.

And, though I knew that the thumping of Daddy's heavy boots outside forecasted a change of atmosphere and conversation, I felt neither frustrated nor relieved; neither held-up nor rushed. I knew beneath conscious thought that, threaded through the gossip and laughter, I'd already been getting those insights from my mother. The laughter especially (I felt certain) guaranteed that there would be more to come.

Then the door opened, bringing Daddy through to fall under our inspection. He stood lanky and solid; a surprising contrast to the old man I'd found waiting his turn to hug me two days before. He held incredibly still as the shadows of leaves passed up and down him, as if probing for a way through his denim shirt, between the buttons, under skin and bone and into his heart. Already he needed a shave. Back from his stroll, he was of the hills and their roots. How could we ever explain our laughter to such an image? We could only stare at him for a moment before tipping back into yet another fit of glee.

To Daddy, half a mind still among the raw trees, the laughter Momma and I were coughing up just sounded like any other hen party. His eyes and mouth were, at first, three round holes of confusion. But as Momma's eyes and mine locked, teared-up and crinkled shut – as we filled the room with rising and falling waves of runaway laughter – his features flattened into the face of any man among women laughing over empty cups.

"I wont ask," he offered. But he'd only fed the flames.

"That's good Joseph," Momma managed as she gasped

for a free breath, "'Cause you don't wanna know," and the laughter rose one last time before finally easing its way down to the sounds of Hanover women clearing their throats. We all shook our heads in wonder.

Daddy poured himself a glass of water, and was drinking it slowly when Momma said, "By the by, you got a phone call while you were out."

His eyes closed as he continued to swallow gulp after gulp. When there was nothing left in the glass he wiped his mouth, stared across the kitchen and den to the cooled, black fireplace and said, "Dick," in a dread low exhalation.

"Yessiree," tittered Momma, not yet ready to give up her good mood.

Daddy called Mr. Bouliard back, and spoke quietly towards the pantry, which obligingly absorbed his words and bounced only a low hum back into the kitchen. I got up to leave him to his conversation, but Momma waved me back into my seat.

"If he really wants to make it private, he can go into the pantry."

Daddy took the hint, and pulled the receiver with him deeper into the shadowed doorway; stretching the spiraled cord to long, thin curlicues. I watched as the curtain was pulled closed to hide from our eyes the man we couldn't hear anyway.

When I turned back to Momma she was giggling again. "What's so funny now?" I asked, feeling a smile push its way onto my face.

"Oh, nothin'," she said. "It's just..." She breathed a deep hiss through her closed-teeth smile, and then slapped her thighs with both hands. "It's just nice to laugh out loud." She paused for a beat, and flashed her eyes at me as she said, "And double-nice to do it with my baby-girl!"

"Momma!" I slapped the table for the second time that day. "You promised! You promised never again!"

Laughing harder now, "Oh, I know, but just this once..."

"Naw!" I tried to turn my face away from her, but could not unlock our eyes; could not hide my half-smile-half-frown.

"...I was pretty good about it through your high school years."

"*Naw*!" I slapped at the dark wood still yet again, smiling against a tone of hurt that couldn't even convince me.

"But you are!"

"Naw, Momma! Come on! You *know* I hate that name! Always have!"

Laughing even louder, threatening to pull me into giggles with her, "Oh, but you are. You are! You *are* my pretty baby-girl." Momma cackled as I rolled my eyes, which only made her laugh harder and say, "Oh-ho-ho! And you did *not* always hate that name. You used to love it when you were pullin' at my apron strings, and learnin' to tie your own."

I remembered that tiny apron she'd made for me when I was only four years old. I'd begged her for one of my own. I wore it to kindergarten and at the dinner table. I even wore it to bed some nights. I used to stomp around the kitchen like it was my own domain, and Tommy, just beginning to toddle, thought he had two mothers. And when my little brother called me Momma, I remembered, I felt a fear I couldn't understand.

And I remembered it was a great relief to remove the apron and to be my mother's pretty baby-girl.

More laughter from Momma, and, for a moment, I was unable to hold my own down. But soon I bit it back, crossed my arms, and stared ahead at the curtain. I watched it hide my daddy, his bottle and the other goods within. I held that pose with an indulgent smile, and waited for the end of the laughter, the phone conversation or both.

We heard Tommy's truck before either ended. Momma was cooling down again as the engine cut off. I saw the phone cord bow slightly from inside the pantry. Momma reached over my crossed arms to touch my face as a door from the truck outside opened and slammed violently shut.

"I'm sorry, darlin'," she said with a smile that was not sorry. A second door opened and closed more softly, and Tommy's boots could be heard crunching toward the house at a furious pace. "It's just that I…" Her mouth held open, but it did not freeze. It slowly frowned, as her gaze passed from me to the screen door over my shoulder. Her eyes locked in that direction; their round shape flattening. The creases at their corners drew together. I turned to see what she saw, but there was nothing through the screen door but blue sky, green grass and dark lumpy hills in between.

Then I noticed Tommy's voice carrying across the rapidly diminishing distance. He was swearing wickedly; something he rarely did even when he was far from our home.

Daddy's phone cord creaked and sagged as he came from behind the curtain. "…call you back if you like." He paused, listening to Dick on the line and Tommy on the approach. "All right, then." Tommy stomped two porch steps, mouth stilled and frowning his chin into an island. "Well, call back if you need. Bye." He slammed receiver to hook, echoed a white-knuckled second later by Tommy's fist to the screen door.

And then came the chorus. Momma intoned the familiar "Thomas Jefferson Hanover, what in the Sam Hill…" It beat out in counterpoint to Daddy's "Tommy, you can't just come bargin'…" which held for a bar or two before Tommy flung his arms out, and drowned them both out with his own Cadenza Espressivo Liberamento.

"It ain't my fault there was nothin' I could'a done Mr. Macleroy would'a killed me then Momma would'a killed me too so you'd best not even try to kill me 'cause I'm ready to kill him or me or someone 'cause there weren't nothin' I could'a done!"

There was a long Silenzio Improviso, and I thought I

heard Daniel's shoes dragging among the gravel stones around the truck. Was that the engine ticking as it cooled? It may have been my imagination.

Momma said, "What?"

Daddy said, "What?"

Another gravel-scrape and engine-tick played across my ear drum, and the image of Daniel's black pants pulling taut against his long legs with each step strutted across my mind's eye. I blinked with surprise. "Wait," I blurted to Tommy, "are you talking to me?"

"Of COURSE I'm talkin' to you! Ain't none'a this is my fault!"

"Tommy, slow down. What in the world are you talking about?"

"I'm talkin' about that!" He pointed to the kitchen wall. The only windows facing the graveled drive and apron to the north being in the pantry and Tommy's room, we all knew he was indicating the truck beyond.

Tommy had chosen to park the truck on the other side of that wall. Had he parked east of the house, we'd have been able to see the truck before he'd even gotten out of it. Apparently he wanted to put up his confusing defense before we got a peek at Daniel and the truck.

Momma and I got up, but Daddy stayed behind and beckoned Tommy come with a backward jerk of the head. Tommy stepped around us, and tried to watch over our shoulders as he went to our father. We poked through the screen door, and looked around to the side of the house. There wasn't much to see. Daniel had dropped a coil of rope to the ground near the passenger side. He was struggling to pull something out of the bed of the truck, but it was impossible to see what he was wrestling.

Daddy's voice could be heard low, but not understood, as he spoke to Tommy.

A corner of white canvas was hanging out of the side, and Daniel seemed to be trying to free it or something underneath it.

"Naw, Dad," we could hear Tommy saying. "I can't right now."

Eventually Daniel pulled the canvas thing free, and canvas was all there was. A large grey tarp now lay across the gravel next to the rope.

"Well, for one thing," Tommy was responding, "the truck still needs to be unloaded."

Daniel reached back into the bed, and withdrew a small mallet and a steel spike.

"Is he lookin' to make a tent?" Momma asked.

Tommy turned from his conversation, turned back to Daddy, gave the universal "come-on" reverse wave and stepped quickly to the doorway. He peeked around to see what we saw. "That ain't no tent stake. That's a chisel, in case he hits something that don't give way to the sledgehammer."

"Sledgehammer?" Momma and I chorused.

Giving no indication that he'd actually heard us, Daniel

reached again into the truck bed, and withdrew a full sized sledgehammer. He was barely sturdy enough to heft it out.

"Yeah, the chisel was Mr. Macleroy's suggestion. Once he saw that Daniel wasn't checkin' the prices, he figured every kind of hammer and pick was a good idea."

Daniel reached into the bed again, and something within clunked heavily as he tried to unearth it.

"By the time I'd gotten a coke from the cooler out front and had a few sips, I came in to find Daniel buyin' up half the store. Mr. Macleroy was beamin' like fouth of July, and he would've surely beaten me red, white and blue if I'd tried to stop the sale by then. I didn't know. I swear, Sarah. I thought he just wanted to see the town again."

"I still don't see how he reckons he's gonna do it with some tarp and rope and a few hammers." I said

"Do what, exactly?" asked Daddy.

PART II

Break Down, Buildup & Breakdown

Chapter 9

Daniel clearly knew how he wanted things to happen. He just didn't know what he was doing. He laid the thick heavy duty canvases around the boulder, tucked them under where stone met turf; as if he was about to feed it, and didn't want anything to spill onto the grass.

When he'd placed tarps all the way around, the boulder was a giant dark brown-gray meatball in the exact center of a light gray paper plate; a giant's spaghetti dinner, abandoned and rained and snowed on for more than fifteen years; the noodles and sauce slipped away. Daniel, it seemed, had come all the way from Vienna to Kentucky to assemble this image, illustrating how Daddy was right: God had hit exactly what He was aiming for. There it was; dead center. Bulls eye!

Up to this point he seemed efficient and competent to my untrained eye, but even this small show was undermined by the first ridiculous swing. He had to quit hammering early. His hands hurt too much from the vibrations of the first few strikes, and he was already afraid of the boulder. I thought he was quitting the whole silly business, but then he started gathering up one of the canvas tarps that had a few bits of stone and dust on it.

When it jumped loose from under The Boulder, spilling most of what he'd accumulated onto the grass, he deflated so visibly that we (Tommy and I) could spot it from the porch. He sank to his knees and refilled the tarp. Finally he gathered the four corners together, and dragged it with its meager load up to the top of The Hill. Truly, this was an expert display of amateurism.

We figured it wasn't even enough debris to fill a flour sack, and that a flour sack would've been less work all around. The heavy canvas itself must have weighed more than the boulder bits he was dragging. Most pathetic was when he "unloaded" the tarp onto the hilltop; pulling and pulling at it until he ran out. He looked down at the pebbles – which Tommy and I couldn't see from the porch – for a good three minutes straight; which, when you think about it, is a long time to stare at rubble. Then he gazed down The Hill, over The Boulder to our direction for another minute or so.

I strained to pick out the features of his face without seeming to stir at all, but Tommy sensed it in me anyway. I looked over to see him smiling – eyes hidden by the bill of his Cincinnati Reds cap.

"What?" I asked, not really asking. "You laughin' at that poor boy commin' down The Hill?" He didn't answer except for the corners of his mouth reaching higher for his cheekbones. "What're you thinkin' Tommy?" Has there ever been a question so important? Is there a question less appropriate for a civil relationship nearly 20 years strong? If I want to say what's on my mind I can open my own mouth. Try to stop me! Tommy's even worse than me. You don't want to guess at the horrors he's revealed to me in reply to that question. But I've never been able to resist asking when curiosity strikes, any more than I can help jumping into puddles despite my advanced years.

"I reckon you like him," Tommy said.

"Psh! You're nearly crazy as he is!"

"S'okay. I like him well enough too. Takes grit, tryin' to pull off a stunt like this."

"I take it back. You're he…" I turned around to peek into the living room through the porch windows. Nobody was in there, but I didn't take any chances. I leaned over to Tommy, and whispered, "You're hell-and-gone *crazier* than him!"

Tommy smiled. "Don't much matter. At this rate he'll break every bone in his hands before he even makes a proper dent in our Boulder."

"You ain't gonna try to help him are you?"

Tommy's mouth puckered and his fair eyebrows pulled together and down viciously. "You know I won't. We're agreed."

Chapter 10

Daddy had not been thrilled at the idea of all this boulder moving business, and I certainly hadn't helped him to get comfortable with it. But I hadn't bothered to try to demonize Daniel either. It was clear from last time that pushing against someone who sited God as their motivation would trigger an inclination in Daddy to defend – or at least become circumspect about – that someone.

When Daddy had asked what exactly Daniel was going to try to do, we began trying to explain over one another. Daddy held his hands up for peace, and eventually got it. "Tommy, help our guest unload his new belongings from the truck. Ruthie, would you mind scratchin' up a snack for the boys? They'll be hungry after their joy ride through town and loading and unloading the truck." He stopped then, and watched my mother; waited for her reply. Her arms had folded somewhere along the way. She unfolded them now, and gave Daddy a kiss on the cheek.

"I reckon I've got a little somethin' the boys'll like."

"Thank you. Sarah." He turned to me. "Let's sit for a

minute and talk." I headed for the couch. "No Sarah," he said. "Let's go sit by the Object of Your Affection." He was pointing out the door. "Ruthie, send Tommy out to us soon, please." He walked out the door, and headed up the gradual slope to the Object of My Affection; The Boulder.

While we waited for Tommy, Daddy asked simple questions: Say again what Daniel intends to do with that equipment? Why would he want to do such a thing? How does he hope to do it with a truck full of hammers?

My answers were likewise simple: Well, sir, he means to move this here boulder to the top of The Hill there. He's hoping it'll make me wanna marry him; long story there. I haven't the foggiest idea. Maybe he thinks he can scare it up the Hill.

Daddy asked for the long story that ended with Daniel hoping for my affection after elevating The Boulder. I obliged as best I could, but Tommy came before I finished. He was carrying a pitcher of water, three glasses, a few dark bread sandwiches in a bag swinging from one wrist and a plaid blanket draped over the other arm.

I wasn't hungry, but Daddy poured and drank another full glass of water before repeating his questions for Tommy. The answers weren't much different from what I'd given. Tommy repeated our conversation perfectly, near as I could tell.

"Did Sarah swear?" Daddy asked.

"Aw Daddy! You know I never cuss!" I said playfully, catching his attention for a moment. But his eyes slid back to Tommy; serious the whole way.

"You know I'm not talkin' about dirty words here, son. Did your sister swear she'd marry the man who puts The Boulder up on The Hill there?" He pointed at the top of The Hill with his left pointer and middle finger, but his eyes did not unlock from Tommy's face.

"No," said Tommy fixing on Daddy with equal stillness. "She didn't swear to it."

But I could have, as easily as not. I knew perfectly well what it meant to swear to something, even in jest, but it was a part of how I talked. Only by grace, luck or fate did it happen that I had not sworn to it on that particular summer day. Daddy's shoulders sank a quarter of an inch, but I only saw it because I was looking for it. I shivered a bit at the sight. What ever would he have done if I had sworn to it?

There were more questions, but I don't remember what they were any more. I do remember the water tasting sweet, and the sandwiches we eventually dug into were salty. I also remember that Daddy was distressed, and that I was sad to see it. But I also remember trying to soak the sunlight in while having a picnic – even an emergency picnic – with Tommy and my father, grown so much older since I'd left for college less than a year before.

If Daddy came to any conclusions after our little talk, he didn't share them with us. He only asked that no one discuss this matter until after he'd gotten a chance to discuss things privately with Daniel and taken a little time to digest it all. I didn't see how any of us was going to pretend nothing was going on, and I said so. Daddy thought it over for a moment, and finally said we could pluck a few weeds out of Momma's garden.

I know that as adults we ought to be above whining about chores, and I held my tongue when I was told to do it. But I couldn't help resenting Daniel just a little bit with each tuft of johnsongrass I had to pull and each purple topped musk thistle I tried to kick loose.

Eventually the screen door creaked, and allowed my parents and Daniel out of the house; Momma with two pairs of her gardening gloves. Daddy and Daniel headed for the tree line. "Here Sarah, you can use my spare gloves. Tommy, leave the musk thistle to us. My gloves won't fit your big ole fingers, and those thistles will cut you up. You just concentrate on the johnsongrass. Go ahead and get a trowel from the tool shed in case you find some with real roots."

Tommy walked towards the shed, and I tipped my head towards the other two men making for the trees. "And where are they going?"

"Your father is taking Daniel for a little walk; showing

him the trees and the hills."

"Well ain't *that* sweet. We're pullin' weeds, and Daniel gets to take a stroll in the woods." I thought without emotion that it was a stupid thing to say. What did I expect? That a guest would be asked to weed our garden?

"You reckon?" said my mother. "You think that boy was hiking in the hills when he wasn't studying in the library? You suppose there's a slope out there that's as gentle as a city street?"

We both knew that the foothills were steep and confusing for most folks from flatter regions. My barely tolerated uncle Robert and his brood from Ohio and its Great Plains always insisted that we were "lost in the mountains" whenever we'd take a light stroll. They'd huff and puff like they were running a marathon. Momma and I smiled at one another, unaware that Vienna is nestled to a mountain and that hiking in the nature is a common form of entertainment there.

"So we're all getting some kind of punishment?" I asked.

"No, your daddy's just keepin' y'all separate for the time being; tryin' to gather all the pieces. See how they fit together. Figure out what to do about it before the three of you come up with something else to gray our hairs."

"Didn't Daniel tell you all about it in the house? OW!" I shook a gardening glove off my right hand, and sucked at my thumb.

"Sure he did. How in the world you came up with such

a ridiculous idea is beyond me, by the way." She gave her disdainful look to the thistle in her gloved hand rather than directly at me. "But it seems that your daddy's got more he wants to say in private."

"It was *supposed* to be ridiculous, Momma! That was the point! Also, it was a joke, and I wasn't even talking to Daniel at the time. I didn't even know I was talkin' *around* him! What do you suppose Daddy wants to tell Daniel that he can't tell his own wife, anyway?"

"Your father isn't keeping secrets from me, Sarah." She stopped pulling and stared at me. "He doesn't want to humiliate Daniel. Whatever you may think of him, he is a human being, and there are things – hard things – you don't tell someone in front of others. That stroll isn't to protect my ears or your father's secrets. It's to protect Daniels manhood."

Theresa, the high school friend who'd called and gossiped with me the day before, would have sniggered at the word "manhood," but my mother and I understood what she'd meant. Gloria, back in Lexington, would have said "his ego," but neither of us in the garden was familiar with that word yet. It was an occasion to understand one another with the vocabulary that dwelled between us. I pulled my thumb out of my mouth, and smiled at her. She smiled back.

Then Tommy came tromping back with the trowel in his hand. Why must men always interrupt us when we're in the middle of something important? "What do y'all reckon they're talkin' about out there?" he called on the approach.

Momma returned her attention back to the thistles with the smile still on her lips. "Mah baby girl" she whispered. I batted at her shoulder with the right-hand glove I was holding in my left hand. She leaned away too late, and giggled like a mischievous twelve-year-old.

Both men returned winded, and ready to sit for a while with a pitcher of iced tea and lemonade. Momma, Tommy and I enjoyed the feeling of cold wet glasses in our red hands. Everyone was quiet and disinterested in talk. Dinner was only an hour away.

Showers were taken. Momma and I got the best of the hot water, and poor Tommy had to dance last in the cold remains. The trade off was that Momma and I, being first to get cleaned, were the first to put our hands to work at dinner: freshly dug vegetables from the garden mixed into the beef stew we'd had the night before with bread heated up in the oven just before serving. Seats at the dinner table were filled, and prayers of gratitude were recited.

We chewed in silence for a while before Daddy spoke up. "I'll be thinking on this Boulder situation overnight, and we'll all talk about it after breakfast in the morning." Nothing left for any of us to say, we returned to silent chewing.

Daniel headed off to his room right after the meal, leaving me and Tommy to clean up. Daddy seemed satisfied with that so Tommy and I didn't complain. Daddy arranged some cord wood next to the fireplace while Tommy and I helped Momma wash and dry dishes in the kitchen, but he didn't build a fire. I mentioned to Tommy that the whole thing seemed clear to me, and I didn't see that Daddy needed a whole night to think it over.

"C'mon Sarah, you know he's gotta consult his Higher Authority before he decides what to do."

"'Higher Authority'?" said Momma, standing right next to us. "Why Tommy, you do tread the line between flattery and blasphemy, but I'll say thank ya' anyway." Then she pinched his shoulder, and gave me a wink. We just stared, and she laughed like she had in the garden. I took too long trying to decide between being amazed at her own near blasphemy, annoyed at how amused she was when I was irritated at her husband's delay or to just give in to the urge to laugh with her. By the time I thought of something to say, the moment was gone. Just as well, I suppose.

Sleep didn't come easily that night, and when the sun hit the morning seemed to have come too soon.

We all helped to clear the table after breakfast (along with fried eggs and potatoes, Momma served toast with a kind of apricot marmalade I'd never tasted before. It was delicious, despite my anxiety and sleepiness,) but Momma wouldn't let us do any of the wiping and washing up. She ordered us to sit by the fireplace so Daddy could have a word with us.

Daddy shot Daniel a few warning glances while he said, that he would allow him to try to move The Boulder to the top of The Hill. "My patience with all of this is stretched near to breaking," he said, "but it hasn't broken yet." There were additional stipulations. None of the Hanovers would help him, or even advise him. Of course, as our guest, he would continue to receive room and board. If he hurt himself, we'd do our best to patch him up or – if we couldn't – get him to someone who could. These were basic civilities, and they would remain. But God alone was to aid Daniel in the actual movement of The Boulder ("if He sees fit to do so.") Daniel maintained eye contact with my father, and nodded solemnly as he went.

Turning to me and Tommy he added that, however any of us may feel about Daniel's progress or lack of it – "because," he turned briefly back to Daniel "I honestly don't think you know what you're getting yourself into, Daniel," – there would be "no cajolin', mockin' or any other sort of nonsense to discourage his progress." He looked at us hard; eyebrow-ridge a single deep line shadowing his eyes despite the morning sun. "This is deadly serious, children. There is precedence on this. Do not mock this young man, or anyone for that matter, as he tries to act in the service of The Almighty. I know Sarah; you see things otherwise. Believe what you will, and leave it to God show us who's right.

"I'm not happy at how things have gotten," he continued looking among the three of us, "and I won't put up with much more. You're hangin' by the threads of my faith and hospitality, here, Daniel."

Momma cleared her throat as she tossed a damp hand towel over the edge of the sink; the kitchen was spotless. Daddy looked over at her, and shook his head to himself. "Right. I think you all understand well enough." He rubbed the back of his neck. "My belly is full, and my legs need a stretch. Anyone want to come with me for a little walk in the woods?"

"As the kitchen is clean and you're done talkin', I'd love a stroll with you." Momma seemed to annunciate the words like a stage actor; spoken too loud for the small room, but there seemed to be real feeling in them.

"Well, I think I'd rather stretch out on the porch and catch some fresh air," said Tommy.

"I'm too tired to walk. I'll probably just sit with Tommy for a spell." I said.

"I must my work tings getting," said Daniel stiffly.

Chapter 11

So Tommy and I sat and waited. Eventually Daniel began carrying and dragging his equipment out to the boulder, and we sat and watched him. We watched his display of ineptitude, and neither guided nor scoffed. And, as we sat and watched and waited, we began to understand Daniel's plan for The Boulder:

He was going to demolish it by hand, and drag the remains to the top of The Hill with rope and canvas tarp. He was going to get it up there bit by bit; piece by piece. And he was going to make the pieces with hammer and chisel. I wanted to cry foul, but I worried that Daddy would see it as interfering against his word. Our family honor was at stake, and I knew better than to trespass over those boundaries. Radish red, I held on. Just you wait, Daniel, 'till my father comes home!

✦ ✦ ✦

But Daddy already knew. He had already approved. Our Boulder. *My* Boulder.

His hands were red, and not just on the palms. His fingers trembled until a few hours after dinner. The following morning he was so stiff he could barely move, and staring at The Boulder – largely unchanged – could not have been much encouragement.

I pitied him from the part of me that pities any suffering animal, but I knew better than to let it show. I didn't want to risk encouraging him, and if my pretended indifference made me seem ugly and unkind I figured that it would most likely help him loose interest.

After breakfast Momma presented Daniel with a jar of oil with dark red silt resting at the bottom. She shook it furiously until there was an angry cloud turning slowly inside. "It's an old remedy for knotted muscles from a branch of my family calling from the middle of Louisiana to the eastern corner of Texas. Make sure it's well mixed up like it is now. Use a rag to wipe it on," she held a clean rag in her free hand. "Not too thick, mind. Those are crazy hot peppers ground up in there, and they'll burn like the devil's grip!"

Tommy wouldn't even look at the jar. I'd never used the mixture, but he knew it far better than anyone would have wished. He wasn't even in high school yet when it happened.

There was a cave-in in one of the mine shafts, and every man available showed up to help. Daddy refused to come home for three days straight. He lugged stones, new and spare drill bits; any kind of work he could do to help in the rescue he did. Of course no one would let him go in for the buried miners. Daddy was no spring chicken, and everyone knew that he would be more help leading and lending a hand outside than getting in the way of younger more able-bodied men in the crippled tunnels. When he slept he slept on a blanket on the floor of his office. When all possible survivors were recovered and there was no hope for the rest Daddy was willing to let Momma take him home.

She was the only person in or out of town who wasn't impressed by the old man. She only fretted that he'd better not try to be some kind of hero. "Jesus may forgive him if he goes and gets himself killed," I heard her grumbling to a friend on the phone the second night Daddy was out, "but I won't! It'll take a real good apology up in heaven, and I can't come rushin' after him for it. I've still got babies to care for." Never mind that Tommy and I were both teenagers, and Daddy had promised several times not to try to go into the shaft.

Momma knew that Daddy would be stiff once he got home, so she ground up the sharpest peppers she could find and engineered her Louisiana-Texas-connection-concoction sore-muscle-oil. Then she left us at home so she could go into town, pick him up and – according to Daddy – chew him out the whole ride up to the house.

Tommy discovered the jar while she was out. A teenage boy's search for food is constant and waits for almost nothing. He was strutting around the house like Richard the Lionhearted in his private castle; showing off for his big sister, I suppose. He opened the jar, sniffed, looked at me and said "Spicy!" while wriggling his eyebrows up and down Groucho Marx style. He poured it over some diced vegetables he'd found in the refrigerator, and took a bite. He smiled at me for a count of two before spitting half chewed carrot, cucumber and tomato into the bowl. His smile turned into a grimace of pain as his eyes rounded with baby like incomprehension of what was going on in his mouth.

"Ba!" he cried, consistent with the baby theme. "Ba! BA!" he started shrieking, and began blowing spittle into his bowl and onto the table. That didn't help much, so he started clawing at his tongue with his fingertips; also to no avail. Worse, he told me much later, after a few minutes his fingertips would begin burning, especially under the nails.

Of course I was laughing too hard to do anything to aid him beyond pointing at the bread basket. At least I think it was the bread basket. I was tearing up a bit.

Tommy's tongue didn't work right for a few days; he could only eat cold foods, and could barely taste them for the first day. Momma was furious that he'd ruined the vegetables she'd prepared for a quick stew upon Daddy's return; not to mention that he'd wasted some of her muscle balm. "It's not for eating Tommy!" she'd shouted at him. I just shook my head at the things mothers say sometimes. Who in the world needed to hear that less than poor Tommy?

Daniel accepted the jar, uncertainty painted across his face. Momma pantomimed tipping the jar onto the rag and rubbing onto her own shoulder.

"For muscle!" said Momma slowly, and too loudly.

"Sharp!" said Daddy, remembering that it might be close to a similar German word.

I said nothing – playing at indifference – but Tommy had watched enough war movies to surprise us all with the best advice of all: Looking over the jar into Daniel's face, he said simply, "Achtung!"

It was hot. It was summer, so of course it was hot. Who wants lemonade in cold weather? Did man make lemonade for the summer heat, or did God give us the heat to inspire man to make ice cold lemonade? The wind held off enough to let the sun justify the crushing of lemons and the clacking of a wooden spoon in a thick glass pitcher.

Outside, Daniel soon stripped off his shirt in the stilled heat, sweating from the peppered oil as much as from solar rays. Such a handsome face and such a nice lean build he had. I wrestled with myself over taking a peek, and lost. (O.K. I didn't fight *that* hard.) I looked out the window, and was genuinely disappointed by the view. He was thin; almost bony. There have been boys with skinny bodies I've liked, but where Daniel's skin wasn't irritated red by peppers, he was pasty; destined to burn. Do all lawyers look like that under their shirts and ties?

It had taken us just over an hour to wish Daddy a pleasant walk in the woods, agree with one another to make lemonade, gather the necessary materials and equipment and to actually make the blessed drink. Daniel must've been swinging away for about 45 minutes to an hour by this time, and he'd already worked up a sweat enough to justify uncovering his blotchy torso.

I turned away from the window, and sipped at my glass. Momma was watching me with a full-face smile that rounded her cheeks to shiny little ping pong balls.

"What?" I asked, hoping she wouldn't answer.

She didn't answer. Instead she moseyed (there's no other word for it. She was one of the last few women in the world who could mosey) over to the window where I had observed Daniel. "How's he doin' out there?" This time *I* didn't bother answering.

She sipped and stared out the window, and time slowed almost to a stop for me as I watched her watching her corner of the world. Momma didn't smoke (though there were stories of her trying a cigarette or two in her youth…you know…when people wrote stories on tree bark or dried leaves) but the late morning light illuminated the dust motes all around her making it look like she was folded among silent running clouds.

Women's liberation was hot on the lips of many a mouth back on campus in Lexington (including my own by the end of my freshman year,) and here I was deifying a housewife stuck in the foothills. She was, to any outside eye, a living embodiment of a woman held to a patriarchal society's "traditional woman's role." But she was my mother, and I loved her. She was still a model woman in my mind; tall and straight, serene with ice cubes clinking as she sipped at her drink and took in the view from the window. Light beamed on her face as she turned to me. There was a look of peaceful – almost holy – enlightenment on her face: her forehead was smooth, and a slight smile turned her lips. Something had dawned on her looking out the window, and she was happily going to share it with me.

She opened her mouth to speak. The distant thud of the hammer of the man outside softened, deferential to the revelation about to come. She was about to bust that housewife image, I was sure. Tommy was nowhere to be seen, whisked away so that this woman could empower her daughter without any outside interference.

Instead, she said, "You should bring some lemonade out to Daniel."

I still wonder if it would have become an official rule if I'd just done it the first time without complaining. Perhaps then it would have been possible to say it was Tommy's turn the next time Momma decided that Daniel needed a drink. But Momma very quickly became convinced that I was to be the official Hanover water-girl.

I'd laughed for a moment, hoping that Momma was only joking. But, of course, she wasn't. "Why in the world should

I bring him a glass of lemonade?"

"Because it's hot, and he'll dehydrate out there if he doesn't have something to drink from time to time."

"But, I mean why *me*? Why don't you bring it out to him? Or Tommy!" Tommy had taken his glass to his room, and was as easy a target as he would ever be.

She looked up and to the right, and pursed her lips in thought. "Mmmmmnnnno. This is for you to do."

"What?! Why?"

"I think we just covered that."

"*What*?! When?!"

"Sarah, I love you, but throwin' out question words will not get you out of this. This is a job for you to do becaaauuuuse," she held up a finger and tilted her head to the side, warning, as she drew out that word, "I have *said* that it is your job. Now fill a glass with ice and lemonade, bring it out to that boy and we can discuss it later. And that will be when I *say* it is time. Really, Sarah, have you've forgotten the ways of our house in order to make room for all the new stuff the university's been teachin' you?"

She was right. It was stupid to argue. Making a fuss gave my parents occasion to think about it, and that rarely lead to things I liked. I filled a glass as instructed, and stomped out to the boulder. Daniel heard the screen door flapping behind me and stopped hammering to watch me approach.

In my mind I saw myself thrusting the glass at him

violently enough to spill half of the sweet drink on his shoes, and felt annoyed at the day-dreamed loss of perfectly good lemonade. So when I got close enough, I directed my nose to the clouds as I carefully held the glass in his general vicinity. I felt, but did not see, his hand grasp the glass, and quickly turned to walk down the hill.

"Thank you very much." He said perfectly to my back with a school learned British accent.

I imagined his eyes were on my rear end as I went, and I cursed the downward trajectory of my course for what it made my hips do. "Should've let the stupid drink spill," I grumbled to myself.

But I knew better than to approach Daddy about this. He would back Momma up. I was going to have to bring water or lemonade twice a day to this loon. I would have to accept the humiliation. For now.

This went on for two days before I decided to talk to Tommy, and I wish that I could say that it became less humiliating over time. I wouldn't let it be less. I was furious, and meant to stay that way. I made sure to stomp as I carried Daniel's drink; never step. I would sometimes hand the glass off and keep walking, veering off into the woods nearby for a visit to my little stream and a moment of calm.

The second day of bringing him refreshments at The Boulder, was Friday. At dinner Daniel asked that someone pass him the water jug. It was closest to me. I poked at a random potato, and would not look up from it. "I think I've given him quite enough to drink today, thank you very much," I said to no one in particular.

Momma "asked" me to help her in the pantry a finger snap after I'd finished speaking. "Up to now you've been childish and petty, but that was plain rude," she whispered. It was nothing unexpected, and I knew – even then – that she was right. I felt that I couldn't help myself, and that feeling of helplessness made me even madder. But there was no time to think about that. I gave the appropriate responses of agreement one gives one's mother, and retained my anger.

None of the men at the table asked why it took two grown women to bring a small package of salt to refill a half-full salt shaker smack in the middle of dinner. I poured the grains carefully into the shaker.

As I poured I planned.

I knew Tommy would refuse to help at first. He was always one to say "No," first, and think about it later. He'd been like that even before trying to use muscle balm for salad dressing. I had to approach him in a roundabout way; offer him some food for thought.

Saturday morning, the morning after I helped Momma top off the salt shaker, I didn't ask Tommy to join me at the over-the-road tree, but I told him I was going for another walk in the woods. "I'll be by the over-the-road tree in about an hour and a half if you want to find me."

He looked up from his book. The cover showed a generically handsome black-haired man with his head in a bubble. He was pointing a bowling pin shaped (or was it more like a zeppelin?) laser gun thing at a swamp monster or an alien or some such nonsense. Tommy liked that trash, but it didn't seem to make him dumb or dreamy. "'Kay," he said, "See ya later."

I dropped Daniel's glass off, like a precision bomber; slowing just enough to deliver the ordinance before banking left. Daniel's voice intoned, "Thank you very much," softly from behind as I headed to my running waters.

The way down got steep fast, but I enjoyed the tall silent protection of tulip trees, American beeches, white basswoods and sweet buckeyes. The red oaks, white oaks and sugar maples also attended as the descending angle of my passage transformed me into another sort of animal: back arched, hips pushed forwards, calves drawn behind me with each step. Rather than actually walking, I simply allowed one foot to hang back while the other braced against the impact of the ground. My arcing body plummeted 6 to 15 inches down with each step.

I went slowly, but any steeper and one might debate between a high speed controlled sliding-fall or climbing down ladder style. The controlled fall is extremely dangerous among so many trees, but it's less strain on the muscles (assuming one doesn't accidentally hug a tree or misstep too badly.) The ladder style is exhausting, and it makes one look and feel stupid. This is because it isn't a vertical surface, so it feels a bit like crawling like a baby. Backwards. And you're more than 20 years old. Plus, you aren't crawling on a simple rug or an open floor. The mulch you're dragging yourself through is thick with loose earth, damp shreds of fallen leaves from the previous Fall, bits of peeled bark, twigs and sticks of infinitely various sizes, shapes and pointiness. Also, your odds are good that you will come across the bones and/or droppings of some animal or park ranger. Just kidding about the park ranger.

A controlled fall was necessary just before reaching the stream, and a final small jump to actually reach the stony bank.

I dallied and stretched and meditated by and over the water in much the same way I had less than a week before. And I prayed. God didn't talk to me in any way that I could sense, and I wasn't waiting for a heavenly light to penetrate the forest canopy or a booming voice to advise, admonish or promise anything. I don't pray like that.

When I was nine, I knew a girl in our church named Alice Smith. She was a sweet little girl, and an on-again-off-again best friend, as girls often oscillate between swearing lifetime allegiance, hatefully excluding one another and becoming best friends forever…again.

The beginning of one of our off-again periods was marked by a day in Sunday school when Alice told our teacher, whose name I forgot long ago, that she'd prayed the night before, and could hear Jesus talking back to her. The teacher, who was an energetic girl herself, got excited and asked what The Lord had told her. Alice said that He had said "Rest now, little lamb," and the teacher went into a flurry. Suzanne Taylor became Alice's new best friend (for the third time that school year) by saying that Jesus had said the same thing to her the previous night too, offering, we all thought, legitimacy and support to Alice's claim. The class got too whipped up then to see that our teacher had become a bit less impressed, and finally switched to trying to shout us down into orderly quiet.

Whatever our teacher thought, my classmates and I believed Alice. I excused myself to the toilet first chance I got and wept, bitterly confused. Why, I asked myself, would God talk to Alice and not me?

I didn't begrudge Alice getting His personal attention (She hadn't told me yet that she hated me again in order to make room for Suzanne. For some reason, 9 year old girls can only be a trio of friends when there is an offensive boy around. Otherwise, only two can be best friends, and the third must be cast out. We had cast Suzanne out some time before this, and Suzanne and I would cast Alice out at least once before Suzanne's family would move to Chicago; breaking my heart, and cementing my friendship with Alice. Until middle school.) I just wondered why I couldn't hear Him.

I came home, and went to my room to cry all over again. My father would eventually begin to avoid me when I was crying, leaving my mother to deal with "woman stuff." But I was not quite old enough yet, so he knocked gently at my door, and waited until I welcomed him in. I told him of Alice's revelations, and that it turned out that more than half of the nine-year-olds in our church were hearing God's voice.

I remember how he smiled when I told him about

the way eight different kids erupted with their identical revelations. He smiled and hugged me. He even chuckled a little bit, cradling my little frame in his arms. He released me, stroked my hair, and told me that I just didn't pray like they did. "Everybody prays in their own way," he told me. "Everybody needs to find the way that works for them. I've known a man who heard God even when he wasn't praying, and he wasn't the happiest or luckiest. I don't hear a voice when I pray either."

"You *don't*!" I croaked, swallowing the last of my tears.

"He talks to me, and I reckon He talks to you too. But I don't hear any voices, so I don't think you need to worry about that."

"How do you know he talks to you?"

"I can't rightly explain it, Sarah. Maybe when you're older I'll tell you, but I don't think I could make you understand yet. I'm not sure it would matter if I could. What's important is that you want to hear Him, and I'm sure that you'll find your way. Just remember that you're looking for *your* way to pray. Not everyone prays in the same way. Look for the way that works for you."

Years later, in high school, I was in a biology class with Alice, and she confided to me over frog's guts that she had never heard any voice either. But by then it didn't matter to me nearly as much as it did to her.

✦ ✦ ✦

I prayed for serenity and the will to fight Tommy's inevitable hesitance. I prayed for patience so that I could hold my tongue when my little brother might be stubborn, stupid or both. I suppose, if you boiled it all down, I prayed to get my way. It's not the most mature or pious prayer I've ever made, but I've never heard of God having difficulty saying "No" when a request didn't suit Him.

I dipped my fingertips in the water again, and thought about the madness of my situation; that I was about to go ask my brother to talk a good looking lawyer out of trying to marry me.

Marry me!

I thought about marriage, a vow to keep forever.

I tried to imagine what forever means. The thing about forever is that it doesn't just take all the time in the world to pass. It takes a lot of time to think about it, even if you've pondered it before. It was time to head to the over-the-road tree before I'd really managed to grasp it. Forever had run out of time.

There was no choice but to shake my extremities, and use wet fingers to pull dry socks over wet toes. I stuffed my socked feet into my dirty old pair of Pumas and took one last sip from that perpetual stream before I tromped-almost-climbed the steep way to the appointed tree at the agreed upon time.

This time, coming up the incline with knuckles nearly dragging on the sod and grasping at saplings to aid my ascent,

I felt like some kind of primitive hunter; ducking and pulling. I was tearing, I imagined, through the flora in pursuit of my quarry.

The only hiccup in the fantasy was that my "quarry" was a date to ask my big little-brother for a favor. And there was no guarantee he'd even be there. But praying about the meet had focused my mind, and the climb got my blood pumping. Sarah the warrior queen was in hot pursuit of the elusive "favor" treasure, held fast by its possessor and guardian, Tommy.

I pulled my body up with the help of a young sugar maple, and said to myself, "Hope he's there."

He was. He was already lounging up there, watching the road. I stomped and dragged my feet a bit to be noticed. Sneaking up on him and scaring him out of the tree might have undermined what I was trying to do. The last thing I needed was him thinking of me as a sneak who could outdo him.

"Hey," he said as I stepped within ten feet the tree. I responded in kind. "Don't bounce up here, shakin' all the limbs when you come up. I got me the comfortable spot, and I don't wan't you rattlin' half the leaves off just so you can get up."

"'Kay," I said, trying to sound humble, but not suspiciously so. *The huntress moves quietly as she approaches her prey.* "Daniel still out by the boulder?"

"Was when I headed out here." I noticed that his book

was stuffed deep into his pocket, and made a rectangular bulge near his hip.

I didn't want to jump in too quickly, so I said, "Book's fallin' out," to fill the quiet. Tommy slapped at the book on his hip without looking away from the road.

"No it ain't."

What was I doing? Playing made-you-look? *Should I try hitting him twice on the shoulder for flinching?* I was a woman in my 20's, for crying out loud, not a ten year old boy. "Why do you read that trash, anyway?" Oh, that was much better. Big improvement.

Tommy looked over at me. "Why do you like lemonade so much?"

"Fair point." I couldn't believe how spectacularly I was botching this whole thing. I was definitely acting weird now. Tommy had to know that someth…

"I won't ask what's eatin' you, Sarah, seein' as how there's a man from Vienna down by our house tryin' to turn The Boulder into slag for your hand in marriage. But…well, is there somethin' you wanted, or did you just tell me that you'd be here so I'd know in case I was lookin' for a fight?"

I wanted to bluff and deny it all; accuse Tommy of thinking he was the center of the world, and act like I didn't need a thing from anybody. Sarah the huntress didn't want to play maiden in distress! What came out of my mouth was, "You've gotta help me. Get Daniel to cut out this nonsense. Please!"

The first three times he said "no" didn't faze me at all. I admit that the fourth "no" had me beginning to doubt myself. With the fifth refusal I thought I saw a glimmer of hope because he actually made an argument, rather than just flat out refusing. "It goes against the agreement, Sarah."

"No it doesn't." I'd expected this. In fact, it was the objection I was trying to work around in my mind when I came up with the simple solution. "It ain't like we're sawing the heads off the hammers or haranguin' him or cementing pieces back onto The Boulder in the middle of the night." These weren't the only ideas I'd considered and rejected, but they were my favorites; the one's I'd still have done if they wouldn't so obviously point to me. "We'd be openly asking him to see reason, and stop this business. It ain't the same thing, and the difference matters."

"Come on! That's *worse* than interferin'."

"No it isn't! You won't lay a finger on him or his hammers. You wont do anything to make it hard for him to do what he wants. The choice will still be his, and you won't be making it harder. You'll just be asking him to… reconsider."

"Psh." He shook his head down at the road, and then looked back at me. "You've got it all figured out, don'cha? So go ahead. I don't see why *I* should do it."

"Have you seen the way he looks at me when I bring

him his drink?" I closed my eyes, frowned and pretended to shudder. "You don't know what it feels like. I don't like it Tommy." I told myself that I was only bending things a bit; protecting myself and persuading my brother.

"Hooee. You really have got it all figured out, doncha'," he said a second time. "Got your arguments all lined up."

"Yeah, I figure…"

"Too bad!" he crowed. "I still ain't doin' it!"

That fake out threw me off balance a bit. That was number six by my count, and I was just about ready to blubber. "Oh Tommy, you've gotta. You've just gotta…" I said, gearing up for a real award winning tear jerker performance.

But then he said, "You're just gonna harp on me 'till I give in outta sheer weariness." That complaint, number seven, was the sign I was looking for; the offer to surrender without actually surrendering yet. It would've been easy to tip him then with a hearty "'Till the end of your days Thomas Jefferson!" or even a cutesy "Well, that was kinda' the plan." He would've laughed then and agreed to help, but the victory would have been short lived.

Like I've said, Tommy says "no" first, and thinks about it second. After surrendering, he'd think about it. He'd think about how he doesn't much like being rolled over like a rotten log. Who does? He'd think about how he didn't really want to face the fires of our parents' disapproval just because he was too weak to outlast his sister. He'd think about these things, and remember that his gut had said "no" from the start. Then he'd decide to change his mind, and *that* decision would be final; deaf to reason, and interested in nothing but endurance.

But in this moment of his willingness to give in I held my tongue. Let him think about it while he's open; not feeling like he'd simply lost a fight.

I looked down at my fingers, and kept a serious face. The stream hadn't done much to clean them or else the trees I'd grabbed on the way back up had left their mark. The fingertips were smudged with soot, and the nails – shortened before heading out for the bus home – were uneven with bite marks along the edges. Thin arcs of grit were semi-visible underneath. They seemed so different from the well scrubbed fingers in my classes. I imagined my toes were somehow different from the manicured toes in the Patterson Hall showers; perhaps longer than the digits of the other girls. Permanently dirtier. I slid my dirty left thumb nail under my dirty right pointer, and thought of my roommate Gloria's pink fingernail polish.

Then I remembered that I was sitting in a tree.

Tommy was watching me with intense concentration and a slight frown. Silently, I slid and eased my way out of the tree, not bouncing his bough one bit. "Just think about it Tommy. Okay?" Like there was ever a chance he might *not* think about it. I walked away without looking back once, and, when I was sure he would stay behind to read his book, split into a wicked smile.

He'll think about it. He'll think about how he was ready to give in. In the end he'll want to give in, and agreeing to help me will be his own free decision.

He said nothing at lunch (thick slices of salami, thicker slices of heavy doughy bread, ketchup, mustard, relish, pickles, raw onions rings, tomato slices and mayonnaise laid out so everyone could build his own sandwich! Drinks included Lemon-iced-tea, straight lemonade, ice water and beer "for the boys.") Daniel shocked us all as he chugged a tall frosted mug of beer in no time flat. He slammed the empty vessel onto the table with an open smile, lamp-lit eyes and an "Ahhhh!" that no one could resist laughing at.

But Tommy was decided by dinner time. He mumbled his agreement while we were setting the table. I thanked him earnestly. Manipulations forgotten, I meant it.

Chapter 14

Tommy put off approaching Daniel for another two days. After the first day it occurred to me that, to Tommy's mind, The Boulder had become Daniel's, even as he slowly destroyed it. It was only an idea I had, but the thought left me sleepless with rage. That boulder was ours, not his. We'd survived its fall, not him. It was our magic, and in my heart of hearts it was mine most of all. If Daniel would move the boulder or even demolish it on account of what I said, that was one thing. That was *my* will being carried out on *my* piece of the eternal. But that he would sneak-thief it from our possession was an outrage. A violation!

I thrashed around in my bed until I couldn't even pretend to have a hope of sleep. I tip toed over to Tommy's room. I was so blindingly mad that it didn't occur to me to knock. I walked to his bed and shook him. As he began to make sounds of wakefulness I began to say his name in what could technically be called a whisper, but was almost a shriek.

Tommy finally sat up, and looked at me like I was the walking dead. I didn't wait for him to collect his thoughts.

"Why haven't you talked to him about The Boulder!?" I said with such mindless fervor that it sounded more like *Wha havencha tawlked ta heem 'bout tha boulder!?!*

"Whmmehhh?" was the best Tommy could come up with for a reply. It was not good enough. Naturally, I began punching him all over his torso and arms as fast and hard as I could. I'd be lying if I said that my goal was to get him more awake, but it was helpful in that way too. He got a hold of my wrists before I could get worked up enough to start actually slapping him in the face, and said "Sarah? What d'you think yer doin'?"

I wanted to scream, and I wanted to pound twin holes into the wall with my bare hands. But I didn't want to wake anyone else up. I thought my head would split in two. "Why?" I whisper-yelled. *Wha!*

"Whah what?" Tommy said. This was also an unacceptable reply. "Woah! Hey! Wait! I'm gonna break both'a your arms if you don't settle down, and it may even be by accident. What are you askin' me?"

I breathed. "Why haven't you talked to Daniel yet?" I said in a voice that was shaky; the steadiest I could manage. I watched his face closely as he considered and dismissed, it seemed to me, the idea pretending not to know what I was talking about, then the idea of taking an insulted defensive stance and, finally, taking a settled look as he let go of my wrists. Moonlight from the widow disappeared from his face as he looked down to his lap.

"I'll talk to him tomorrow afternoon." His voice came from the darkness between his hanging curtains of hair, and before I could spit my expectations at him he said, "Afternoon Sarah. Don't argue with me. I've said it, and by my name I'll do it." I knew the promise was good because he sounded like Daddy on the rare times he ever swore to anything.

After lunch ended, the next day, Tommy cleared the table and washed up. Daniel had only been allowed to put his plate and glass in the sink, and had then gone out to The Boulder to begin his second shift at the sledge that day. When everything was straightened up Tommy looked directly at me. "I'll be right back. I'm going to go see how Daniel's doing." Daddy didn't even look up from his book, and Momma only smiled and nodded.

Tommy turned and walked out the door, fixing to make our visitor clear on just one or two things.

I went to the door to see what would come. I looked past Tommy to the moving image of Daniel and his hammer at the boulder. He had just tossed his shirt onto the ground, and was bracing the hammer in his hands as he prepared to take his first new swing.

I felt a weakness in my thighs. His body still wasn't beautiful. He was beginning to get some muscle tone, but nothing to drool over. In that moment, though, *he* was beautiful; his hair wild, chest heaving and that mallet heavy and still in his long fingers. I wanted to be that shaft in his hands. I wanted to be that rock under his glare. I wanted to be the air going through his mouth and the sun bouncing off his burning shoulders. I wanted to be burning in his skin. I wanted to bite him with my whole mouth. I wanted to eat him alive!

I braced myself on the door post in a way that looked like I was trying to block out the afternoon sun. *What the heck is this?!* It hit me so quickly, and totally uninvited. I wanted to fall completely into what I was seeing; to feel and smell and taste all of it. In my mind I fought the ambush flood. I closed my eyes, and took a deep breath. When I opened my eyes, I saw that Tommy had nearly reached him.

Daniel turned from his work to Tommy, approaching from downhill. His glance seemed to jump to me in the doorway and back to Tommy; adding it up. But at that distance it was just as likely my imagination as not. Deep low inside I suddenly wanted to run out there and stop Tommy, but I needed to clear my head. What was going on?

So, I was attracted to him. I was attracted to a madman; a man who thought I was going to marry him after he finished pounding and dragging a boulder up a hill. As an idea it sounded quirky and sweet. When a real person is there trying to do it, though, that person seems more sad and unnerving than anything else.

But my reaction to sun drenched Daniel was far from

sad or sweet. From the doorway there was something more to what I'd seen; something that pushed my insides all around. But I didn't want to think in that direction. That was the wrong way. This was about my life being committed based on someone's ridiculous whim.

Trying to regain my focus, I thought of how Daddy always said that God looks out for crazy people and that we ought to always take our lead from Him. I needed to remember that Daniel clearly fit into that category. He may have stirred something physical in me, but he was still a poor crazy fool; lost and lonely enough to be hearing voices, and thinking God was playing matchmaker. That must've been the reason why I wanted to stop Tommy; out of pity for Daniel. That wasn't such a bad thing.

I punched the screen door open, and chased after Tommy. I knew that I had steered him at Daniel, and I wanted to make sure that he wasn't too rough on him. It would be cruel to completely unhinge him, like kicking the cane out from under an old man.

"Of course," Daniel was saying as I caught up to them, "I am happy to be speaking vit you Tommy. Vat is the problem?"

"I want you to…"

"Easy Tommy." I said; breathing a little deeper than usual from the sprint, but not much. Tommy turned to look at me like I was the craziest of the three people standing there under the sun. I guess that's understandable. "Tell him, but don't be too hard on him." I explained.

"How please?" said Daniel weakly. "Eh, I mean to say… vat is happening?"

"You wanna tell him after all?" Tommy offered. He may have gotten himself revved up to tell Daniel off for his little big-sister, but he looked happy to hand it off to me in a pinch.

"Naw. I think…" I started, feeling pity well up inside as Daniel watched us go back and forth without a clue. "Please Tommy. I'm sorry to interrupt. Go ahead." *I'll have to thank Tommy for this later* I thought *but it's best I shut up, and let him get on with it already.*

"Oookaaay." Tommy said, getting his bearings again. "It's like this, Daniel: Ya'…you. You've got to stop this." He opened his left palm toward the sledgehammer and The Boulder. Daniel looked over at it, but said nothing. "It's over. You must end it. Now."

Eyes still glued to The Boulder, Daniel let out a breath, and I thought for a second that he was already giving up; that it could maybe be that easy. Then he spoke. "I suppose zat I am being optimistik to be hoping dat Sarah is decided to marry me with no boulder moving?"

Tommy spat, and took a breath of his own. "No, Daniel. No. You've gotta stop this because you're embarrasin' yourself here."

"I am feeling fine Tommy."

I bit my lip hard.

"Well we ain't feelin' fine." My ears registered Tommy's temper climbing, but I couldn't feel any anger over this. This wasn't frustrating for me any more. It was too sad to make me angry. "We want you to stop!"

"Who is 'Vee'?"

"What?!"

"You say 'Vee vant you to stop.' Has your fahter asked you to speak for him here? Is 'Vee' the whole Hanoffer family? Your fahtter? Your mutter?"

Tommy hesitated, but finally chose. "No." The truth always did come easiest for him.

Daniel finally looked up from the boulder for the first time and looked at Tommy. "Den 'Vee' is you and…" he turned his eyes on me, and I was caught in the brushfire again. I burned. I blushed. I could not run. I could only look down at my bare feet and clench my teeth to keep my tongue in my mouth. "…Sarah," he said.

His voice shook a little as he said it. Just a little. "Sarah" became "Sahara," and Sahara I was. I was just as desperate for the rain, and just as deadly. I was a woman and a desert at once in the lush wilds of Kentucky.

Hidden by my hair, tears popped from eyes clenched shut with no memory of closing. *Nnngh! What is this?! I thought I'd managed to control this!* No sooner did I think the word "control," and I heard someone somewhere laughing.

"That's right Daniel." Tommy replied. "Sarah and I want you to cut this whole thing out."

"I am sorry Tommy, but you know already dat I cannot."

"I don't know that at all. I only know that you say that God told you that somethin' was gonna be."

"Yes, and…"

"I'm not finished. So you heard a voice. How do you know it was Him?"

Daniel half chuckled. "How did Ah-brah-hahm know? Or Moses?"

"So now you think you're like Moses? Those are some mighty big shoes you're steppin' into my friend."

"I am not certain that I understand the second thing you haf said, but, no, I do not say that I am equal of Moses. I do say that I understand some things from his story."

I thought to myself that Tommy was ready for this swim. Daddy hadn't forced the Bible or God down our throats, but they were household subjects. They were members of the family, and Tommy knows his kin. "And just what do you think you've learned?" Tommy was fond of saying that every time the Bible could be used to point in one direction it could be countered by something else in that same Good Book. The Bible, he used to say, always points both ways.

"I learned that when you meet Gott, there is no questioning, Tommy. You know it is Him. When pharaohs question it, they fall under His hand. This is beyond question for me. I know. You may believe what you like, but it will not change my…my…" As Daniel struggled for his word, Tommy stepped in.

"Haw! Moses didn't know any such thing! When he heard God, he asked who was there. If he knew it was God then why would he ask.?"

"For the power of His name."

"What do you mean by that?"

"In the times of Moses, it was thought that when a man knew the name of a god he had a kind of power. It was a power to be able to call this god for help. Moses was clear that he was in a holy place with someone beyond man."

"I don't remember reading any such thing."

"But it is true. This is why Gott answers only 'I am that I am.' He will not give Moses that power. Gott performs his *wunder*…" I picked the word "wonder" from the sound of the word, "…as He chooses. Moses may not choose for Him."

"Can't choose for Him? What about what you *can* choose? Don't you believe that you can choose to stop doing this crazy thing?" This was one of Tommy's favorite angles. It wouldn't matter which track Daniel chose. Tommy could argue both Fatalism and Free Will until anyone ran away screaming. I knew the running and screaming part from personal experience. But in five short words, Daniel demolished Tommy's trap.

"Choose? I choose to obey Gott."

That answer and the resulting silence finally drew my gaze up from my feet. Daniel had my brother pinned with his eyes, same as his answer had done. Without ever having discussed it with Tommy I knew that if he'd try to tell Daniel to go against God, he would not have been able to stomach sleeping under our father's roof. His only choice was to back track.

"Well, *I* don't know that you heard God. Let me tell you what I *do* know. I know that your choice is makin' a fool outta you, and you're draggin' my sister down with you!"

Daniel made a look of puzzlement, but I didn't trust it.

"Vaht do you mean?"

"People are laughin' at you Daniel!" Tommy said, his voice finally starting to rise. He put his hand up to stop Daniel's reply. "I know that may not matter much to you. You're ready to bear any scorn. Don't worry 'bout what that means. I understand that it don't matter to you that they're laughin' at you. You don't know them, and you believe you're following God, so it don't matter to you. But the men drinkin' and laughin in town are laughin' at Sarah too, and these are the folks we grew up with. I don't know what kinda village you grew up in, but you gotta trust me that it's hard to have people you've known and cared for your whole life laughin' at you. That's a pain that you are makin' Sarah carry…you and your choice - what you're choosin' to believe – is makin' a fool of her to her own friends and neighbors."

Daniel looked away, over the boulder and up the hill.

"Now, I'm willin' to believe that you truly like and care about Sarah," Tommy pressed. "Embarrassing her in front of her community ain't a good way to treat someone you care about. And it certainly ain't gonna help you to win her hand in marriage neither."

We stood in silence for a time, the three of us in a triangle. Daniel had heard what Tommy had said, no mistake. He stood there as silent and still as any man I've ever seen, and Tommy stood with an open stance; waiting for the next round. All that sexual flushing had completely passed from my body. Tommy's words had run ice water over me, and I stung with the realization of just how humiliating all this was for us. For me.

I spent that pause thinking about the power of those words. Daddy used to talk to us about the power of words; about how things – good things or bad things – could be "spoken into existence." I'd always thought about magic words like "*Alakazam*" and imagined speaking bunny rabbits into existence. During my year in college I came to see it as a description of how we can make people feel something by how we treat them. But standing there I was rethinking it all.

I hadn't thought for a moment about the chance that anyone was laughing at me. It was a dimension I hadn't even considered. But with Tommy's words the awful reality of it appeared and chilled my heart.

In my momentary imaginings, Tommy hadn't just spoken my feelings into existence; his words had populated the bars. Before he'd spoken, my old high school hang outs were empty, and now they were filled with distant cousins, old teachers, old friends and old enemies. And they were laughing at me. *Alakazam!* I was…

"**JUMP!**" Daniel had whipped around and shouted it right at me, and it was so loud and quick and staccato that the echoes could be heard for a long time after…or at least I'm told it could. I was busy for those first few seconds trying my best not to fall over dead from shock. *Alakazam!* Again!

Tommy jumped between us, though Daniel hadn't actually taken a step towards me. His, Tommy's, fists were clenched, and I was sure that Daniel was going to get a closed fist second lesson about how the Hanover children were taught to follow through when they strike.

By the time my heart quieted down enough for me to hear anything, I heard Tommy saying something along the lines of "…SWEAR I WILL! WHAT KINDA FOOL BUSINEES ARE YA' TRYIN' TO PULL!?!? I OUGHTTA…" And as loud and furious as Tommy was shouting it still wasn't as loud as Daniel's shout had been. What had come from Daniels mouth was…just unbelievable.

Daniel's reply, though, was so quiet by comparison that it was practically a mumble.

"WHAT?!" shouted Tommy.

Daniel just stood there, silent and still like he'd been before his great yawp, while Tommy took a couple of breaths to calm down. "What?" he asked again, not quiet but not hysterical. Frankly, I was grateful that Tommy's blood was up.

"I told Sarah to jump, and she jumped." I looked around and found that – sure enough – I was at least a foot back from where I'd been standing before. Suddenly I could remember having been about three feet or so in the air for a moment there too. "Will you laugh at her tonight at supper?" Daniel said quietly, but with a slight shake to his voice.

"She wasn't doin' what you told her to do! She woulda' done that even if you'd said 'soup'!" Tommy was still kind of shouting, but I could hear the screen door creaking a ways behind me at the house. I knew that at least my father was there, but no one was coming up the hill to investigate the shouting. Yet.

I had the strangely random thought that I didn't want these men talking about me like I wasn't there or else was too dumb to understand. But I had to remember that I'd asked Tommy to speak for me.

"Yes. This is true," Daniel replied to Tommy, "but 'Jump' *is* the command I chose to give, and that *was* the way I had chosen to give it. Will you laugh at Sarah for jumping?"

"'Course not. She had no…" Tommy scrunched up his face, seeing clearly where he'd been lead.

"*Keine Wahl. Ja.* No choice. I have known people in Vienna who would laugh, even knowing this. But even they would not really be…mocking?" We nodded. There was no point in not nodding. "Yes? Mocking? Yes. They would not really be mocking her. Their laughter would be mocking me, because I have given the command. I made something strange. Not Sarah." Tommy was looking at his feet, and I had to fight not to do the same. "Perhaps tonight we will all laugh at what I have now made Sarah to do. We will laugh at me. That would be very fine. But when people laugh at what I do here," He pointed at the boulder without looking at it, "they do not laugh at me or Sarah; even if they do not know it. They laugh at The One who commanded it to be so, and He has never been One to be mocked."

Daddy was back there in the doorway, and he wasn't laughing. But I could hear him chuckle in my mind anyway.

Chapter 15

Tommy and I made our way back to the house. We didn't have to face Daddy right away. He was looking up past us at Daniel, and he and Momma headed up the hill just as we got to the porch. Tommy and I turned around, and saw that Daniel was on the ground. He shook his head, and tried to wave off Momma while Daddy crouched down beside him to see if he was okay.

A four letter word was the best comment Tommy could muster.

"His English got better just then, did you notice?"

"No." It seemed, at the moment, that Tommy's eloquence for the day had been spent on Daniel. Fruitlessly.

"It was better. I'm sure of it."

"What d'you reckon it means? Y'think he's a German spy, and he slipped up or somethin'?" It would take Tommy a few more years before he'd look at a proper map of Europe, and see which country actually holds Vienna.

"Pshhh! Yeah, Tommy. The back hills of Kentucky are a real hot spot for international espionage."

"Maybe they don't know *what's* in Kentucky. Or," he started shaking his head. "Nah."

"What?"

"Just thinkin' stupid. I was thinkin'…well, y'know… maybe it's something to do with Pop."

Daniel lost the rest of that day's work. Momma and Daddy wouldn't listen to his insistence that he was well enough. "Dehydration sneaks up on you," Daddy explained. "One minute you're fine, and then the next thing you know you're too weak to drag yourself out of the latrine and open your canteen."

"That sounds like something with a story behind it," I declared.

Daddy glanced an icicle my way. "I think you and your brother are the ones who're gonna need to tell a story or two, Sarah." Indeed we did. Tommy told his own abbreviated version of our talk with Daniel, and Daniel offered no corrections. "You violated my word," he said in a soft tone that made me wish he was screaming. "In my own house."

And it was my turn to go to work with the defense. Daddy's mouth was a flat line. His eyebrows crinkled downwards and towards each other, and, where they met, the wrinkles spelled out the words "not buying it."

But Daniel began to smile as he listened. "She is right,"

he said before Daddy could shake his head for a third time. "They did not inter...eh…interfere." I had used the word about five times in my backpedaling defense. "They asked me to stop. Tommy said his not belief I hear from Gott, and that I am hurting Sarah with my…what I do. But I felt no Disrepekt from them. There was no trick. It was fair." When he pronounced the last word, it sounded like *fey-ah*, but everyone understood. The whole wanting to eat him up thing was passed, but right then I did want to give him a big fat smooch.

My father looked around the room, and ended with my mother. She raised her eyebrows, and her shoulders went the same way. He matched her gesture, and began to get up to leave the room without another word.

"Waitaminute Daddy!" I called out, meaning to take a bossy tone, but the voice I heard from my mouth was eager and hopeful; almost breathless. "What was that about latrines and canteens and dehydration?" Tommy, to my right, made the first sighing chuckle I'd ever heard; a sigh with a few extra exhalations. I made eye contact from Daddy's straight face to Momma's open curiosity to Daniel's smile left over from earlier to Tommy's smiling face back to Daddy with a smile I'd grown on the way round.

"What, you think army training is a bunch of guys layin' around in swimming pools drinkin' daiquiris?"

✦ ✦ ✦

And that was all he'd offer before leaving the room. Only now, remembering that summer, do I realize that this was the first time he'd mentioned his time in the army since Daniel's arrival. The Hanover Stonewall had begun to crumble, and none of us had noticed.

Chapter 16

Nobody likes the word "beg." It's an ugly word with an ugly meaning. It even sounds ugly, like the mewling of a sick goat with a grunt at the end. When I was in seventh grade I heard a sermon about submission, but to me it was all about different people begging; the woman who threw herself at Jesus' feet that he would heal her son, the lame man who was healed when he begged Peter and John for money and even the whole Hebrew people on their hands and knees for hundreds of years in Egyptian bondage, begging for help from On High.

The pastor used these and other examples to illustrate the different meanings, uses and results of begging. Sure, begging is essentially asking for something, but it can also be used to show regret or suffering. It could be meant to indicate loyalty or fealty when knees are put to the ground. It can be a way of acknowledging the power of one over oneself. Catholics, the pastor told us, get on their knees a few times a week! He went on about questions of sincerity when you're forced by an authority…blah, blah, blah. He rolled into the Book of

Esther, and lost me there.

All I could think of was hands and knees, hands and knees, hands and knees; on the dusty ground, like a dog, muddy from sweat and tears. Some pastors can be a bit repetitive. Our pastor was one such speaker. When I left the church, I could close my eyes and see scene after invented scene of humiliated begging.

The next day, I lost half a point on my Monday morning vocabulary review quiz. I defined "begin," (an easy throw-away word teachers put in to let you build up your score!) as "What you do on your hands and knees." Mr. Stosser, the English teacher, put a red "X" next to the answer, then wrote "+¼ pt. for color, +¼ pt. for philosophy."

It disgusted me to do it, but, since Daniel wouldn't choose to stop, I was going to have to beg my father to put an end to this nonsense.

Chapter 17

The morning after Daniel's "dehydration" scare I was set back to work as the Official Austrian's Water Bearer. It was too much. I tried pinching my tongue between my teeth to keep from swallowing it, and nearly bit it off in the bargain.

"Thank you very much," said Daniel's open lips before they were moistened by the water I'd provided. I turned away in a hurry.

A short ways before I reached the house my tongue was released at the sight of my father just swung out the screen door. He was setting his hat on his head, and scanning the trees for a likely direction.

"Daddy!" I called out, and trotted the rest of my way down to him. "Would you like some company for your walk?"

He started a bit at the suggestion. It was an idea he'd never considered before, I guess. "Well sure, Sarah, but you'll have to slip outta' those pretty sandals and into a proper pair of walkin' shoes or boots."

I looked down at the sandals, then back up at Daddy

with a red smile, then up to where Daniel was just putting his glass down and reaching for his sledge hammer and back to Daddy again. "Okay," I said and dashed into the house.

He was smiling up at the treetops and robin's egg sky when I came back out. We said "Ready," to one another, and then nothing more until we were in the shade of our trees.

"It's nice havin' you along, Sarah," he said, looking down and to his right to make eye contact. His hat tipped and dipped like a flying saucer about to crash.

"Thanks Daddy," I returned. Then I grabbed his arm and hugged it like I was four years old again. Or twelve. Or sixteen. Or just a few weeks younger. Or a few years older. "I'm really glad I came. *Ah come teh see where you got all the bodies hid!"* I added in a low gravelly B movie voice.

He chuckled that way that marked him as my father; that marked my heart. I squeezed his arm with both of mine. "I reckon it'll do you some good," he said to the trees.

"How so?" I asked, this time with a casual tone I'd stolen from Audrey Hepburn in a movie I'd seen a few years before.

"Walkin' out and about helps clear your head. Helps to make peace with whatever ails you."

"Like some crazy man beating on a boulder to show how much he cares?" I honestly couldn't tell if it came out playful or bitter, but, either way, he looked at me seriously.

"Yeah," he said. "Like that." And he faced the path we were walking again.

"Well, you've been out under the leaves and needles

every day, Daddy. What's buggin' *you* so much? Or is Daniel what's bothering you too?"

"Naw," he smiled, and then he inhaled, putting the words together.

But I stepped in before he was ready to speak. "Is it that business with Mr. Bouliard?" I almost said "Dick."

His head dipped twice just barely out of step with his foot falls. "Yeah, Sarah. I'm out here thinkin' about things back at the plant."

"Momma told me about how Mr. Bouliard's been acting; makin' like you're…like you can't let go of things at work; like you're the one always callin' him." Daddy's eyes searched the high branches as we continued silently together. They searched the low branches. They never fell on me, and he said nothing. I asked, "Why do you let him do that Daddy?"

"It's complicated."

I looked down at the path, watching out for stray roots and loose stones. "Complicated how?" I smiled to the shady black-brown earth and leaves laid before and beneath me. "I mean it *must be* pretty complicated if it's got you out here every morning, and putting up with Mr. Bouliard's calls nearly every day."

Exactly eight minutes and twelve seconds before that moment, the sun cast a beam among many in the direction of where Kentucky would be exactly eight minutes and twelve seconds later. The beam traveled across space and time, as we all do. It fell through our atmosphere, like so many before it, and eluded the green exhaling clutches of mountain silverbell leaves – like a bouquet fallen between the grasping hands of waving bridesmaids – and fell upon my father's face.

He squinted.

"Yup."

"Yup," I agreed. I put my hands in my pockets and nodded with frustration fueled exaggeration. My lips pressed together until they nearly turned white. I started gearing up to bob my head faster and to talk longer until he forced a change of conversation, spilled his story or sent me home. But he'd been my father all my life, and he knew me well enough. He started talking – really talking – just a moment or two after I'd begun nodding so fiercely. He must've recognized my stubborn face, whatever *that* looks like. Or maybe the swaying treetops bent in just the right way to usher us forward, conversation and all. Maybe he read encouragement in their wind moves and posture: Go ahead. Go on and tell her.

Whatever it was, his talk began with a name other than Mr. Bouliard.

"It's about Roland James. You've heard me talk about him at dinner plenty of times."

"Yeah, I remember Mr. James," but I'd never met him. Daddy would rant to Momma about Mr. James the way other men would bang on about Hank Aaron. "He's a really good digger, right?"

Daddy scrunched his eyes for a step, but managed to

keep from actually wincing. He hated when people used the word "digger" to describe his men, like they were just scratching around in a sandbox in the P. Rogers Elementary School yard. I hadn't forgotten. "Has he started making trouble? Or has he been slackin' off?"

"No!" he said with real offense in his voice. "Just the opposite!" You would think I'd just asked if Tommy was a midget or if Momma was a devil worshiper.

"The other men getting tired of him showin' them up? Mr. James making everybody look bad?"

"No Sarah, but you're getting closer to the problem. Remember a few years back when we had that collapse at the mine? That was the time Tommy ate your momma's muscle balm."

"Yeah. I think I remember." *Ba! BA BA!*

"Well you remember I was down at the mine for a few days but I never went in after the men trapped down there, on account of Momma made me promise."

I said only "Yeah."

"Roland James lead one of the three rescue parties. That party was him and some of the other colored fellas; saved five men the first time they went in. One of those five was Giacomo Pagnucci. When Giacomo came up, all he wanted to know was where Filipo, his brother, was. You know those boys left their whole family behind in Italy, and all they have is each other. They work different shifts, so Filipo wasn't workin' yet when the shaft collapsed. But Giacomo wanted to be sure that his brother hadn't started early or anything.

"Problem was that Filipo had gone in with Dale Landry's crew hoping to find his brother and any others.

"Landry's a good man, and he doesn't like taking risks with the lives of his men. So, when James wanted to search a tunnel that Landry figured was likely too dangerous in light of the collapse, Landry refused to take his men. That's where James' team found Giacomo and the other survivors of his crew.

"Landry's team came up empty, and Philipo demanded that he be allowed to switch to James' party when he saw who had rescued his blood and why. Landry and his men saved the lives of nine family men over the next two days, but Filipo stood behind Roland James wherever he went."

"Wow," I said. "How many men did Mr. James find in all?"

Daddy squinted up at the trees. "Mmm. I believe he found two other men. One of them was Jackie McCarthy. You remember he lost an arm that day." I didn't remember, but my father never forgot such things.

I couldn't stop the thought that nine is more then seven, and that Mr. Landry fared well enough in that story. But I knew that this wasn't about Mr. Landry, and that the saving of lives isn't the sort of thing Daddy would approve of keeping score on. Besides, I was still waiting for my chance to beg for my own rescue. So I went for something that Daddy might find a bit more pleasing. "Sounds like you've got a few heroes workin' down at your plant. What's wrong with that?"

"Ain't a thing wrong with that. What's wrong is what I didn't do."

"Oh come on, Daddy. You know perfectly well that you would'a had no business going down into those tunnels."

"No, Sarah. Of course not. It ain't about me goin' into tunnels. You think I don't know that I'm an old man? I'd look almost as silly as Daniel does back yonder with a hammer or a drill in my hand." It was an opening, but I let it pass. I still wanted to see where Daddy was going with all of this. "James is one of the finest workin' men I've ever known. You know that. You've heard about him enough over the last few years. When he rescued those men, and won the loyalty of those Pagnucci boys – not to mention the respect of every man and woman at the plant – I knew that my last reason for not promoting him was a lie." He sighed looking off into the steady flora, and then down at his moving shoes. "And still I didn't promote him."

"What?" That was all I could say.

It was enough. "I've seen lots of hard workers," my father continued. "It's the only sort of worker who can survive in a job like that. Too often the guys who get the promotions have been the best workers, but the best drill man isn't always the one who should lead a team of drill men."

"What do you mean?"

"Good workers ain't always good leaders. Sometimes the most talented engineers I've met – men who could get their jobs done in half the time of most others – have ruined whole projects because, as skilled as they are with the math, they were no good with the men below them. Same goes with drillers, jackhammer workers, soldiers and every other line of work I've ever touched."

"But Mr. James *is* a good leader?"

"I watched men, *white* men, follow him literally into depths filled with the dead. Yes. He is a good leader."

But, like he'd already told me, he didn't promote Roland James. For more than three years he'd sat on the knowledge that Mr. James was better than the position he held.

"And what was the lie again?" I was getting confused. I wasn't sure that this question would help any, but I figured it was worth a shot.

"I told myself for some time that the white men wouldn't follow him, and that someone was bound to get stupid. And when people get stupid in a mine…"

"…someone might not make it out of that mine, I know, but how do you figure someone's going to get stupid just because of who you make assistant shift manager?"

"Maybe someone disagrees that a black man should be allowed to tell a white man what to do or how to do his job. Maybe someone will do a bad job just to make his new boss look bad; leave a piece of equipment so that it malfunctions or even blows up."

"Would someone here really do something like that?"

"Maybe. Maybe they'd just show up at his home on his

day off or the middle of the night. Beat him up or even just scare him and his family."

"That sounds like somethin' uncle Robert and his weird friends would do."

Daddy stopped and turned away from me. His whole body stiffened. He wouldn't face me until he'd taken a deep breath. "Yeah, Sarah, that's right. He's family and he'd do something like that. I don't want one of my men doin' it. I certainly don't want it for Roland James."

He spat to his left, away from me, and we continued walking. Our mouths held, and our thoughts wandered for a few minutes. He was shaking his head a lot, and finally I had to ask, "But Daddy, if Mr. James is a good worker and a good leader, don't you think he'd be able to handle…you know… whatever they'd do?"

He chewed on it for a moment before answering. "The stuff on the job, I reckon he could handle. A mob showing up on your doorstep, I don't expect anyone could be expected to handle. Not even a man as big as Roland."

"Do you think that there's a good chance of that happenin' if you were to give Mr. James that promotion?"

"No. I reckon that sort of thing ain't too likely, especially if Roland don't go around lookin' for a fight – and we all know perfectly well that he's got more than enough sense and charm to know better – and if the people in authority handle it properly."

"Well that's you Daddy, and Mr. Bouliard."

"Now we ain't the *only* ones in authority, but that's right, Sarah, Me and Dick are the one's I was talkin' about."

"So…so *that's* why it was a lie? Promotin' Mr. James doesn't really put anyone in danger?"

"Well, there's no way to be sure, but, yeah, you've got the idea."

"Why'd you go and believe that lie for so long? How can you keep on living with it if you know it's a lie? What are you goin' on vacation like this for, with all that goin' on? Aren't you the one always quotin' Leviticus 15:somethin', 'Justice! Justice! Go get Justice!' or somethin' like that?"

Daddy laughed. He's probably the only one in our church who laughs when I butcher Scripture. Most of the preachers and all of the teachers would look at me like I'd spat on someone's baby or someone's grave. "It's *Deuteronomy 16: 20*, Sarah," he said with a chuckle still in his throat. "And, you *did* ask me why I'm out here every day. I've held off so long out of fear, plain and simple." He'd stopped walking now, and turned to face me holding his hands up in front of him with the palms up. Then he pointed out a few green boulders, mossy mountain teeth just off of our way, sticking out for us to sit for a moment or two.

We didn't talk climbing onto the boulders, but Daddy kept shaking his head and chuckling to himself. "Like one of them cheerleader chants," he was saying to himself, "Goooo Justice!"

I punched him in the shoulder, smiling as I did it. "But,

wait a minute," I said, pointing at his chest like I'd spotted a stain. "I still don't understand what Mr. Bouliard callin' all the time has to do with Mr. James and all that."

"Well, let me see how I can put it all together for you, so it'll be clear." He swung his heels against the spongy green surface of our sitting place, like a kid balanced atop a set of monkey bars. Watching him act so boyish, I remembered – or maybe I just put it together from several different memories – being a very little girl, and Daddy telling me that we're all just babies next to these hills. "I reckon it starts this spring. My annual bottle came right around Easter, like always; this year about two weeks before. But this time it came with a letter.

"'You don't know me, and I don't know you. I suppose this is the reason for this letter…' That's how Daniel's letter started."

"So you invited him on over for a visit?"

"Actually, I was a little suspicious 'cause the letterhead on the letter was from a different address than his law firm." He looked at me sideways with his left eyebrow raised, and the left side of his mouth grinning. Detective Daddy had found a clue.

"What!?" I acted scandalized; the kind of conversational pretending we all do to keep the story coming.

"Yeah, but his letter explained things pretty good. I guess he got an English teacher to help him out. Anyway, we eventually arranged for Daniel to visit us this summer. That, plus the imminent arrival of my own little college woman seemed like a good reason to use the few weeks of holiday time I've accumulated."

"I think my arrival should be reason enough by itself." I said in the least convincing huff of my many unconvincing huffs.

"Of *course,* darlin'."

"So you told Mr. Bouliard to take your post, and he's makin' a mess of things?" I said, still not seeing what any of it could have to do with Roland James.

"Not exactly. Like I said, it's complicated." I raised my eyebrows, and bit my tongue. "You see, Dick is handling my job, but – whatever you may've heard – there's more to the job than sitting around with your feet on the desk and puffin' away on a big cigar. So, Hank Macleroy (He got promoted last fall. He always was too big for his Daddy's little hardware shop) has to cover Dick's desk, which means all the way down the hierarchy people gotta take jobs above their usual stations."

"Really? All that's necessary just because you're taking a vacation"

"Necessary?" He palmed the stubble across his face, "Actually, no. Normally the responsibility bump only goes down one…two levels at most, and the extra work just gets spread among a few people at the effected levels."

"But this summer you've got this…bump…this job bump thing going all the way down."

"Just for a few weeks until I come back."

"A *temporary* bump…going all the way down…" I repeated, hoping it would start to make sense.

"All the way down," he said, nodding to himself, "to Roland James."

He'd arranged it all with Dick Bouliard, and his holiday leave made it all temporary to see how the men would handle it. Not exactly the greatest leap of faith, but he put a lot of trust in Mr. Boullard and it must have taken some belief in all of the men who worked under him. He'd brought Mr. James into his office too to ask if he'd want to fill in as assistant shift supervisor, and Mr. James only thought for a moment before taking the offer.

Mr. James thanked Daddy for the opportunity, and Daddy looked him in the eye and said he was sorry it hadn't come much much sooner. They both knew what this meant, and the dangers it might pose. They shook hands, and Daddy had said "Good luck."

"Good luck to us all," Mr. James had responded.

"If Roland can hold his end together, and Dick tells me he was able to keep things from exploding then I'll send Hank Macleroy over to work under Don Wheelus in…" the names and departments swam around me, but I got the point. Room would be made so that Mr. James' promotion would stick.

We continued our walk. I spotted a tiny brook ahead, and pointed it out. We agreed wordlessly to head there, and have a sip.

Things were still unsteady at the plant according to Mr. Bouliard. I asked Daddy if he thought that he could be trusted. "I mean, maybe Mr. Bouliard, you know, doesn't *want* a man like Mr. James getting that job."

"Dick already knows that if he can keep this situation under control, then it'll be a feather in his cap. If things fall apart under his lead, then it'll make him look bad. He's got plenty of motivation to make it work, and to say so. But if it's a mess he won't be able to hide it."

"Well that's a pretty tough spot you've put him in."

"It's not so different from the spot I'm in every day I go to work. Yeah, Sarah, you don't need to roll your eyes. I know it's a bit tougher with the changes, but I like to think I'm a pretty fair boss. If things go bad Dick won't be hurt that bad. But these changes are already happening all over the country, and we need men who can lead in all sorts of adversity."

I noticed that he didn't seem to see the need for women who could lead in adversity, but I was looking for a favor not a fight. "And this business with you being seen as the one who always calls and never the one Dick calls for help?"

Daddy frowned, and rolled his eyes. Then he seemed to think better of it, and simply turned away from me to squat down by the brook and pick up a smooth blue-grey stone. "That was his idea," he growled the end of the last word as he tried to sidearm the stone along the line of moving freshwater, "and we've had a little chat about that already."

I crouched beside the stream, and dropped the four fingers of my right hand into the water. I looked up and to my left at Daddy. "But he's still callin'."

"I still want him to call if there's a problem he needs help with. He just knows now not to make a big scene out of my return calls. He's told a few of the boys in the office that he's thought about things, and that he figures it's good that I'm keepin' up to date on things. Better than if I just abandoned the place, and came back without a clue. As long as he doesn't clown around like that any more things ought to smooth themselves out."

My fingertips were getting numb already, so I pulled them out, and spread the icy moisture across both hands; rubbing them together like I was hatching a master plan. I stared at him, and he stared at the water. Who knows how long it had been burbling before we came to hear it. "*Are* things smoothing out? He didn't call yesterday or two days before that."

"You can never be sure with some men, Sarah. 'Jealousy is as cruel as the grave,' according to the Song of Solomon."

I nodded like I knew what he was talking about; like we were sharing some deep understanding. But what did I really know about men or hatred? There had been three "colored" kids in my high school, two girls and a boy. I never even bothered to learn their names. They seemed angry and aloof to me, though, in the years since I've come to see how frightened and frustrated they must really have been. In that year of college that preceded Mr. James' promotion I had easily maintained the same distance and opinions I'd kept in high school. I saw them, and believed that they were simply nothing to do with me. If I hated them, I did not know it. What did I know about men and hatred? Nothing at all.

I was out of my depth. It was time to change the subject. It was nearly time to beg.

Chapter 18

Trying to ease my way into it, I scooped up a handful of the water that was running by us, and slurped at it. "mmmm *mmm*! This water is delicious!"

Daddy seemed to welcome the distraction. His eyebrows rose along with the corners of his mouth. "Y'don't say."

"Yeah! Hunker down and try some." I offered. We were like some kind of living half-baked commercial for free water. He hunkered, and tried the water as advised.

"Yup. That's pretty good." He said, hamming it up along with me.

"But you know what makes this water extra sweet for me?"

"What's that?"

"I mean, what makes it double-triple good!?"

"I'm dyin' to know." He chuckled.

"It's that I went and got it for myself." After a moment's consideration he seemed to realize where this was meant to go, and this time he did wince. "Really!" I pressed on, "Knowing that I walked to the water with my own two feet really makes…"

"Sarah…"

"…the whole experience of drinking this water extra *extra* good…"

"*Sarah…*"

"Don't you think our guest should be introduced to such a…"

"Sarah, cut it out." He was still smiling, but there was a seriousness to his tone. "As a hard working old man who was once a hard working young man, let me assure you," he shifted to a sitting position "that no water, no matter how hard earned it may be, tastes as good as a glass brought to you by a beautiful young woman with a fresh white smile." .

"Well I've never smiled when I've brought him his water, and I never will."

"A frowning beauty is a close enough second. Our guest is being well taken care of, and you will continue to do your part."

"But Daddy! You've gotta make him stop." It was a rough gear change, and I don't suppose it had anything to do with him getting his own drink. But I'd never really expected that to work anyway. "It's terrible." I felt like I was going to choke as I said it.

"Terrible, how?" he asked. I would normally have expected some concern from him, but all I read from him – palms-up outstretched arms, raised voice, and rocking back as he said it – was that he couldn't believe that I'd said such a ridiculous thing.

Terrible because that's my *Boulder he's smashin', and because he's gonna cart me off to Europe when he's done.* But those words, of course, never left my mouth. I knew in my heart that I was right, but I also knew that he'd be right. I knew he'd be right that the boulder is more his than mine, and not just legally. I was already off in college most of the year, and I'd completely fly the coop before long. He'd stay, and have The Boulder on his land for the rest of his days. I didn't want to hear him say that. I didn't want to hear in his voice that I was just a silly girl.

And of course he and Momma and Tommy wouldn't let Daniel take me away with him. But, silly as I knew it would sound to my father, a seed in my heart worried that Daniel somehow *would* take me with him; that he was conjuring a power with every chunk of rock he dragged. I didn't know who had planted that seed or how, but I was certain that I wouldn't be able to explain it to my father as we sat together sipping freshwater from his own land.

A different answer had to be given. I grabbed at the water flowing by my side. "Because he'll dehydrate. You said it yourself. He's already dropped once, and he's bound to drop again. Who knows if anyone will be looking the next time. We've gotta tell him to stop. For his. Own. Health."

His hat hid his face as he looked down and to his left at the water. I guessed he was thinking. But then the hat pendulumed, hiding his left shoulder, then swinging over to hide his right and then back again. He looked up at me smiling. "You're absolutely right Sarah." I noticed the mischievous glint in his eye, but I didn't really need it to know that I was about to hear something I'd dislike. It was way too easy, and if he were really worried, he wouldn't be smiling. "Daniel is still puttin' himself in grave danger." The smile didn't budge. This was going to be bad. "I guess you'd better bring him water four times a day instead of just the two times you've been doin' so far."

From the fire, that old frying pan looked downright comfortable. I reckoned that was Daddy's intention, but it only made me desperate. "How can you make me chase after him like that?"

"Chase…? Sarah, you're only just bringin' him a glass of water now and then. I don't think that's so much to ask."

"I don't know which is worse, him tryin' to make me his wife or y'all tryin' to make me into his servant." Secretly, I cursed myself. I'd promised myself that I wouldn't say that one. It's a prime opening for Daddy's God-serves-us-all-but-is-no-servant routine.

"I know that this is hard for you Sarah, I do. But we trust you to do what is right, and, even though Daniel's doing something that makes us uncomfortable, we still need to make sure he…"

"Make sure he can have a good ole' laugh at Sarah

Hanover."

"Is that what you think?"

"Look, Daddy, I wish that you would make him stop. I wish you'd throw all of his hammerin' stuff away, and tell him that he misheard or misunderstood The Lord." Daddy made to speak, but I cut him off at the pass. "I wish it! I'm begging you to do it. You and momma didn't raise me to beg, but I'm begging you to do this."

He'd stood up in the middle of my little speech, and, since I was begging, I stayed on the ground. Daddy knelt down beside me, and took my dry hand. "He ain't crazy, Sarah. He's just..." He looked over my shoulder and up the little stream for the right word, and caught it, "...enthusiastic. He let his tongue swing when he should've held it in his mouth. He's still young and a bit wild in his faith. I know! I thought of myself as a reckless bulldog for God back when I was a few years younger than him, back when dinosaurs roamed these parts." His smile dragged mine to the surface, and we both laughed for a two count. "He's got some growing up to do, I'll grant you. But the best thing to do here is to let him show his faith by hammering that Boulder to oblivion and putting the remains on top of The Hill, let him see what happens when the dust has settled and let him learn what he can.

"If we throw him out now he'll learn nothing. He'll just tell himself that he's a believer where we're a bunch of heathens. I can live with him thinkin' that about us except that he'll see it as part of his cross to bear, and he won't really grow. But if he does his task, and then sees that the results ain't what he expected, well then he'll be able to start really learning and growing."

"How can that help him to grow?"

"He's gonna have to ask himself, and The Almighty, what really happened, since no acts of men came between him and his goal. He's gonna have to start considering what he really heard and what was the purpose for it all. Trust me when I tell you, darlin', that there's no danger here. This young man came here to learn a few things. He said as much to me in his letters. There's a chance for him to learn a lot now. I want that for him, and I want us to be the sort of family that can allow him to have it." A light was in his eye. His cheekbones rounded as if he were smiling, though the corners of his mouth held level.

I imagined, in a passing second, the moon rising and falling to the light of the dawning sun; my father and me arguing the whole way through. And, even in my imagination, he still wouldn't give.

"I just don't…" I shook my head at my knees. "Why me?" My voice was soft; desperate in surrender.

"Because you're connected to all of this," he said, giving my hand a squeeze, a smile threatening to surface. "And because I've learned to trust your mother's intuition." Now he really did smile. "She's always kept an ear to her spirit's lips."

I kept my mouth from twisting, but my eyes rolled before I could think to stop them. Between her spirit, the ground, her heart, the ear she's got for a lie, the one for a tune and all the other ears she's been said to have, Momma must have more ears than the Hindu goddess, Kali, has arms; a virtual Swiss army knife of ears.

Chapter 19

I chewed and swallowed dinner, thinking nothing of salt shakers or lemonade jugs. I poked at my plate (I couldn't have said later that evening what the main course had been) thinking about fairness, chances and resistance. I thought of the chance that Mr. James was being given despite the resistance of the white men around him. I thought about the chance Daniel was being given despite my resistance.

I saw that the two men didn't match up. Mr. James was being resisted because of his appearance, despite his abilities. My resistance to Daniel was based on his fool mouth, despite his appearance. Mr. James, held back for what he was, and Daniel, held back for what he'd done. I decided, wiping my mouth, that my resistance was more fair and righteous.

But, spreading butter on a roll I didn't have an appetite for, I saw Daddy in the middle of it, handing out these opportunities to both men. What was he to each of them? Why was he in a position to hand out chances? What did it mean that he took so long to give Mr. James the chance he obviously deserved, but was so quick to give Daniel the chance to play at nonsense that no man needed or deserved to do? Just why in the mountains and valleys of Appalachia was Daniel even here?

I found myself swallowing part of the roll, surprised to find that I'd spread mustard on it rather than butter. Everyone else was clearing the table.

I stood up, and silently wiped the table down. Tommy and Daddy helped with the dishes until Momma shooed Daddy to join Daniel – whose help had been refused, as usual – among the stuffed chairs and sofa by the unused fireplace. When Tommy, Momma and I finished the kitchen, I excused myself to my room. I lay down, stared at the ceiling and juggled these thoughts until the time for bed clothes and deep sleep arrived.

If anyone tried talking to me that evening I don't remember it, and if my silent thinking had bothered anyone no one told me. But I thought I saw something in how Momma prepared Daniel a massive breakfast the next morning; eggs, toast, bacon, grits, coffee, water, orange juice, a second helping of grits and an insistence that could not be refused. It seemed that, despite her many ears, she couldn't hear Daniel say, "No, thank you very much."

Maybe it was my imagination, but I had the feeling that the plates and glasses she set before him beat out a chant as they hit the table, sounding out the theme "Get on out there and get it done already!"

"Here's your protein!" clacked the plate of eggs over easy, "swing that hammer!"

"Vitamins!" tinked the glass of orange juice, "to keep you going till it's done!"

"Wake up and eat up!" plunked the mug of coffee, "Forget about being tired! Time to smash and drag!"

"Sop it up," crunched the dark toast under the spreading butter knife, "and get it over with."

The only way Daniel was going to avoid a busted gut was through the screen door and out to the sanctuary of the Boulder and his hammers; crafted to destroy stone as you worked off a well-filled belly.

The bacon sizzled a fond farewell from their pan. They'd wait for his lunchtime sandwiches.

Three hours passed. There was a clean kitchen, a few pages of Tommy's "Something Wicked This Way Comes" passed under my dubious gaze (it wasn't bad!) and the Hanover men were absent; Daddy into the tree line and Tommy into town to make a delivery for Mr. Macleroy for pocket money. And, of course, the heat came and hung on our faces and crept into our mouths and down to our lungs.

It was time to bring Daniel the first water of his second

Saturday in Kentucky.

I opened the screen door with a quick steady motion to keep it from squeaking. I closed it slowly behind myself to avoid the flappity-flapping back-and-forth of the double hinges. Door sounds always seemed to catch Daniel's ear, and I'd found that he would stop hammering at the first sign of my approach to watch me.

He always watched me as much as his ideas of courtesy would allow during those water runs. I tried each time to convince myself that the intensity with which he watched me was creepy; that there was madness in those eyes. And the harder I tried not to get excited by the force of his attention the more electricity seemed to run from the backs of my knees to the hollows of my collar bone…and back down to my knees again.

Maybe it made me a hypocrite, but I didn't mind watching him strike the stone, unaware of my approach. It was like catching him in a private act done out under the sun.

Also I'd begun to notice that Daniel was getting better at handling the great hammer; making strong blows without committing all of his strength to any one strike. It had been a gradual improvement. That first day he'd toted the great blunt tool like a cocky baseball player, testing his bat; trying to bounce the head of the thing in his hand. He'd tried the first few swings as if he'd picked up Thor's Mjölnir at Macleroy's Hardware Store, and that he'd reduce the boulder to rubble with one mighty swing. His feet actually left the ground on the first and second attempts; pulled skywards from the force of the big sledge's falling arc.

Whatever one may say of his foolishness, he certainly did believe.

My brain said to cough up a good mocking laugh to discourage him, but, not only would it have violated the terms of the agreement, my heart and stomach weren't into it. I decided that it would be beneath me.

After those ineffective first strikes nearly vibrated his hands and wrists to pieces, he made his test run with the tarp and those few bits of rubble. That he was afraid of the boulder showed he had brains enough to learn. His next strategy, however, showed that he didn't learn quickly.

He tried a kind of windmilling approach for the next two days. After a strike, he would drag the head of his hammer off the boulder and try to let the momentum of the fall carry the hammer into a large circle, pivoting around the ball joint of his shoulder at the center. "He's gonna pull his arm right outta the socket at that rate," Daddy had said, observing Daniel through the window.

The momentum only provided a minor help at getting the hammer back up to a striking position; even less help in completing a full circle. Worse still, trying to make a grand continuous circle like that left him with nearly no control of where the head would strike. I observed three separate times, when the hammer actually bounced back along the arc from which it had come. It surprised Daniel and forced him to jump out of his hammer's path before starting again at his foolish scheme. Even when the hammer struck true, there was no momentum to be gained, and he'd have to jerk at the hammer, making more strain on his shoulder to get it going again. All through that second and third day of failed demolition he'd tried variations on the windmill theme; smaller arcs, making fewer circular strikes at a time before starting again and standing at varying distances and stances in relation to The Boulder.

None of them had worked, and Sunday morning Momma's muscle balm had Daniel's shoulder glowing red like it was fresh from Vesuvius. It was the Sabbath, and Daniel rested. The Boulder was missing only a few lumps from its bulk, and a correspondingly tiny pile of chips and dust could be found at the top of The Hill.

My parents went to church without waking any of us to go with them. I guessed that they wanted Daniel to get some rest; lick his wounds, both physical and spiritual. I'd hoped that he would spend the day looking out at The Boulder, how little had come of his struggles and strategies, and realize that it was time to say "When."

Tommy and I had been left behind for more practical reasons. A folded note with our two names on it read, "Make breakfast for Daniel and yourselves." I made sure it was cold cereal for the lot of us.

But the next day Daniel was out there slugging away at The Boulder, hopeless but intractable. His blows were weak and ineffective. He'd surrendered to The Boulder's endurance. That Monday was when I approached Tommy, and secured his promise to try to talk Daniel into quitting the whole business.

Daniel was still swinging without hope or effect Tuesday and Wednesday as well, but he showed no signs of quitting. Wednesday night, despite Daniel's slow going, I slipped into Tommy's room (after a full day of serving Daniel water and lemon-iced-tea) and beat a promise out of him to talk to Daniel like he'd said he would on Monday.

The boys had their theological debate Thursday afternoon, and, thanks to his swooning (or whatever that was) Daniel didn't swing at all in the afternoon.

Friday morning I didn't really watch how Daniel was swinging; as I was gearing myself up to beg Daddy. When we came back from our walk & talk in the woods Daniel was still bashing away at The Boulder, but it was different. There was none of the wild arcing, ping-rebounding or wearily hateful glaring at the boulder. The hammer was impacting with a solid SPACK, and – though it was still just minutes before lunch time – a pile of humbled fragments lay at Daniel's feet. He was making steady blows. He was expecting no momentum. He was banking on no miracles. He was slugging The Boulder patiently; just doing his best with carefully measured strength.

I should've seen trouble there.

Nothing was mentioned at lunch or dinner. My head

was too full – of Daddy's stories of injustice and justice for Mr. James and of Momma's intuitive eardrums – to mention Daniel's progress to anyone…or even to think very seriously about it.

On Saturday Daniel ate the enormous breakfast my mother served him, likely unaware of how the eggs and the toast urged him on his way, and three hours later I squeezed out through the screen door silently; bearing his water, and watching him battle The Boulder alone as I ascended to him.

I planned clearly in my mind that I'd refuse to speak to him. I gave him his water, but he didn't try to push for conversation. He said only "Thank you very much," in a well prepared sort of way, and then drank as he watched me.

And so it was for the rest of Saturday until the Sabbath.

Chapter 20

And so it was for the weekdays that followed the Sabbath. Daniel progressed slowly; hammering, gathering, dragging, dumping and heading back down The Hill to start all over again. And with his progress my anxiety increased. Always he gave me a friendly smile. Always, "Thank you very much," like he was reciting it in a classroom. I locked my jaw tight, refusing to let anyone know how my irises fit to his form – bronzing, burning, hardening his arms and callusing his hands over me – as I presented him his refreshment.

I planned that I wouldn't break.

Then, on Thursday, I spied Tommy sharing a few beers with Daniel beside a much reduced Boulder; just barely more than half of its original size.

I held out until Saturday. Then I broke.

"This ain't gonna work you know. I ain't gonna marry you just because you…you drag some…some *rock* up a hill!"

He continued drinking his glass through the outburst. It made me think vaguely of Dick Bouliard, though I wasn't sure why. When he finished drinking the glass dry I expected him to say something, but he didn't. He stared at me with a silent serious frown.

"This is stupid," I continued. "Crazy! Just look at what you're doing! It doesn't make any sense!"

He nodded, and said, "Yes, I understand."

"You understand? You *Understand*!? If you understand that what you're doing doesn't make any sense then how do you know that you can even know what *does* make sense? You *can't*! So maybe you don't *really understand* what you're even doing, and I don't just mean standin' out in the sun hammering a rock. I mean what you're really *doing*."

"Na…eh…yes?"

"Yes?!"

"Yes," He repeated, but his face looked more hopeful than affirmative. My eyes slit. "I…yes…I am more than hammering stones." I could feel my jaws bulging as I mashed them, and Daniel held out a hand towards me, placating. "And I understand that you say you will not marry me when The Boulder is of The Hill."

"When it's *on* The Hill," I corrected.

"Yes. When it is *on* The Hill." And so now we'd basically said it three times aloud, that The Boulder *would* end up on top of The Hill. In my mind I could see the full pile up there for me, and warmth spread into my torso from my breastbone.

Wait. No!

"Wait! No, Daniel. No!" I was shaking my head at the

ground. *How did he do that?* "You don't understand."

"Yes."

"What? No!" I stomped my foot, but the soft earth swallowed any sound it might have otherwise made. "You've got to understand that I'm…no…I mean…" Just what the heck *did* I mean? I started over. "No Boulder on Hill. Okay?"

His smile flattened. *I'm finally getting through to him* I thought.

"No, Sarah. I must do this."

I went on, trying and failing to restrain my tone and volume, but he just stood there and let me talk. I tried reason, and I tried rage. I tried to bargain, and – eventually – I even tried to beg. All my best weapons were failing me that summer.

He didn't try to practice any new English words. He just kept sticking to "No, Sarah. I must do this." No one came out to investigate the ruckus.

I was groggy waking up Sunday morning. I didn't expect to hear Momma's call to prayer, considering the previous two Sabbaths. But Tommy and I were called, and we came, dizzy with forgotten dreams.

"I thought you were leavin' us to rest on this Day of Rest." croaked Tommy.

"It's a day of reflection too, you know perfectly well." Momma retorted plunking a thick brown and green ceramic mug of coffee in front of him. This was an exchange I hadn't heard in a little under a year. I didn't feel like giving my traditional retort – "I can reflect real good in my bed," – so I stared at the wall just left of the screen door until the thick brown and red ceramic mug of coffee plunked down before me.

Tommy gave his own variation, "I was already doin' some award winnin' reflectin' in my bed." I guess he'd put that together since I'd left for college. It wasn't a comedy routine. It was our chance to complain without trouble. It was long ago established that there was no actual way to get out of attending church Sunday mornings, but airing our grievance let us express it without souring the whole holy day. And doing so pretty much every week for more than ten years had become a custom in its own right.

Tommy's version of my part still left room for Momma's final answer, "Be sure to tell Jesus all about it while we're in church." And finally it was the first true Sunday morning in the Hanover household since my return to Coal Fields.

Daddy entered the kitchen, face shaved clean enough to pass inspection. It seems funny now, how we never wondered whether it was God's inspection or Momma's that he was preparing for. The thick brown and blue ceramic mug of coffee hit the table the same time his butt hit his chair. "I reckon he should at least be given the *choice* to go." He said.

"Really?" Tommy said. "I can choose?"

"Don't be silly, Tommy." said Momma, then she turned to Daddy. "He's too tired and worn out."

I took a deeper sip of my coffee, hoping to clear the confusion chemically.

"He's a grown man, Ruthie. He should be given the choice; a chance to decide if he's too worn out."

"I'm definitely too worn out." Tommy said in a soft high whine; so quiet that I couldn't tell if he was talking to our parents or himself. I don't think he was sure either.

"He's been swingin' a jackhammer for six days straight,"

Oh.

"Oh," Tommy said with an exhalation like a split bag of flour.

"Of course he's too tired." Momma continued.

"Sledgehammer, Ruthie, not a jackhammer. And I can name a hundred men who work as hard as Daniel has and still decide that they're strong enough to sit a pew on Sunday."

"Those are men who have been workin' stone all their lives. Daniel hasn't ever lifted anything heavier than a few big books, or maybe his bicycle." Daddy opened his mouth to reply, but, "We discussed this last night. Let the boy have a rest." Daddy closed his mouth. We prepared for church in silence. For our parents it was a stubborn silence. For me and Tommy it was a confused one.

Our parents took Daddy's old clunker to church. I rode with Tommy in his truck. I tried asking him if he knew what the exchange had been about, but he said "No idea" before I could even finish my sentence. We sat and rocked quietly as Tommy turned corners and braked occasionally to keep us from skidding off the gravel back road. The gas pedal went unloved in our descent. Finally I remembered something to talk to him about.

"Tommy!"

"Mmm." He hooked us a right so sharp that we were practically headed in the opposite direction (hence the term "switchback.")

"What was that about on Thursday?"

His eyebrows wrinkled for a moment or two. Then he said, "Well, Sarah, Wednesday was plum finished, and everybody agreed that calling the next twenty four hours Cindy would be cute, but that someone was bound to be confused. So we all just decided to call it Thursday like we always have for the last…"

"I mean the beers you were drinkin' with Daniel Mr. Funny Pants." It's not that I was above harsher language. It was more that we were headed for church, and it just felt weird swearing on the way to God's house. Besides, I'd been calling Tommy "Mr. Funny Pants" since his first year in middle school. It used to drive him nuts.

Tommy rolled his eyes in mock disbelief. "Oh that. On Cindy…I mean on *Thursday* I brought a few cold ones up to Daniel, 'cause I figured, 'how much water and lemonade can one man be expected to stand?' It was murderous hot out there, and…”

“But why did you go out there, Tommy. Were you tryin’ to get him drunk or somethin’?”

“We each just had one beer, Sarah. You’ve seen him chug it down. You know that wouldn’t make him drunk. Man, those lawyers in Vienna must…”

“Tommy.”

“I was just trying for a friendlier approach, y’know? When I brought up the beers he said he wasn’t sure if he should take one. ‘Beer does many bad sings, you know’ he says.

“‘You mean like giving you a big belly?’ I asked.

“‘No, zat is not vaht I am meanink.’”

“Tommy,” I interrupted, “would you mind telling the rest of this without the accent. It’s terrible, and you’re hurting my ears.”

“Sure. So I ask him, ‘Well, what *do* you mean, then?’

“‘Forgetfulness is the second sign that drinking beer is a problem for you’ he says. I nod.” Tommy nodded to illustrate, in case I somehow managed to misunderstand what a nod is. “‘Okay, I’ll bite. What’s the *first* sign that beer is a problem for you?’ And he just starts smilin’ at me. I asked him, ‘What?’ and he just smiles even bigger than before.”

I remember rubbing my eyes at this point.

“Took me a long time before I got it, but it was worth the laugh.”

“So you two just joked around like old chums?”

"Chums?" His left eyebrow rose, independent of the rest of his face. I'd picked up the word from Gloria. I'll never know why the cabin of Tommy's truck inspires the college student in me. "No, my deah guhrl," he said in a British accent so awful that the words were difficult to identify as belonging to the English language. "I didn't just jewk about with him like chums."

"Was there something in your coffee that wasn't in mine, or are you just more annoying when you're in your truck?"

"Oh, is Mr. Funny Pants too funny for you?"

"Alright. I apologize for calling you Mr. Funny Pants. I'm sorry." *Mr. Grumple Butt!* "Will you please continue without trying to be British, Austrian or any other sort of international person?"

"Alright," he said with a look of satisfaction that was too glib to be real. "Well, once I got him a little more loosened up I tried another angle. I told him, 'One day, even if you get Sarah, you'll look back at what you're doing and feel stupid.'" Get *me? What am I here? An autographed picture of Elvis?* But I held my tongue, and let my brother ramble as he drove.

"He says, 'It will be a good story. Yes Tommy, even if it is a story that makes me sick.'

"Next I said somethin' like 'Stories, eh? Stories are important to you?' You know, I was tryin' to get a clearer picture of what we're dealing with here. So I was askin' questions to get him talkin' about his *motives*." I wondered to myself when the Hanover men decided to be detectives.

"Then he goes, 'I can guess, because of your father, that you have read The Bible, or?' I remember how he ended with 'or?" like that. Maybe it was the beer, but it seemed funny to me at the time.

"'Cover to cover, my friend.' I answered.

"'If you must read one of the books from The Bible, What do you wish to read? Genesis, or numbers or one of *Pauls'* letters?' I guess that's what they call Paul.

"'I catch your meaning. The stories are better reading,' I tell him.

"'Yes,' he says, 'and I have always learned best with the stories. There are always so many different things you learn from one simple story or parable.' He didn't really say it that good. We had a devil of a time figuring out that he meant parable; but that's basically what he said.

"'So,' I say to him after we've looked up the word 'parable' in this tiny German/English dictionary he brought with him from Vienna, 'you're really doing this just to make a story?'"

"He's sick!" I said. "See? He's crazy!"

"Let me finish, will ya'? He told me his life is already a story."

"He said that?" I could hear the old rhythms of my high school gossip mongering, but I didn't care.

"Yep. 'My life *is* a story,' he said, 'and so is yours,'"

"Mine?"

"No, mine, but I expect he would say yours too. He

said 'There is much we learn from stories of The Bible, much we learn from the stories of we. That is the meaning of *Weis-heit.*' We looked that one up too. It means wisdom. Anyway, we started swappin' Bible stories; Shadrack, Meshack & Abednego, some of those Elisha stories, you know. Stories of might and tests of faith. Samson. It all seemed to fit with those tarps next to The Boulder and surrounded by hammers and chisels." He smiled to himself, and then, "I guess those stories are where he came up with the idea of having a contest."

"A what?"

He shook his head, keeping his eyes on the road. "He suggested this cockamamie idea of a challenge. A test of our faiths. One against the other. See who can make a fire, and who'll get eaten by bears."

"What…Bears? What!?"

He waved it off. "Never mind. The point is that he wanted to do a challenge like you read about."

"What was the challenge?"

"What? Oh. Uh, the idea was that we'd each take a swing at the boulder, and whoever knocks off the biggest piece wins."

"Wins what? My hand in marriage? You're a lovely boy, Tommy, but you *are* my brother."

He chuckled. "Yeah. He said that if I win he'll stop tryin' to get The Boulder up The Hill bit by bit. If he wins, then I talk to you about cutting him a break and trying to be friendly with him."

"Naw!"

"Yes Ma'am. I told him that I was already doin' him a favor in refusin' to do the whole thing, 'cause he'd regret it if I…"

"You turned him down?" Of course he'd turned Daniel down. This is Tommy we're talking about.

"Of course I turned him down." He was staring at the windshield like it had just turned a stupid color.

"Tommy, I know that you're not one to agree to just anything any time it's thrown at you, but why would you turn *this* down? You can't loose. Now what I'm about to say, I mean in a nice way: You're big as a bull. Don't be as thick as one too!"

"I ain't bein' thick, Sarah. It's a setup." We were on flat paved road by this time; not far from town.

"A…how…what're you talking about?"

"Daniel isn't expecting a miraculous victory here, Sarah. Didn't you see how he swung at The Boulder the first few times? He thought God Almighty was commin' down from heaven to personally split The Boulder in two for him. It didn't happen that way, but he's still been out there the last two and a half weeks. He knows that he's gonna have to do this job himself. He may be crazy, but he sure ain't stupid. He can see that I could pick him up and swing *him* at The Boulder if I wanted, but he offered the challenge anyway. Some clever idea slipped into his head while he was sippin' my beer. I don't know what it is, but I'm not offering myself up to be made a fool of." He was shaking his head at the sporadic run down houses popping up on either side of the road. The church was less than a mile or so away now.

"You've gotta do it Tommy," I started to say. He tried to say "Naw," but I shouted over him, "Yes yes yes yes *yes*! At least try! You and I both know you're smarter than he thinks. Chances are you'll see his trick commin'." We were pulling into the parking lot of the Savior's Own Christian Fellowship Church. I had to talk fast. "What's the worst thing that happens? You fall for whatever trick it is. You can tell me what a great guy Daniel is, and I'll just ignore you like I always do." We were parked, and he was just staring straight ahead. That last bit wasn't helping.

Tommy cut the engine. I looked at the parishioners: Friends and cousins I hadn't seen in nearly a year shuffling their way towards the chapel entrance. Tommy was reaching for the driver-side door handle. "Tommy." He gripped the lever, but turned to show me the face of an unconvinced young man. Over Tommy's shoulder I could see Momma walking across the parking lot, smiling and hanging on Daddy's arm. My final bid hit me. I looked in Tommy's eyes.

"Pray on it, okay?"

It happens sometimes. We can't always pay perfect

attention to every word of every sermon we attend. It was especially difficult in light of the information Tommy had just dropped. Why had Daniel offered up this bet, and what did he hope to achieve even if he won? How would I feel if he won? Was this an attempt to show off, or was he looking for a way to get out of the whole screwball situation while saving some face? No. I couldn't see how loosing this bet could help him out of the whole Boulder thing in a less humiliating way.

And humiliation seemed to be at the root of this whole ordeal. Wasn't it?

The pastor hadn't begun yet. There were still a few hymns warming up the congregation. I tuned them out. This was important mental and spiritual exploration I was doing here. Let the others chant. I'd join them once they'd caught up with me.

Where was I? Oh yeah, humiliation. I certainly felt humiliated when Daniel told me I'd be his wife, though, sitting in that pew, I couldn't figure why it was so *so* bad. I mean, he'd said it. I knew I wouldn't marry him. It was weird, and surreal. But, humiliating? The very idea that he could claim me was demeaning, and that's close enough. Only my slap prevented it from being humiliating.

Who else? Momma? No. She'd been smiling and giggling all the way through this stupidity. It seemed that I should've been more annoyed with her, but her cheer won me over again and again. Not Tommy, of course. If anything, he seemed more annoyed with me than Daniel.

Was it humiliating for Daddy? It seemed to me that Daniel was playing some strange games in Daddy's house. Remembering the talk Daddy and I'd had the morning after I'd gotten home, how he was unsure of where God was in all of this, I could see how he must still be riding that fence. Wasn't that reason enough to feel humiliated? *Shouldn't my father*, I wondered, *be outraged?*

But he wasn't. He hadn't kicked Daniel out, and, more, our conversation in the forest seemed to suggest that Daddy knew some things Daniel wanted or needed to know. Come to think of it, on the day I returned home Daniel actually said he'd come to learn some things, and I know Daddy never told me or Tommy what those European bottles of wine were about. Daddy and Daniel had stayed up all that first night. Had the war veteran told the young Austrian what he was looking to learn that night? Or was he keeping Daniel hanging on the same string from which my brother and I had been dangling since we'd grown old enough to wonder?

Daddy, I thought as the last hymn wound down around me, wasn't being humiliated at all. He was holding all the cards; all the stories that Daniel was looking to hear. They were stories Tommy and I had been hoping to hear for more than a decade. Daniel had been in our home for three weeks now. He'd come hand delivering that bilingual bottle, and asking a few questions. Had he been laboring these weeks without any answers? Was Daniel being humiliated? Was *Daddy* humiliating him?

The pastor's voice was low and soft – typical to his introductions – but none of his meaning penetrated. Could my father be acting like some kind of manipulative sadist? I looked over to him. He looked so fragile and open staring up at the pastor.

I scrunched my eyes and shook my head. No, I wouldn't believe it, first because it was an unbelievable idea. Second, Daddy had had no hand in Daniel's labors. That was our doing; Daniel's and mine. Tommy, to a lesser extent. Daddy had simply tolerated it. If Daniel felt humiliated, it wasn't Daddy's doing. In fact, why was I even including myself and Tommy in this? If Daniel had only held his tongue then…

…Well, I wondered (the pastor began striking a rhythm, and he started to repeat himself over and over in earnest,) how *would* things have developed if he'd kept his prophetic revelation to himself? What if he'd believed he'd gotten that divine thumbs up, but instead of doing something stupid (telling me all about it) he'd just taken it as a green light from On High to smile nice and pretty? What if, instead of interposing his personal prophesy, he'd put on a little charm?

I closed my eyes, and saw him hammering at The Boulder. Then I made The Boulder disappear. With nothing to strike, he dropped his mallet to the soft ground. Then there was me approaching the foot of The Hill, a sweating yellow glass in each hand. I handed him a lemonade and sipped my own. The question *How does this feel?* passed through my mind, and the un-hammered Daniel smiled at me. The sun dipped behind The Hill like in a cartoon (In reality the sun rises from behind The Hill, but that didn't occur to me. I was too busy tuning out the pastor to worry about such particulars.) The sudden dusk darkened his already tanned face; only his white smile and yellow lemonade could be seen. *How does this feel?* It became a white flame over a yellow candle, and the boulder could be seen whole at the top of The Hill beyond. Darker. I could still taste sugar and lemon juice on my tongue, but I could see only three shapes now: Lemon candle, sugar-white-hot flame and, hovering above the flame, a ruddy blushing shape that had been the boulder. How long could it hang over the flame like that? Wasn't it burning? *How does this...*

The swept boards beneath my father's foot boomed. I jumped slightly, and turned to see his face blotched red, his jaws flexing; radiating with fury. I thanked heaven he wasn't shooting that glare my way. His hostility was all for the front of the room: the pastor, apparently as unaware of my father's indignant glowering, as Daddy had been of my wandering thoughts.

He stood up, a one man fire drill. Momma, on the other side of his perfectly vertical form, lightly stroked his forearm, and took his hand. Her eyes pulled down in a look of pain at his face. He was turned slightly towards her, away from me, so I couldn't see his face. But I could see Momma's hand as she squeezed his, and she whispered, "D'you see now?"

He released her hand, and reached for the back of the

pew in front of ours. "Excuse me, Ruthie," he grumbled in a not unkind tone. Then he pulled himself across her into the isle.

We three Hanovers tracked his retreating shoulders until he ducked around a corner that lead to the men's room. Tommy and I turned to face one another with cuckoo-clock synchronization. "What was that?" I mouthed, and then, before Tommy could answer I whispered, "What was the pastor sayin'?"

"Not sure," he said in a hush, mouth hung open like breathing through his nose wasn't an option. "I was only half listening. Somethin' about idolaters."

We stared at each other until it felt weird, and then I turned to Momma. She was still frowning nervously back down the hall as if Daddy had left a blur trail.

Daniel was waiting with cold cuts, sliced bread, lemonade and a set table.

I tried my best not to pester Tommy too much about the challenge. Yes, he insisted, he was thinking about it. No, this wasn't going to drag on like before. Yes, he would have an answer soon, tomorrow most likely. No, I could *not* help him along in his decision. Yes, I was getting on his nerves, and had best leave him alone.

I didn't bring it up any more that day, but we both

knew my eyeballs would be shooting off question marks and exclamation points over oatmeal the next morning.

Chapter 21

Tommy's sunny-side-ups were very interesting. At least they interested him a great deal that Monday morning. He concentrated with perfect diligence (completely avoiding eye contact with me) as he cut the yolks free of their whites with patience and precision that would have earned the respect of mathematicians, engineers, surgeons and archaeologists the world over. Next he sucked the grits off his spoon before carefully transferring the liberated yolks to the bowl of the spoon using the edge of the butter knife to ease the patient onto its concave gurney. From the spoon the yolks were delivered to individual slices of buttered toast with a jeweler's care.

Much satisfied, he turned to his coffee (brown and blue mug this morning.) Safe behind ceramic cover, he scanned the rest of us at the table. Daniel and Daddy were equally busy, if less compulsive, eating. Momma was watching Tommy's new little hobby (or was this a new ritual?) but returned to her hash browns when she saw his mug touch his lips; he *was* going to eat after all. I was staring at him flatly.

My fork clanked on my plate when our eyes met. Tommy's eyes immediately dropped to the dregs of his mug.

He put the mug down with such concentrated care that it made no sound at all. Then he dropped his hands to his sides and stared at his yellow-eyed toast. He kept up that staring contest, like a living statue, for so long that I began to think that the yolks on the toast would find a way to blink first.

"Should I get you my camera, Tommy?" I offered.

"You okay, Sweetheart?" Momma asked him.

"Yeah. Just thinkin'."

"Thinkin' what?" she wanted to know.

"Just *thinkin'*." He said with authentic teenage grief.

Daddy looked up from his food, but said nothing.

"Alright," Momma soothed, "just don't let it get cold, now."

The parents returned to their plates, and Tommy glared over my way. "Sorry," I said, hushed but loud enough for him to catch it.

He went back to contemplating his plate of protein. After about 300 years he reached up, took a toast mounted yolk and bit right through to the center of his sculpture. He looked over at me and significantly – making sure he had my attention –nodded one slow nod as he chewed.

Either the wait made those eggs and toast taste unusually good I thought to myself, *or he's gonna take Daniel up on his challenge.*

Tommy stalled for another hour or two in typical Tommy fashion, but he did eventually go up to the boulder to talk to Daniel. He brought a couple of iced-teas with him (it still being morning; too early for beer,) and looked to be shooting the breeze with our guest. Eventually I saw Tommy gesture over his back with his thumb (*remember back on the other day…,*) point at the boulder, swing an imaginary hammer and finally hold his hands up making wide brackets over his head (*big.*) Daniel could be seen nodding near the end of this *Handspielen*, and then they were shaking; the deal parenthetically sealed between their gripping hands.

"He'll need all his strength, so we're gonna do it tomorrow morning," Tommy said back at the house. Over his shoulder Daniel could be seen digging among his tools with frantic energy. Waiting until tomorrow appealed perfectly to Tommy's put-off-what-he-could-do-today disposition. "It would be pretty unfair for me to come up just before lunch, fresh as sun dried laundry, and expect him to compete when he's been wearing himself out all mornin'."

I guessed he was right, but it seemed suspicious to me. Daniel came late to lunch, and shot off before anyone else was done. Tommy became suspicious too, so we stood silently together at the window and watched him. For a long time neither of us could figure out what Daniel was trying to do out there. Tommy brightened after a few minutes, though, and started nodding his head. He switched places with me three times without saying why. Unsatisfied, he went to the screen door for yet another angle. Still not seeing what he was looking for, Tommy announced that he was going for a walk.

I opened my mouth to offer to go with him, but I noticed Momma watching us from the entrance to the hallway that leads to the bathroom and bedrooms. After Tommy's oddball performance at breakfast she was looking at him like he was sneaking out in the middle of the night with two dozen eggs and a roll of toilet paper. Not wanting to be lumped in with him I said, "Okay Tommy. Have a nice stroll. Hey Momma. Where's Daddy?"

Properly distracted, she let Tommy slip away, and answered, "He's takin' a nap."

"Eatin' lunch really tuckers a man out, huh?"

She smiled, and blinked slowly. "What're y'all up to?"

"Up to?"

Momma just stared, eyebrows high up.

I huffed. "Can we at least wait for Tommy and Daddy?"

"Daniel suggested this?" Daddy seemed to be straining to see us through a fog.

"Yes!" Tommy declared, and I nodded ferociously as if I'd been there personally.

"And it came from a discussion about Bible stories."

Daddy reached up, and gripped the top of his head with his right hand; trying to keep it all in and straight.

"Yes!" Tommy proclaimed, and I swung my head up and down like a bell on a running cow.

"Whoever or wherever it comes from," Momma opined, "it sounds like gambling to me. Sarah will you please cut out that head shakin'. It's makin' my neck sore just watching you." She rubbed the back of her neck, and turned to look over her shoulder at the kitchen. "Like a dog with a squirmin' cat between its teeth," she mumbled loudly enough that I heard and still remember.

"It ain't like that, Momma. Dad, it's just like in nearly every Bible story you can name. God shows which side He's on. He gave victory to the Israelites, set fire to piles of wet sticks while keeping sticks doused in oil from burnin', turned away centurions when the time wasn't right for them to come, Heck, the whole first half of Exodus is Pharaoh sayin' 'I do not know this God of yours,' and God introducin' Himself through Moses and the ten plagues! And I don't just mean those super magical stories nie..."

"Super*natural*, Tommy," I blurted.

My brother plugged me up with a look that made me fall back into Daddy's chair, hold my breath and bite down on my tongue. Low and hard he said, "Thank you, Sarah. Supernatural."

He returned to our parents and his argument. "I don't just mean those supernatural moves neither." I bit harder down on my tongue. "'Let he who is without sin cast the first stone.' That one stopped a mob! And…"

"Alright, Tommy." Daddy said shaking his head. "I see where you're coming from. A contest of faiths. But I warned Daniel." Our guest was still out under The Hill, unaware of the conversation. It had been sprung on our father, and he was reeling to get a grip on what was happening. "I mean this is really the last straw! Look, I know that you're a clever boy; cleverer than most give you credit for. But Daniel is more than half a decade older than you, son. I'm an old man, but I'm clear enough to remember. Those five years are a time when a man learns to maneuver."

Tommy and I began to respond at the same time. Much to our surprise, so did Momma. Funnily enough, we all shut up in unison too. "I got none of that. What were you sayin' Ruthie?"

"I said that I'm surprised to hear that maneuverin' bothers you. I seem to remember a young officer maneuverin' round my neighborhood not so long ago." I'd never heard her talk like that to our father, or at least I'd never noticed it before. The hungry mischievous grin she was giving him made me blush.

I'd gathered from the start that Momma was enjoying all the madness of the handsome Austrian's visit, but for the first time it occurred to me that she was even more tolerant of it than Daddy; that Daniel's continued presence was even more thanks to my mother's counsel than my father's saintly patience.

I didn't look over at Tommy, but he was as silent as me. Even my father seemed at a loss for words. Finally Momma restored the room to a proper temperature by saying, "It's the gamblin' that bothers me."

"It's more like a contest than gamblin', Momma," Tommy tried groggily.

"Yeah, Ruthie, I'm inclined to see it as a test of faiths; one against the other. But Daniel's already got permission to move The Boulder. Why in the world would he even offer up such a test? I told him he was out of last chances. I won't have him staying here messin' round with my children any more. I've tolerated enough. There's just no good cause for this."

If only I'd listened to the pastor on Sunday, I wouldn't have already considered the questions Daddy was asking. If I hadn't thought of those questions the day before I doubt I'd have thought right at that moment, *Maybe* he's *not sure that he's on the right side of it all. Maybe he wants to test what he's doing.*

Everyone turned to me and starred. I stopped chewing my thumb nail. "Did that come out…I mean…did I say that out loud?" They all just kept staring at me. I slapped my thigh. "Dangit!"

Chapter 22

Dinner started later than usual because the debate went on for three hours, round and round. (This suited Daniel just fine as he made his final preparations.) Tommy leaned harder on the Old Testament stories than the New Testament, which made Momma suspicious. He retold his conversation to our parents, as he'd told it to me in his truck on Sunday, but he was more specific about the Biblical stories he and Daniel had discussed. Even Momma came around grudgingly.

By the time she'd started preparing dinner Daddy was advising Tommy rather than debating the issue. "Now there's probably gonna be some trick. You'll need to keep your wits."

"There *is* a trick!" Tommy led our father to the window to show what he'd seen. I hopped up and followed them to the window for another look. Everything looked to me exactly the same as it had a few hours ago. Tommy confirmed my thoughts by saying, "He's been workin' with that chisel an' hammer for hours, and The Boulder looked just the same." He went on to explain what he'd seen when he'd gone out for his walk and what it meant.

Chopped onions hissed in hot oil contained by an old pot in the kitchen. My kin were at work, and my fingers itched to be part of the Hanover machine. I thought to myself that one day, perhaps, I'd grow to be a respected author or professor of literature, with a cook at home to prepare my meals. But I knew what was the best role a college sophomore, man or woman, could play in a small house in the mountains. I joined Momma, and chopped what she told me to chop. I laid the table and even swept up. But whatever my hands played at, I kept my ears open as the men I loved planned and schemed.

When Momma sent Tommy out to fetch Daniel for dinner I approached my father.

"Yes, Darlin'?"

"I thought you wanted Daniel to finish so he could learn, you know, and think about God and all that stuff you talked about while we were walking in the woods."

"I did say that, and it's true that I want him to learn. But if he's going to involve my son in contests revolving around discovering God's will, then my first priority is to make sure that my son play his roll as best he can."

"Oh."

"You were in the room Sarah. You heard when I said to Tommy about how to act when it's all done: No crowin' in victory. No bellyachin' in defeat. That isn't just because I don't want him actin' the fool. It's because we're putting this whole thing into God's hands, and you don't want to take credit or complain when God wins and God al..."

"Always wins. Mercy Daddy! Are you really telling me that you don't..." But the energetic stomping of Tommy's feet and the sluggish drag-clomping of Daniel's stopped me up short.

It was time to say grace, break bread and see where the crumbs would fall.

Very few crumbs fell during dinner. Daniel ate and drank until there was nothing left but to scan the empty saucers and check for lost fingers.

"I see you worked extra hours out there" Daddy offered, but Daniel, mouth full of bread and gravy, could only affirm with an "Mmm hmm," and a heavy nod.

"I reckon you're just softening The Boulder up for your little contest with Tommy tomorrow," he said, tipping his cards to gage Daniel's response.

Daniel's chewing slowed for a moment, but never stopped. He nodded, then washed down his mouthful with a quarter of his tall mug of beer. His exhaustion was obvious even before he started falling asleep at the table, so none of us had the heart to trouble him any further. He stumbled off to bed immediately after the meal was over, bidding us *Gutte Nacht* over his shoulder.

I don't know where all that food went, but he woke up the next morning with an equally lionesque appetite. Eggs, toast with butter and jelly, grits with butter and honey, bacon, fresh strawberries, hash browns, sausages, orange juice, apple juice, milk *and* coffee; you name it, it disappeared between his teeth and down his throat.

Even Tommy was impressed. "Jeezooee," he muttered into my ear, "maybe he's just gonna *eat* the rest of the dang boulder."

We gave Daniel an hour and a half to digest, but we were all sure to be standing at The Boulder before lunchtime, lest he eat himself into a coma with what was left in the pantry. We found one sledgehammer waiting for the five of us, a few tarps littered with a great many more or less finger sized stone chips and a shabby piece of rough hewed modern sculpture art where my Boulder used to be.

It was still tall, nearly my height but wider. It was shaped like an ice cream cone turned upside down and cut vertically in half. In fact, I suspect that it was a complete cone before Daniel took chisel and hammer to it, and chipped nearly half of it away. The half cone leaned back, away from where it had been chiseled. But the pitiful remains of the proud stone that marked dynamiting done in my childhood days was not defenseless.

It held before it (even as it leaned away) a shield made

of its own material, fat in the middle and thin around the edges. It was a slab that jutted from the middle, imperfectly round with a diameter as long as my arm from shoulder to wrist. From down in the house it had looked like a regular shelf in the stone, but from the side I could see that almost all of the material connecting that disk shaped slab to the rest of this reduced boulder had been chiseled away. The result was a vestigial out-thrust held tenuously – very tenuously – by two…no there was a third…three adult fist sized blobs of stone; an amoeba nearly at the end of cytokinesis.

Daniel, Tommy and Daddy eyed the hammer warily, nearly salivating over it. Daniel seemed to decide he couldn't pick it up yet, so he snapped his attention up to the rest of us and spoke: "We should review the…eh…terms of the contest, or?"

"Sure," said Tommy.

"Yes, please," annunciated Momma, showing nervousness for the first time since church two days ago. Daddy crossed his arms, folded his hands into his armpits and nodded. I was motionless and totally aware of it. What was it that mesmerized me again, just like when Tommy had tried talking Daniel into quitting? Was it this place? The Boulder? Tommy? Daniel? The intensity of everyone around me? Did God freeze me where I stood for some higher reason?

Daniel's face looked fresh from breakfast, and his chest and arms looked hard and knotted from work. No question, he looked good. I was standing still, as if floating in the liquid center of a block of ice; arms nearly weightless. But, knowing all this, there was one thing I knew for certain: If he tried to tell me to jump – in any tone, at any volume – I would kick his tail steadily down our little mountain to the bus stop, buy his ticket with my own tip money, phone home for Tommy to bring down Daniel's bags and leave the ticket atop his crumpled form.

"Tommy and I each take one turn *mit dem hammer, ja?*" We all nodded, and Daniel continued. "Whoever makes the stone or stones with the most surface area wins."

"Why surface area?" Daddy asked. Tommy had only ever said *the biggest*; nothing about surface area.

"It's to make sure it's fair," Tommy piped up. "Suppose Daniel knocks off a big chunk." We all looked at the UFO shaped extension. It was safe to say that *I* could have knocked off a big chunk, given a chance. "But then," Tommy continued, "I knock off two rocks with one swing, and each of those rocks are only a little bit smaller than Daniel's one big stone. We agreed that it would be unfair for his one piece to win when my two have more surface area together. The rocks with a greater sum-surface-area win."

"'...greater sum-surface-area...?" Momma repeated, "Looks like you got somethin' from science class after all!" Tommy reddened. He'd often complained about how hard he had to study for Science, but he'd never said he wasn't learning.

"Why don't you just go by what's heaviest?" I asked.

Daddy shook his head.

"This can be unfair," *Oon-fayah* Daniel said. "The boulder is made from many different types of rock, so a piece can be heavier without being bigger. If I win because my smaller rock is heavier than your bigger one, you will feel I'm cheating on you."

"That's possible," Daddy put in "but I'm not too sure how likely it is. More importantly, *some* slabs of stone," he looked off to the trees rather than glare at The Boulder's protrusion, which may as well have been decorated with a kick me sign, "might be too heavy to weigh with our little bathroom scale. We could take the stones down to the plant where we have scales that could handle the job, no problem, but we won't for three reasons:

"First," he declared pushing one pointer back with the other, "the stones could roll around in the truck bed and lose chips while being transported, and then you get all sorts of contention about tampering and so forth. Second, it's too much hassle, and third, I ain't goin' down there 'cause I'm on vacation!

"Besides, there are easier ways to judge surface area with a bucket, water and a crayon."

"Eh…I am not so sure of this water method," said Daniel. "It can be a question about how much one or the other rock is…eh…" He began snapping his fingers for the word. "Ah! If one is like a…eh…" He held his hand out absently, palm up, and opened and closed to a fist – making squeezing gestures – before finally taking a tiny yellow German/English dictionary out of his pocket. All stood staring as the little pages flipipipped from one thumb to the other. Finally he made the sound "Spun-geh? The stone might be like a spun-geh."

Tommy leaned over to look, and Daniel pointed.

"Sponge. I don't get it. The rock may be like a sponge?"

"Porous," said Daddy.

For crying out loud! I thought. *How could two guys thumping a rock be so complicated?*

Daddy tried to continue, "I see your point, but…"

"I am sorry," Daniel interrupted, holding up his hands and shaking his head. "I am sure we will need no *messer*ing. I think it will be clear with no buckets or trucks or scales." We all made sounds of agreement with varying levels of confidence and sarcasm. "I was being…stupid." Momma never cared for that word, "stupid," but even she let it go in this case. Maybe she thought a good hostess doesn't correct guests in that situation or maybe just not on that word specifically. Or maybe she just agreed.

Both of the young men stepped toward the hammer simultaneously, and – seeing each other's movement – backed off simultaneously. They tried a second time, mirror images reaching out as they leaned toward the blunt instrument between them; and straightening up.

"I am going first, okay?"

"No, Daniel, I'd like to be first, and I think it's only fair."

"Fair?"

"Yeah. You suggested the terms. The whole surface area thing was your idea and I agreed to all of it. Don't get me wrong, I think it's a fun idea and I believe it's fair. But it *was* all your…all yours. Now I'm making this one condition: I swing first." This was the principle idea that Tommy and Daddy had come up with before dinner the previous day. The trick was obvious once you got a side view of the boulder; whoever struck first would easily knock that huge extended slab loose from the greater bulk of the remaining lump of Boulder. The plan was simple: agree to all else, as long as you go first. "Take it or leave it…that means I go first or we forget about the whole thing."

"Yes, I see," said Daniel. "Thank you." He was staring at the hammer as though he was tracking the descent of a diamond ring as it toppled away from him and down a black hole. "Yes," he kept his eyes down on the sledgehammer. "I see. You have right. I mean…" He shrugged his shoulders, arms akimbo for a moment before letting them fall, slapping his thighs softly. "I must agree. What you say is fair." He turned away, and looked off to the right of the house; where our gravel driveway met the gravel road which led down to town, the bus stop and away from here.

I may have felt sorry for him.

Tommy Picked up the hammer, and – as ever and always – he was not rash. He crept around the rock-blob. He marked carefully where the fat disk shape connected with the rest of the stone. He judged exactly where (a flat angled surface in the thick middle) and how hard (as hard as possible to be sure of shattering the three connecting points) to strike.

Daniel looked out at the driveway and the road as Tommy drew back and struck. He turned around in time to watch the slab slide down the slope of the remaining boulder; a slope he'd created. The slab nose dived into the earth, and stopped. Daddy grabbed the edge that was pointing up. He pulled so that it flopped down, exposing the convex surface, interrupted by three misshapen prongs – placed closer to the center than to the circumference – by which it had been held to The Boulder. Tommy jumped out of the way as it landed in his place on the tarp in one enormous, irreproducible piece.

No one crowed, and no one bellyached.

Chapter 23

Tommy offered Daniel the sledge, and, to our surprise, Daniel accepted it. "I would like to stand there please," he said pointing at the slab. He tossed the hammer to the ground and began tugging at the tarp pinned under the slab. He grunted and strained and made a snail's progress. Finally Tommy and Daddy grabbed an edge and began to help. Seeing that we were near the end, I decided to pitch in too.

Daniel gave me a look of such fresh surprise and pleasure that I nearly let go of the tarp. "Thank you, Sarah," he beamed.

I felt heat rushing to my face, and, in resentment (or embarrassment,) a half dozen snotty retorts – most of these about Daniel's imminent failure – came to my mind. I said nothing. I just pulled.

We dragged the slab until it rested about three feet from it's greater sister cell. "Thank you very much," Daniel recited to the Hanover men. They nodded in response, and we backed away to give Daniel a fair space and a fair try at the impossible. No one bothered laying a fresh tarp under The Boulder, and Daniel requested none. Even he realized that there was no way he would off knock a larger block than the three-eyed wedge of granite that was staring blindly at the sky from those broken connection points.

He stood where he'd said he wanted to stand, staring at the long handle, held out parallel to his hips. The hammer's head pointed without hope or doubt at The Boulder. Our eyes followed it in the wrong direction.

He was silent. We suspected – though later musings would find me doubting it – that he was praying. We held still and quiet for him.

Then his hips shifted, and, for the first time, I realized that something was off. I couldn't have said what in that one count, but I can tell you now: He shifted his weight the wrong way for the beginning of a swing; towards The Boulder rather than away from it.

The head of the sledge nearly glanced the surface of The Boulder before he lifted it into the beginning of its arc. Up to his shoulder, above it (his hips now shifting away from The Boulder) over his head (he'd begun shouting along the way, "EEEYYAA…") and then slicing down, away from The Boulder ("…AAAU…") slamming with tectonic, crushing force into the heart of the slab that lay on the tarp we'd dragged. Splitting it into three uneven pieces. Momentarily it was folded slightly in on the central point of impact, three-ways cross-eyed. Then the pieces fell away from one another; finally three-ways wall-eyed.

My "Wha?" came out just above whisper, and was drowned out by Daniel's breathy chuckles.

"Heh heh." He dragged the hammer off the still large fragments. "That is not exactly where I meant to strike," he confessed, smiling and pointing at his handiwork. I thought it to be some European version of extreme irony, but then he said, "I meant to strike closer to this edge here, to be sure to break off a piece." His smile broadened, and his eyes brightened. "But this is much better, or?"

"Is this some weird way of saying you give up?" asked Tommy, and Daniel chuckled louder in response. Daddy stared, wordless, at the fragments; still trying to puzzle it all out. Momma watched both young men with crossed arms and a look of frank suspicion. I was beginning to entertain the notion that Daniel had finally gone completely crackers.

"No, Tommy," gushed Daniel with a warmth that struck me as totally inappropriate, strengthening my crackers theory. "I give *not* up. It means I win!" Yep. Like a busted box of Saltines.

"What? You didn't even *hit* The Boulder." Tommy said.

His tone triggered an automatic response in me. I felt my temper begin to itch, but I ignored it. Daniel's contention that he'd won was too ridiculous to hold water.

But it didn't sink.

"We never agreed that each swing must hit The Boulder." Daniel argued, still smiling.

"What are you talkin' about? You didn't knock anything off the boulder." Tommy searched among us for comprehension, something he maybe missed. He found none from me.

"No," smiled Daniel, finally dropping the sledgehammer to the ground, "but I win *trotzdem*…eh…nevertheless."

"How in your German-talkin' world do you figure *you* win?"

"Surface area," answered Daddy from the sidelines, giving everyone a jolt.

But Daniel recovered quickly, kneeling beside the slab fragments. Wedging one knee under the largest fragment, he drew the other two to it – meshing the three back into one – and managed to hold them in place with one long fingered hand. He held his free hand over the fractured whole, fingers splayed and palm down. He made the free hand orbit the top of the slab, and said, "This is the surface area from your hit, Tommy. This and the under part. The pieces I made too have this area, but also…" He released the fragments to fall apart again. "these areas," he pointed to the newly created edges where the fragments had previously been joined. "My area is your area," he reiterated, "plus this in the middle."

My jaw dipped, and my temper jumped another few notches.

"I'm not sure that holds, Daniel," Daddy finally said. "Tommy knocked that whole big chunk free, and you only exposed those edges you just pointed at. I don't reckon it's fair of you, takin' credit for that whole slab a second time; seein' as how it was already exposed."

Daniel stood, and watched my father as he spoke, his face relaxed except for a slight frown. It appeared more concentration than displeasure. When Daddy concluded, Daniel nodded, as he had at Tommy's argument before.

"I can aczept this way of measuring," he said, and knelt back beside the fragments. "These new exposed edges *only* are mine," he began.

"That's right," Daddy said, arms crossed. Head nodding.

"But then only these three points," Daniel dragged the pad of a pointer finger across each of the three nubs that pushed up from the greater surface of the fragments, "can be credited to Tommy."

"What?" cried Tommy, his prize suddenly stolen from him right before his eyes.

"No," stated Daddy, shaking his head with steady, swift turns.

"No," echoed Daniel in a thoughtful tone, tapping his bottom lip with the dusty pointer that had brushed the stones. "No, that is oonfair," he continued. "It would be these three 'new exposed surfaces,' but two times. There must be matching 'new exposed surfaces,' on The Boulder. They should be counted too. But I believe that your six dots are still not more than my six large edges. I still win."

"No way!" red faced, pale haired Tommy's voice broke on the second syllable. "I knocked that whole slab free. No way you're gonna say I didn't."

"But, Tommy," Daniel said with the first hints of condescension, "your father has said that we are judging by 'new exposed surfaces,' and I sink every person here knows that I exposed all but those six points yesterday with hammer and chisel. Zo, to say as Mr. Hanover, I do not reckon it's fair of you, taking credit for that whole slab a second time."

I very nearly managed to not explode.

Chapter 25

But then I did. Big and messy. I think my arms were flapping around a lot. I called him a dirty, rotten, lying, cheating…something…it might have been "thief." I hope I said "thief."

He sited the story of Jacob and Esau as an example of – he must have looked this word up the night before, but I swear he used it – "guile" being allowed or tolerated.

I don't remember that whole episode too well.

I think, but I'm not sure, that I blasphemed right in front of my parents. I said that Jacob was a low down S.O.B. (I hope to heaven that I only used the letters,) and that I was right to say so because his mother helped him sucker his own brother. "**His own brother!**" I remember shouting. That was one of those arm-waving moments. Oh yeah. I followed that up with something like, "Is that the sort of man you suppose I'd marry?! The sort of man who cheats my brother, and then acts like he's got permission from The Bible because some rotten sneak got help from his own *mother* to steal the blessing of his *father* from his own *brother*?! Is that the sort of girl you think I am?" And in a sudden rush of my own sneakiness, I added, "Is that the sort of *women* you think to find from the *Hanover family*?!"

I'm not proud of how I acted, but I was happy to find that Daniel was right as far as the whole stories-being-easier-to-remember-and-use thing goes. I remembered that story just right. And that old bit of mischief happened back in Genesis! I didn't think anyone but our pastor and my parents remembered anything from The Old Testament. Maybe the Sunday school teachers too. Turns out they weren't the only ones.

Somewhere along the line, Daddy called me off. Momma was red as a Rome Apple, clearly furious rather than embarrassed. I never asked her who, specifically, she was angry at, and I don't plan to.

Daddy said that Daniel made some interesting points. He wasn't convinced by those interesting points, but he wasn't convinced that Tommy had won any more either. He shook his head at the whole ordeal, and finally said that the boys should drag the three shards of rock up to the slag heap that had been formed on top of The Hill over the last weeks. "Then," he said with deep steady tones, "I want y'all to come into the house, and get cleaned up. We'll make lunch together, however Ruthie will let us, and eat it in fellowship. After that, Daniel, I want you to put your tools away for the day. I'm not sayin' you can't finish the job. Just call a halt for today.

"The three of us, Ruthie, Daniel and I will head into town to get some more provisions. We're runnin' low."

"What about me and Sarah?"

"You two can go on and do what you like after lunch, Tommy. I know you've still got some pages you wanna turn, and Sarah can stroll to cool off by one of her streams."

"You know about my…"

"I introduced you to most of them, Sarah," he interrupted. "You two just be sure to be cleaned up and fresh for dinner. We're gonna have a special meal tonight. Why? Because I want us all feeling good after dinner. Why? Because enough is enough, and it's time to swap some stories already. Why are we waiting until tonight? Well, we don't make a habit of drinking during daylight hours unless it's a beer, and it's only appropriate that these particular stories be swapped over a certain bottle of wine."

The kind with two languages on the label.

PART III

The Wine, The Stories & The Fire

Chapter 26

Daddy came back from his bedroom with a small, faded green cloth bag that looked military issue. He sat down, facing the yellow-red glare of the fireplace across the coffee table. Tommy and I sat on the couch to his right. I held my dark, half-filled wine glass out low in front of my lap with both hands, forearms crossing thighs. I leaned forward, over my glass, allowing the fragrance of the red to drift up to my nose. Tommy leaned back into the couch, his glass resting on his leg. Daniel sat in the chair to my father's left. Their wine glasses shared the coffee table, situated in the middle of the ring formed by the couch, chairs and fireplace. Momma hovered back in the kitchen; cleaning up the last signs of the Spaghetti Bolognese we'd enjoyed with salad, warm rolls and apple cider. Bearing the remnants of a chocolate cake bought in town, small saucers and forks dotted the counter; waiting for the soap, the sponge and her attention.

Daddy stared into the fire for a minute - Stonewall Hanover holding out on us one last moment before finally telling his tale.

"I reckon it's best to start with this here cross," he said as he withdrew from his shirt a polished metal cross on a dark leather cord. I'd never seen him without it, but now he took it from around his neck, and put it into his lap. "And with this here Bible." He took from the cloth satchel a generic looking copy of The Holy Bible; severely beaten, singed and swollen from long passed water damage. It was smaller than my hand, but still managed to look heavy in Daddy's.

He gently bobbed the fat, black barely bound wad of rice paper. "These were the ingredients of my sin," he said looking from the Bible to the cross "and my salvation."

He set the Bible on the cloth bag, which had been laid on the tiny square table to his left. Taking the leather cord in his hands, Daddy leaned forward – elbows on his knees. He held it so that the cross lay across his bent knuckles. It reflected the light dully, and tiny black spots could be seen near the edges.

"This thing used to shine like a light bulb. My pastor in Berea gave me both the cross and the Bible before I went off to volunteer for service."

"That means before he joined the army, Daniel," Tommy said, not unkindly.

"Yes. Thank you," Daniel replied evenly; not indicating that he'd had any trouble understanding in the first place. He stared at Daddy with intense focus.

Daddy, for his part, stared at the cross – into the story it held – and shook his head slowly and blindly. "He told me…well, he told me all sorts of stuff. Mostly Old Testament stuff; God protects his servants, and the unbeatable force of the Israelites with God's blessing, The Bible being mightier than any gun, and the cross a guarantee of success even in death. The Nazis, he said, were a Godless bunch of idolaters, and so we were guaranteed victory. They were destined to damnation…you get the idea. He was just a preacher in a small town. All he knew about the Germans or the Nazi's was what the papers and the newsreels told him, so it was the best he could give me. It all seems scattered to me now. But back then I had every word memorized, and I believed it with all the force and conviction that young men put into those things they're called upon to believe.

"In boot camp, they broke me down, and trained me up to declare my gun to be my closest friend. I kept it close, and learned its every part with an intimacy, ferocity and professionalism that a soldier must have to have a hope of surviving the training; not to mention the war.

"I did my best to never neglect the Bible, but there were times that it simply wasn't possible. When I couldn't read it, I recited my pastor's words in my thoughts 'till I fell asleep.

"I learned to trust the men in my platoon, and that they relied on me. We all came close during the training, but I'd become especially close with a Catholic fella' named Murphy.

"Now, we ain't Catholics in this house, Daniel, and I'd been raised to think of them as practically another religion entirely. We'd gotten close after having a nasty brawl in the barracks one night. I was sittin' there studying the Bible when Murphy came along, and called me a thief. I was already exhausted, and had decided I didn't like bunkin' with a Catholic. So, I didn't hesitate tryin' to knock his block off.

"After the rest of the platoon had pulled us apart Murphy said I was crazy, and that I'd attacked him for no good reason. The Bible had fallen on the floor. When we picked it up and took a look at it we found Murphy's name on the inside page. He said that he'd dropped it onto my footlocker in order to go help a buddy to lug out the garbage.

"I'd come across it, and assumed I'd left it out on the footlocker by accident. I'd taken it as a kind of nudge from The Almighty to turn a page or two. When Murphy'd come back to find me reading his Bible he'd decided to rib me a little, and I'd just exploded all over him.

"We opened my footlocker, and removed my Bible to hold it next to Murphy's. It wasn't exactly the same, but they were close enough that we'd had to double check the 'This Holy Bible belongs to…' pages to be sure which was whose. Naturally there were a few extra books in his version, but you had to put them on scales to find the difference. I don't know, maybe they'd come from the same printer or the printers used the same paper suppliers.

Anyway, the whole platoon laughed at the two of us 'till we had no choice but to laugh at ourselves. It may sound silly to you, Sarah, but sometimes it's a fight like that that'll bring fighting men together. Not every time, mind you, but it did with us.

"Well, I don't wanna put y'all to sleep with every detail, so I'll skip on to the first dead Nazi I ever had time to look at up close."

"It was in France, and he was wearin' a cross. Not the Iron Cross. A crucifix. It was just a necklace, sort of like this one here 'cept it was made of some dark wood and had a tiny figure nailed to it. It was too simple and plain to be a decoration. This was a symbol of faith.

"I tried to fall back on what I'd always been told about Catholics, and told myself that this man had been praying in the wrong directions. He had nothing to do with me. But I felt uneasy anyway.

"First I tried to tell myself that I was just shaken up that I'd seen a dead man up close. I prayed about it. I prayed for peace over and over, but it wouldn't come. As we pressed through France I started arguing more and more with Murphy, and neither of us could understand why he was getting under my skin so easily.

"He died there in France, and I wept for him when the fighting let up enough. Our Sergeant gave me Murphy's Bible as a remembrance."

"Daddy, what's Murphy's Bible there got to do with bottles of wine from Europe?" I asked while he swallowed back the memory.

He looked mildly startled at my question. Then he looked at the Bible and back at me before saying, "Oh. No, darlin'. This ain't Murphy's Bible. It's mine. I couldn't stand to hold onto it, and besides in Boot Camp he'd given me an addressed goodbye letter for his family back in Tennessee in case somethin' happened to him. We'd all swapped that sort of thing before goin' into action. I mailed that book back stateside first chance I got.

"But I did look at it for a long time before getting someplace where I could mail it off. I looked at it nearly every night, and I rubbed the cover under my thumbs when it was too dangerous to make a light. I thought for a long time about Murphy, that Bible and that first dead Nazi soldier I'd seen; first of many.

"I guess it all seems clear as a sunny day to y'all kids, but it took me a long time to see what was botherin' me. That Nazi had his crucifix because sometime in his life he'd touched a book just like that one, and believed. Sure, his Bible was probably in German, and who can say whether he really believed or not. But in the end it didn't matter. The connection was there. He was flesh and blood, and had likely prayed to the same God as Murphy had; the same God as I had. It was too likely a possibility to ignore, no matter how hard I tried. And believe me, I tried.

"Murphy's Bible and letter had been mailed off a long time before our unit was moved to Germany. By that time I really understood what was buggin' me. But by then knowin' didn't help anymore. My faith had been slipping with every dead man, woman and child I saw. I didn't fall easy. I prayed and begged for help, mercy, protection and forgiveness. I prayed for peace inside and out. None of it seemed to come. My faith wiled away bit by bit, but it didn't die.

"At least not until we liberated the death camp."

We broke to refill our glasses, and grab some snacks that Momma had been warming up for us. I was hesitant to eat, but Daddy promised that his story wouldn't bring our food back up.

"I ain't goin' into none of the gory details," he said. "You can pick up a book when you're back in Lexington if you want to learn about what I saw. It's enough that y'all already know that what we saw there was as bad or worse than anything seen by any man alive today. Those death camps were ugliest part of the ugliest thing mankind does."

He rubbed his eyes, and we returned to our places around his chair without saying a word. Questions bubbled in my mind, but I chose sipping over squawking. I could see in Tommy's eyes that he was holding back questions too, and he watched our father closely as he strode quietly from some private conference with our mother to his seat. Daniel seemed to be holding his peace without too much trouble, but I don't suppose he'd learned much yet that meant anything to him.

Daddy sat and took a bite from a toasted roll Momma

had pushed on him. He wiped melted butter from his mouth with his sleeve before continuing. I saw that my own glass was nearly empty, and accepted a toasted roll and a slice of cheese that Momma had placed on the coffee table. I could hear her pouring glasses of water in the kitchen. She was keeping us sober for some reason.

"My faith was already weak as a sick bird by the time I walked through the gates of *Mauthausen*. What I saw there crushed it, and I was among those who bent to vomit before the evening fell.

"I puked and wept for my own faith and soul as much as for the poor bastards we'd found in there. I ain't proud of it, but it's the truth. After a campaign through France – and being in the middle of one in German territory – most of us had hardened enough to hold our lunches. But my faith, burned in the ovens along wi…sorry Sarah. The loss of my faith had peeled away those calluses that keep men at war sane. I was softened and lost in the darkest and most purely evil place I have ever known in my life.

"My platoon dragged me out of there, half crazy with despair. I wouldn't eat, and by the time we'd pitched camp I couldn't bear the company of the others. I wandered off with some firewood and a canister of gasoline I stole from a nearby jeep, and I made a fire.

"I didn't know what I was building that fire for, but the idea grew in my mind as the gasoline used itself up and the wood burned without further help. It was a modest but hot fire by the time I began to pray what I intended to be my final prayer.

"I told God that I'd had enough. I called Him sick; an unforgivable monster. I said that I didn't want anything to do with Him. I said that I wasn't gonna play along in His 'filthy little sandbox' no more. Aw, Tommy, close your mouth for cryin' out loud. I said all sorts of things you never heard from my lips, and ordered Him out of my life like I had some kind of authority to make Him do it.

"I ripped this here cross off my neck, and threw it in the fire." With that he tossed the cross to me. I caught it automatically, and froze in the pose in which I'd caught it. "This here Bible followed it not five seconds later." He underhanded it into Tommy's lap, and Tommy nearly jumped out of his skin like the book might still be burning.

"You're a cruel hard man, Joseph Hanover, to be makin' sport about such a thing; and at your children's expense no less!" Momma called from the kitchen.

His mouth was a perfectly horizontal line. "I wasn't teasin' them, Ruthie," he said with his eyes checking back and forth between me and Tommy, "They're entitled to know what they're inheriting, blessings and curses alike."

Tommy was the first to recover. "But you're forgiven, Daddy, aintcha? I mean, here's the Bible in my hand. It was saved from the fire. And the cross too!" He pointed at me and the cross I held. "Besides, you must've repented. I know you well enough to know that."

"We'll get to that, son. But you should understand the temperament you've inherited. I've tried to raise you to be the masters of your tempers, both of you. But you need to know that the same blood that pushed a Bible and a cross into the fire runs through your veins."

A moment of silence swelled around us as we took in what my father had said. I sat there and thought about all the times and ways I'd screamed, cajoled, whined, schemed and fought just in those last few weeks I'd been home. I closed my eyes with the shame of knowing how I'd failed; how I'd let my blood boil up out of my mouth and all over people I knew and cared about. I saw myself, in my mind's eye, spitting fire and blood all over the furniture of the house in which I'd grown, learned and loved.

I wished that it wasn't already dark so I could run to that little brook I'd found the day after I'd returned. I wanted to lie on that new flat boulder in the middle. I wanted to dip my finger tips and toes in the water. In my mind I saw myself there, and as I touched the water steam rose up. The steam smelled like the sweet wine I'd been holding under my nose.

I opened my eyes, shocked by the vision.

"But you must've grabbed a hold of yourself, Daddy," Tommy finally said. "You saved the cross and the Bible." He held the singed rice paper Bible out between them as if someone in the room needed proof that it was still there.

"No, I didn't, Tommy. I threw them into the fire to burn, melt and to go away forever from my life."

"So, was there a miracle or somethin'? Was this book like The Burning Bush? It wouldn't be consumed?"

"Watch your tone when you're speaking of such things Thomas," Momma warned.

"I reckon you *could* say there was a miracle."

I looked over at Daniel to see if he was being taken in by my father's pace and evasions. His eyes were glued to the conversation, but he was still sitting back in his chair and waiting from a distance. He hadn't been waiting these weeks for this story. He was waiting for something else.

Tommy was looking around the room to see if anybody was getting as flummoxed as he was. Momma was in the kitchen with her back turned to us all, and Daniel sat there like he had ice in his veins. I don't know how I looked, but I reckon I wanted to know where all this was leading as badly as Tommy.

"You *reckon*?!? How do *you reckon*? Enough's enough, Dad. Tell us what happened already. If you threw a Bible in a fire more than twenty years ago, and never took it out how come I'm holding it in my hand?"

Daddy's eyes gleamed. This all may not have been a good memory for him, but he'd turned it into a good enough yarn to rile one of us up. He and Momma always did tell us to count our blessings.

"Take a sip of wine Tommy, and try to calm yourself down. I'm just barely half way through. The cross and the Bible sat in the middle of the fire for about five seconds before I heard someone not far off in the darkness cry out '*Nein*!'" Daddy imitated a ragged and shaky voice.

"All of a sudden, this gray haired Jew came runnin' outta the darkness, and threw himself onto the fire! He was screaming out all kinds of German I didn't stand a chance of understanding. He grabbed the Bible with his bare hands, and used it to flip the cross outta' the fire. Then he jumped out of the fire, and rolled around on the ground holding the Bible against his chest.

"He smothered the flames, saving the Bible and himself. I was too surprised to do much of anything but watch that crazy sonofa…" the water thumped to a stop in the kitchen, and Daddy hesitated. "Well that crazy *Jew*."

"How'd you know it was a Jewish man, Daddy?"

"The prisoner uniform with the yellow star on the chest, the first aid blanket that fell from his shoulders and the fact that he was starved to the shape of a lamp post. Besides, the fact that he was screaming in German and not trying to surrender was a pretty good sign by that point in the war."

"Never mind how you knew," Tommy said "why'd a Jew run, literally, through flames to save a Christian Bible and a cross?"

"Yes," added Daniel. Even Momma turned at the sound of his voice, held silent for so long until this point. "Why did

Herr Bergmann do this?"

Daddy met Daniel's eyes for a handful of heartbeats, before saying, "That's what I wanted to know, Daniel; after I finished calling him a damn fool and checking him for burns, that is."

Momma set down a tray with five glasses of water, and poured herself a splash of wine into a fresh glass. She sat down in the last chair nearest the fireplace, and took a sip. She smiled at my daddy, and he smiled back at her. The fire grew by a few degrees.

Daniel sat catlike still except for his long right-hand pointer absently scratching the pad of his thumb.

"What do you know about him?" this time it was Daddy.

Daniel seemed to look around at the four of us, trying to make a decision. The firelight bounced warm off his polished dark oak colored eyes. It was a softer brown than the hard dark shade they took in the sunlight, more welcoming than the wide open pupils he'd shown the first day we'd met. He looked different; tired and worn down in a very good way.

Chapter 27

I couldn't help watching Daniel over the weeks that had passed. I had seen him overeager and fresh those first days, gleaming with sweat as he swatted at the boulder and collapsing in exhaustion at the end of most of the days he'd been with us. It was always too much. He was always pushing and trying so hard that he'd made himself unreal. Sinewy and beautiful. And yet terrible. There seemed to be no shades of gray with him, nothing subtle.

But the firelight, the wine or finally being close to finished with his task had softened his whole face. I saw for the first time in Daniel the look my father had brought home most nights from the plant. He always came home tired, of course. Mining's no job for the weak or lazy, and those with lazy minds don't usually survive long enough to be as old as my father.

We used to have an unofficial routine that always told us his mood. When he came home I'd ask if he was tired. If he just took off his hat and tossed it onto a chair or table, saying "Yeah," we knew to stay clear. Walk quietly. But most nights he'd give the same answer: "Yeah I'm tired!" he'd cry out. Then he'd split into a smile, and say "But it's a good tired."

Daniel looked us over, trying to decide if he could divulge what he knew, and I finally got to see what he looked like with a good tired. It wasn't hard to look at. No trouble at all. You couldn't have dared me to stop looking.

Chapter 28

"I have never met with Mr. Bergmann personally," Daniel began, "but I have handled documents pertaining to him. They were always perfectly thorough. There was never a detail missed. This would be normal for the files of a longstanding client, but it was unusual to me because it was all written by hand. This alone was enough to make me curious, but most strange was the fact that it was not the handwriting of my employer. I asked him about it once in an offhanded way, and learned that it was the handwriting of Mr. Bergmann himself!

"I commented that Mr. Bergmann must have been a great lawyer before leaving the country."

"So this Mr. Bergman doesn't live in Vienna anymore," I thought out loud.

"Of course not, Sarah," he looked at me, lips thick and relaxed, with his face half glowing in firelight, and half black with shadow. "If he lived in Vienna he would be able to buy the Kosher L'Pesach wine himself, and avoid our fees. We do not charge much for such a simple service, but it is not gratis."

"Where does he practice now?" asked Tommy. "I'll bet he's still prosecuting ex-Nazis and following paper trails to stolen Jewish money and art!"

"You've seen too many war movies, Tommy," I muttered.

"He does not practice," answered Daniel "and never did."

"What do you mean?" I called for Daniel's eyes to return, and I drank the view with my own. "Was he a professor or somethin'?"

"When I ask my employer, he tells me that Mr. Bergmann was not a lawyer of any sort and has never been."

"But you said…"

"And so I ask my chef…"

"Chief." Daddy intoned.

"…how Mr. Bergmann could have composed such perfect legal documents by hand if he is not a lawyer." And Daniel finished right there, looking around the room as if he'd told a complete story of righteous indignation, and was waiting to be rained upon with calls of sympathy and support.

Tommy cleared his throat gently, "Umm, Daniel, what did your boss tell you?"

"He does not know, of course! He says that it was quite amazing to him as well, and that the documents I'm seeing were all single drafts. They had never been rewritten or corrected, and no changes had ever been needed. Mr. Bergmann would simply sit down with his ink pen and scribble out a perfectly legible, well ordered, thorough and legally sound document without pause or hesitation!" Again, Daniel looked around the room for sympathy and support, but, again, we had no idea what for.

"So, why was he able to do it?" Tommy tried again.

"I do not know Tommy! *Zat* is one of the *sings* I have come here to learn! My chef…chief" looking briefly at my father "could only recall a joke Mr. Bergmann told when asked about this extraordinary…eh…thing he does."

"What was the joke?"

"It is not funny in English," he said, waving the question off. "At the time I just found the whole thing to be an interesting small story from my office, but it begins to interfere with my private life. The strangeness of it pushes into my thoughts when I pray. I try to forget it, and connect with God. But every time I open myself to Him, I open a dam, and it rushes in upon my thoughts. Other questions about Mr. Bergmann begin to come into my mind whenever I pray; or simply sitting on the tram."

Now Daddy was leaning forward onto his knees again. We all were.

"I begin to feel that I am being somehow persecuted by this mystery. I know it is only a small mystery, but it makes clouds in my praying. The more I think about it, the more I pray to be released from it. The more I pray for release, the more I think about Mr. Bergmann. Finally, one night, I give my sister a fist full of shillings and ask her to go out from our apartment for some hours. When she has gone I turn off all of the lights and fall on my knees on my bedroom floor. I pray with all my strength. Why is The Devil sending such strange distractions to keep me from God?"

He looked at my father to his right, then straight into my eyes. He then skipped over Tommy to look at my mother on his left, and said, "It was then I receive a great understanding. The Devil sent none of it. It was God. It was when I'd open myself to Him that *He* would put these questions to my mind." Daniel turned to face the rest of us. "When I finally accepted it in this way, I found great peace. I felt that this was something that I was being lead to investigate.

"Over the next months I ask my *boss*" nodding at Tommy "about it, but no matter how I ask, he always remembers himself of some funny joke or story Mr. Bergmann had told him. When I press he shrugs his shoulders and says that he'd never gotten around to finding out. *Alzo*, in those days shortly after the war…" He paused to begin shaking is head at his glass. "Even today – one does not ask too many questions in Vienna about another's past.

"Eventually, my frustration leads me to mailing a letter to the address in Kentucky where I have been sending the bottles. After dropping the letter off at the Post, I whisper a prayer to God that this is all I can do and that I am leaving the rest to Him. It was not the sort of hard prayer one makes alone in one's room or in the church. It was a simple thing one says, like 'Ahhhh' after the first *schluck* of a good coffee. It was not really meant to do anything, but it did something doing. I felt different. I felt the questions wash away, like a pipe being made clear.

"I knew that it was the last thing I could do to find answers to my questions. I thought it was this knowledge that made things better, but now I do not think it was only that." He looked at me. I thought that he looked sad, and my chest ached. He blinked, and looked around the room. "After that my prayers seem to fly to God, and my connection seems stronger than ever." He looked, for the first time, at his knees. "It was shortly after sending the letter that I was told that I would meet my future wife in the U.S.

"I hoped," he continued after raising his head back up with new energy, "That Mr. Hanover might be able to explain how Mr. Bergmann had come to have his talent, why he would hide his story in jokes and funny tales, why he would pay us to send a wine from Vienna that he could probably send more easily from his own home and – now as I have begun to hear this story – why a Jewish survivor would dive into a fire for a Christian Bible!"

"Take it easy, Daniel," Daddy said. "I'll tell you what I can. His reason for jumping into that fire comes near the end of another story. Come to think of it, like most things, it almost certainly marked the beginning of still another story for him too. But the stories are his stories, so I'll tell them to you as faithfully as I can manage. I'll tell you everything now."

Chapter 29

"Bergmann was cryin' and saying in pretty good English, 'You must not do this! It is my guilt!' while tryin' to push the Bible and cross on me like *I* was the one all skin and bones and he was gonna feed me whether I liked it or not."

"Sounds like Auntie Norice at dinner time." I whispered to Tommy, but he didn't respond.

"I asked him, 'Why the heck does a Christian Bible mean so much to a Jew?' Get this: He *chuckled.* He chuckled and said, 'I guess we just don't like to see books burning. Especially not in these times.' Haw! My jaw dropped open, and he used the opportunity to try pushing the cross and Bible on me again.

"I told him he could keep it if it meant so much to him, because I was done with it. Me and God, I said, were quits for good.

"Well he just started wailing even louder than before, and kept saying that it was all a terrible mistake; all his fault. He kept tellin' me how sorry he was, and that I should take it back. I told him that if he'd cut his screamin' out it'd give him a chance to say why he cares whether a Christian Bible burns or not.

"'In our tradition,' he told me, 'We never burn a book, most surely never a book about God. If a book of God is so old that it cannot be used we bury it with the respect given to a dead person.'"

"'Do you burn yourselves alive to *save* them in your tradition?' I said. He pulled a play-guilty face like he knew he'd been caught out. I still think he must be crazy as a foaming dog or stronger than steel. What kinda' man comes out of a place like that and can still laugh and joke? He admitted that there was more to the story than a distaste for book burning. After he'd told me his story - and after we'd had a chance to share company from time to time over the next few days - I realized that laughter and jokes were the key to his survival; literally his bread and water."

Jonathan Bergmann (he pronounced it Yonatan, but Daddy only ever thought of him as Jonathan) had been a proud member of the German army before Hitler came to power. He'd been born and raised a Jew, and educated in their ways. But he'd never cared for it much. He'd found a true home in the military, and would have happily served it to his death.

It's a funny attitude for a pencil pusher like Jonathan.

You expect to find it in a fighting soldier, or at least you're not really surprised when a grunt shows it. But Jonathan was a supply officer. He was one of those lowly men trusted with the awesome responsibilities: Finding Stuff and Moving Stuff. This sounded to me and Tommy like small potatoes, but Daddy explained that, when you needed a new pair of boots to help you slog through Italy or France and the men below you will live or die based on whether or not they get their ammunition and subsistence, there's no one more important than the quartermaster.

Jonathan had shown himself to be strong in the two basic requirements for the job: He was a great scavenger and a great diplomat. He also had an ability to read and move densely written legalistic paperwork as needed in order to scratch up whatever is being looked for. He said it was probably from all the densely written texts he'd been forced to study by his rabbi. He had a sense of humor that kept those above and below him content; happy when supplied or assured of continued effort when not. His jokes and anecdotes greased the wheels no matter which way they spun.

"When Hitler rose to power," Daddy explained, "Jonathan was declared unfit for service, and, over time, unfit for living among other Germans. Like millions of Jews – some passionately faithful and some not even aware that there had been Jews hanging out in their family trees – he was sent to die by working himself to death through exhaustion, starvation, giving a good enough excuse to be shot, any of a generous list of diseases or whatever creative methods his guards and handlers (men he had once called his compatriots) could think of.

"Just the fact that he managed to stay alive in that place was an accomplishment. There must be a story worth telling there, but I don't know it. All he'd say about it was that knowing the ways of the soldiers, officers and the army in general helped him to know how to say what; and to whom he ought to say it.

"'Not long ago,' he told me, 'I was lying in my shelf.' I didn't try to correct him. Those sure weren't beds they'd been sleeping in. 'I was trying to think of a joke, but I was only succeeding at falling asleep because falling asleep was the only easy thing there. But, before I began to fall away, I heard someone calling my name. I stayed quiet, waiting for someone to shush whoever was making noise. The only sound to follow was the same voice calling to me. *Ja.* I said *here I am.*

"'The voice told me to come to the center of the room. Doing what one is ordered to do is the way of life in the Army, and it was part of the only small chance for survival in the camp. So I went to the middle of the room, but I saw no person there with me. I waited for some time because I didn't know what to do. There was very little chance that a prisoner was playing a joke on me, and a guard or officer would not tolerate me to speak unless told to do so. But after some time I decided to mumble out *I am here* again.

"'*You may sit, Jonathan. It is I, the God of your fathers* the voice said. I was already sitting by the time the second sentence was said, so, sitting, I looked around the room. It was too dark to be sure, but it looked like everyone was asleep. I knew then that it was not a guard or officer, because – even for a joke – they would only say that they are a god over me, perhaps even God, Himself. But they would never make their mouths dirty saying that they are the God of my fathers.

"'*Either one of you is playing a joke on me with their eyes closed, or I have finally lost my mind,* I said softly to the sleeping others in the room. No one moved. I speculated that I was much more likely going crazy, and almost hoped that this was right. *What would you need to believe I am that I am?* the voice asked. *I never heard that God was cheeky*, I said, but there was no response. The question seemed to be rhetoric, but still needed to be answered.

"'I was so tired, and did not want to let my obvious insanity make me too tired for the next day's labors, so I just said, *Okay. If you are God, have Schmidt give me a double portion tomorrow.*'"

"Who's Schmidt?" Tommy and I asked in unison.

"Funny you should ask that."

"Why?"

"Because that's exactly what I asked Jonathan when he was tellin' me the story. 'Who's Schmidt?' I asked. 'Schmidt,' he told me, 'was one of the guards at the camp. I knew him when I was a quartermaster in the army. About two weeks after I'd arrived, I was walking back to my barracks when he began to walk next to me.

"'*Tell me a joke* Jude, he said.

I knew better, but I could not help looking over at him. He gave me a second to recognize him before hitting me in the face with the butt of his rifle. On the ground I opened my eyes to see him standing over me, screaming. I tasted my blood in my mouth as he screamed that I should know better than to turn my big nose on a proper Aryan.

"'I believe that he did this as much to protect us both as to punish me for putting us in danger. Had he tolerated a Jew looking him in the eyes and treating him as an equal, his career would have been ended; possibly even his life. My life was standing on the head of a pin anyway, and anything but the beating I got would have been reason enough for the guards to spend a bullet on me.

"'This was the beginning of the relationship where Schmidt would come to walk beside me two or three times a week, and demand that I tell him a joke. If the joke I told was good, he would punch me in the stomach. As I curled around his fist, I would find that he had passed me a half eaten piece of bread. I am not sure that I would have starved without those pieces of bread, and I was still hungry all of the time. But I cannot guess what my awful life would have been like without even those.

"'Well, I told the voice to have Schmidt give me a double

portion. This had never happened before, and I did not really expect it to happen the next day. *Lie down and sleep then, Jonathan* the voice said, and I was happy to do so.

"'But it did happen. The next day, while I lay on the ground for a few seconds to hide the bread in my shirt, I found that I had to roll around an extra moment to slip a second piece under my coat.

"I asked Jonathan if he was convinced after that. 'Yes,' he said, 'I was convinced that I had lost my mind completely. But, even if I was a crazy man, I was a crazy man with two extra pieces of bread under my coat. I had not expected the bread that day, but I was expecting to become crazy for a long time by then.

"'That night, I ate my bread as silently as I could, but I did not say the *motzi.*' That's the prayer Jews say before breaking bread. 'As I was beginning the second piece of bread, the voice came back. *Now will you believe?*

"'*You are God, eh? Don't you know the answer already?* I mumbled. *Yes,* the voice said. *Now, will you believe?*

"'As I have already said to you, sleeping is the only thing that is easy. Getting angry takes a great deal more strength than one can normally spend in the camp, but I could not help it. *If you are God, then get us out of here! Throw open the gates, and I will believe!*

"'Now, here is something funny. No one was surprised or even moved when I said this. It was not worth the strength. It was a prayer almost all of us had said at one time or another.

"'*Lie down and sleep then, Jonathan* the voice said again, and I did again.'

"Well, I suppose y'all can guess what happened the next day. The guards were running around like cockroaches in the toilet when the light goes on. Some were packing up to head for the hills, and others were doing their duty and trying to destroy as much evidence of their crimes as possible. But, by early afternoon, my unit arrived and liberated the camp. The German soldiers were gone before we even got there, and the inmates were already so close to death that it seemed more like we were uncovering a living grave than freeing prisoners.

"That afternoon, while I vomited and surrendered the last of my faith, Jonathan was staggering, dazed, out of the camp, and being given a blanket, some rations, and some helpful advice about where he could go and what he could do.

"'A miracle,' he explained, then laughed. 'I assume that you and your friends did not appear out of nowhere, or that your officers were directed by the voice of God.'

"'Pshh!' I spat into the fire.

"'Who knew,' he said as he leaned towards me and winked like we were sharing a conspiracy, 'that miracles are just clever timing!' He laughed, but I didn't answer.

"'So, I began following your soldiers, as I had been told that you were going to pass Vienna in a few days where I could rest and eat and get more help. As it got dark I pieced everything together. It was a beautiful explanation. I must have noticed the guards like Schmidt acting strangely days before, and – having gone crazy from hunger or I don't know what – I made up God in my head!

"'And then the night came. And the voice came. *I have done my works, and you will believe.* I could not bear it. I wanted to scream. I was insane, or at least I wanted to believe that I was insane. Perhaps I am. But, if I am, I will die with the same insane certainty that I was not alone. There was no one else there, but I was not alone. I wanted to believe that I was insane, but I could not. I wanted to believe. I wanted to not believe. Do you understand this? No. Do not answer.' He laughed for a second, and I could see his eyes were wet in the firelight. 'I am saying these things, and I do not understand them. It is enough to know that I ran into the falling darkness, telling myself that my mind was closing as the day closed.

"'But after the dark came I saw a light ahead, and my mind did not close. It was your fire, and I saw you throwing your cross and Bible into the fire. I thought to myself that this was when the voice would speak to me. It had told me that I would believe, and I knew with the greatest certainty that it would command me to run to the fire to save your Bible and cross. I knew in my heart that this was the true beginning of my madness. Or righteousness? Mad righteousness? The voice would command me to do what is Right, and crazy Jonathan would obey his voices.

"'I waited for the voice to command, and to feel that

presence hovering inside and around me. I bit down hard, and gave in to despair. *Ja*, I told myself. I would obey. I gave up to the madness. This all happened within a heartbeat, but I wanted to fall on the ground and tear at the grass with frustration at what I was sure was about to come.

"'But it didn't come. There was no voice. There was no one there with me. There was only me. Alone. In the dark. And you were watching your faith burn away. The voice was not there. God was not with me.

"'There you stood, Joseph. Your Bible was burning.'

"He cried then. He plopped himself down into the dirt, and rubbed his face in the grass, cryin' out with the abandon of a wild animal. He began to repeat 'Your Bible is burning! Nein! Bitte nicht!' He dissolved into a babbling sound that was all these words all mixed up. I tried to pick him up a few times, but every time he'd pound the Bible into my chest and cry out that it was burning, and that I had to take it back! I finally took it, and the cross. It was the only way I could get him to calm down.

"When he did finally calm down, I said, 'What's all this about, Jonathan? God *was* with you, right? I mean, in the end, He did tell you to come and save this Bible.'

"'You do not understand. *He* said nothing. I knew He was not with me, but that your Bible was being burned. I could not bear the sight. I ran to the fire because *I* could not bear the thought of…' He drifted off for a moment, staring at the flame. His mouth opened and closed occasionally, only making a swallowing, grunting, croaking sound. Even with the fire light reflecting in them, his eyes were as black and cold and hopeless as the emptiest pit of Hell; which fairly describes where he'd lived before my men and I had arrived."

As my father said this he too was staring into the burning fireplace. His face showed us something like what he saw on the visage of Jonathan Bergmann.

I'd sooner God strike me dead than let me see Joseph Hanover in such a state ever again. His mouth was open and frowning deep, and I couldn't see any of his teeth in the low burn of the fireplace. He looked ten thousand years old, and still as a corpse in his horrified remembering. He was an uncovered murder victim, rictus frozen in the middle of his own savage death. It was a relief when a tear streamed down each side of his untwitching face.

"Daddy?" I whisper-whined.

Nothing.

"Oh, Daddy," I breathed, even quieter than before. I wanted to stomp the fire out. I was ready to kick the whole house down around our ears to snuff whatever made my father's face turn that way.

Nothing. Then a slight shiver.

And then Momma was over his left shoulder. "Joseph." her hand cupping his upper arm. "Joseph, my love." She squatted beside his chair, but didn't kneel. "Look at *my* eyes Joseph."

Finally, thank God, he turned to lock eyes, and saw the

strongest woman I have ever known. Her lids were even, easy and unafraid. She stared into that dark hollowed face with a humor bordering on disdain.

His face softened a bit.

"You and I have known war and outrage, Joseph Hanover. It has bloodied our eyes, pierced our ear drums, filled our noses. It has tried to break our every bone, and by God we are carried through." She laced her fingers through his short hair, and touched his brow with her own. "Come on home, baby," she said softly. She closed her eyes. "Your duty's done. Tell the tale."

When had we all stopped breathing?

I had no idea what sort of war and outrage my mother might have known. It seems to me now that we'd always given our father too much credit as a keeper of secrets, and our mother too little. She'd maneuvered us so well that we never even realized she'd had any secrets to keep. How had she done it? How had she kept us from wondering about her side of the family; the grandparents we'd never met or heard about. Was it her quick short answers ("Dead and gone in graves too far off to visit, Sugar,") or was there a message we'd only received between the lines not to ask further? Who was this woman carrying a broken war veteran clear of his memories? What had been my mother's war and outrage?

But that, I knew, was another story for another time.

✦ ✦ ✦

Daddy closed his eyes and took a deep breath through his nose before Momma released him. They looked at each other again, and Daddy thanked her with a salty voice

He reached for his glass, and, inhaled the red without looking at anyone in particular.

"Sorry about that," he said, and sipped as we mumbled our lies about understanding and not being bothered. Our parents had worked hard ensuring that our lives would prohibit comprehension of what war had shown my father, and only a wax statue without even a wax heart could have watched undisturbed.

He nodded, *yeah yeah*, and said, "So anyway, Jonathan was saying that God never told him to jump into that fire. He said, 'I could not bear the thought of…ach. I just could not bear it. He pulled away from me, and I had to run into the fire myself.'

"We both sat silent for a while. Jonathan was staring into the fire and shaking his head, new tears beginning to leak, and I sat looking at the singed edges of that Bible.

"When we did finally speak again, we couldn't talk about the past few hours or days. We settled on the present and the future. For the present, I promised I would hold onto my cross and Bible. For the future, we agreed to talk more over the next days as long as we were headed in the same direction. And we did talk a lot over those days; about a lot of things."

"And he talked you back into believing?" I guessed.

"No, Sarah. Weren't you listening? Jonathan Bergmann,

when in that place and time, ran into that fire himself. I saw it with my own eyes. He didn't need to talk me into anything."

I'd like to say that I understood what he meant by that, but I didn't; and I was too shamefaced to ask. It was only in the telling and retelling of the colliding stories of my father and that man and God that I came to understand the shape of it; to see what it had to do with Daniel's story. To see what it has to do with mine; with how we all must walk.

"We came close to talking about God, I suppose," Daddy continued. He told me about some of the things Jews believe, like *B'shert.*" Neither Tommy nor I remembered him using that word some weeks ago, but Tommy asked what it means anyway. "In a word, son, 'Destiny,' but it's used in reference to people who are supposed to come into your life and have a big effect. To help you change and grow."

"Like you and Mr. Bergmann."

"Well," Daddy chuckled a little, "you could say that without really being wrong, and Jonathan joked to that effect. But it's most common use is to indicate the one you're destined to marry."

My eyes bugged a little. "Really! Do they have some way of knowing if someone's their sherbet?"

"B'shert, darlin'."

"One is like ice-cream, Sarah," added Tommy helpfully, "the other is destiny." We all took a moment to laugh, but I wasn't satisfied.

"Seriously, how does a Jew know when *some*one is *the* one?"

"If Jonathan ever told me I've forgotten it. He probably covered it up with a joke like 'How many Nazis does it take to screw in a light bulb?'"

Tommy wanted to hear the punch line, Momma decidedly did not. I protested in general to the diversion from answering my question by throwing left over bread crumbs and bits of cheese.

But Daniel silenced the room with his steady voice as he said, "In truth there *is* a way they believe they can tell, and it is *very* interesting."

"Really?"

"Yes. I have seen it many times in the second district, where many Jewish people live. It is *very* strange; the most bizarre thing, really. Just crazy what they do to know who is to be their one."

"What is it?"

"Well…eh…but you must know that I do not approve of this practice. Only madmen would do such things! I am only telling you about this because you are curious."

"Okay. What do they do?"

"So! The woman goes and chooses a really...gigantic... boulder…"

After Daniel brushed off the breadcrumbs, cheese, balled up paper napkins and feathers (a pillow Momma had hit him with tore on the second impact) Daddy picked up in the neighborhood where he left off: "I've always reckoned (correctly, it seems) that those bottles were coming from Jonathan. I hope this all settles your curiosity, Daniel."

"Yes. There are still some things about it I am not sure of, though. Perhaps something from one of your talks would help me understand."

"I'll help however I can."

"Do you know about the connection of the sort of wine I must send and the time of year I am instructed to send the bottle?"

"Well, let's see. I know that it's Kosher, though I don't really know what that means except that Jews are only supposed to eat Kosher food. I assumed that the bottles were Kosher so that I'd be likely to know that it was coming from a Jew, and remember Jonathan that way."

"Did you know that it is more than Kosher? It is of a kind called *Kosher L'Pesach.*" The last word ended with a soft throat-clearing sound. "Do you know about this?"

"No. I don't really have much experience with wine, and none with Kosher or Kosher Le pez-ach."

"I see. Did you notice when in the year we were sending the wine?"

"Well, it was always around Easter. Sometimes it arrived a bit before, and sometimes it came well after. Seeing as how it's a gift, I figured it was best to just be thankful and not ask too many questions. There's all sorts of reasons that a package from overseas can arrive at a different time each year. The postal service is the most likely reason."

"Yes, of course. Alzo, the sender could be disorganized or not always have the money at the time the bottle should be sending.

"Hm! Well, I have told you so much that I may just tell you some more. We have been very organized, as you will see one would have to be well organized to carry out the contract, and there has always been enough money. The Post could account a little bit for the different arrival dates, but the real reason it has been on such different dates each year is that our orders have been based on the Hebrew calendar."

"Really? Well I'll be. Jonathan never told me that they have their own calendar."

"Yes. We are instructed to buy and send the bottle each year so that it arrives at your home (or post office) before or on the 15th day of the Jewish month of Nisan."

"That's weird. And specific. Weirdly specific," said Tommy, almost to himself.

"It is not so strange," replied Daniel, "when you understand the connection between the bottle and the Hebrew date. Does any of this sound familiar to you Mr. Hanover?"

"Not a bit. Ain't Nissan a kind of Japanese car?"

"Eh…yes, but I do not believe that there is any

connection there. The connection is that the 15th day of Nisan is the first day of the Jewish Holiday *Pesach*. As in *Kosher L'Pesach,* which means *Kosher for Pesach*. It seems to be some kind of extra-kosher kosher just for this holiday. It is very difficult to find the wine in Vienna except in the weeks just before Nisan fifteen, and then the Kosher store is extremely busy and strange. Whole sections of the store are sealed off where one cannot buy the products on display because they are only normal kosher and not *Kosher L'Pesach*. Does it have any meaning for you?"

"Sorry, Daniel. That was nearly thirty years ago, but I'm pretty sure none of this sort of thing came up during my talks with Jonathan. Likely as not, he came up with the whole bottle sending idea – sending date and all – long after we parted ways. But don't be discouraged if you find out it's some kind of joke. I think it's clear enough that that's his way." He paused to smile, and then asked, "What's the holiday even about? Some kind of spring planting festival, or does it have a story like Easter?"

Daniel blinked in surprise as his lawyer mind picked out the answer. "Ha! I had pushed that out of my mind! I asked the man at the kosher store about it, and he looked at me like I was an idiot. What was I doing in his store buying K*osher L'Pesach* wine if I didn't even know what Pesach was about? I was so embarrassed by his look that I had forgotten that part." We nodded and watched. "Exodus," he finally said. "It is a remembering of the book of Exodus." He pronounced the name *eh-xoh-doos*, but the meaning was clear.

Daddy paused mid-chew. He swallowed hard, and then coughed out a sound that was almost a chuckle while shaking his head at his lap. "Well," he looked up and back into the fire. "If it's a joke then Jonathan's sense of humor's a whole lot drier than kindling in august." Blank stares in return. "Don't you get it? Exodus! That bottle and the holiday it's made for marks the Hebrews' redemption from Egyptian bondage and slavery, and he's sending it to me to mark his exodus from the Nazi camps. Likely a fair comparison."

Another bubble of silence formed around us as I reeled, fitting this piece together with the rest. And once again Daddy popped it in a high by-the-way tone.

"To be honest, even though I still remember a few Hebrew words like *Shalom*, *Motzi* and that they call the Sabbath *Shabbat, B'shert* was the only Hebrew word I really held on to tight 'cause I found it so interesting."

"Yes?" Daniel intones, leading his cooperative witness.

"The thing about B'shert that I found strange is that they believe that you can have more than one in a lifetime."

"How's that supposed to work?" I asked, not sure whether I was offended or tickled at the idea.

"Well, first of all, like I already said, *B'shert* usually means the one you'll marry, but it can be used in a broader way; to include people you were destined to meet for whatever other reasons God has cooked up for you. But also, Judaism allows for divorce."

"What!?"

"Yep. Jonathan said it's strongly discouraged, but it's allowed if good enough reasons are given. Their idea of destiny says that the first husband or wife could be the one meant to help you change in just the right ways so that you're right for the next B'shert…hopefully the final one for life."

"Pshh! How convenient! So you can just go marrying and divorcing all you want and you can just say 'They were all meant to be!'"

"I don't think it's quite like that, Sarah. You've never been married, and none of us here have ever been divorced. But I reckon it's no fun. I suppose Jews take married life as seriously as the rest of us, and no one wants to drop in and out of marriage like ridin' a see saw.

"I just always thought it was interesting, the idea that someone can be destined to meet you, to effect you, to change how you think and believe, and that that same person can be destined to only play that role in life for a short while." He tipped back a sip of water. "Even them goin' *out* of your life can be destiny." He shrugged, and tipped his glass again. "I thought y'all might find that interesting too."

And that, I believed, was the message my father was trying to send; the point, that Daniel didn't have to marry me to consider his destiny fulfilled. That I could consider him in a similar light, without feeling like he was a threat to my freedom. Maybe this handsome lawyer from abroad *was* sent by divine agents, and maybe we could accept that possibility without jumping to drastic conclusions like marriage or insanity. I thought that I could be comfortable with this way of looking at Daniel's visit, and that made me smile.

I wonder if, in the long run, things would have been much different if Daniel had gotten that point too. It might have been worse, come to think of it; in the long run.

Chapter 30

I was too fuzzy headed from sleep to see it when I walked into the kitchen the next morning, but, looking back, I can see that Tommy was the lookout. As soon as he saw me he said, "Good morning, Sarah," loud, flat and dead monotone. Conversation between my parents and Daniel broke immediately with greetings of such enthusiasm that they seemed to be trying to counterbalance Tommy's dull voiced alert. It was enough to chill the blood of an alert person with a suspicious mind.

But I was neither alert nor suspicious that morning. I saw no reason to be after the previous evening's revelations and deeper meanings. I needed a few sips of coffee and a crunch of toast before their grinning clownish attention made me more than mildly suspicious.

"What's going on?" I asked with a smile.

"Oh!" chirped my mother, "She's on to us already!" She was still putting on a show. But no one was trying to pour me a glass of lemonade, so I reckoned things couldn't be all bad. Yet.

"Sarah," said Daddy with a warm smile (which I resisted suspecting,) "We've been talkin' about it this morning, and we've decided that we're takin' you into town today."

"Uh, really?"

"Yep!"

"Oh. Uh…okay." Everyone seemed to freeze. I can't even remember hearing anyone breathe. "Why?" I asked, as much to break the weird silence as to learn more.

Family and guest slowly reanimated as Daddy answered; "You've been home nearly a month now, and no one in town has seen you. I figure it's past time I got to show off my college girl."

"We're gonna go to Mrs. Paul's shop to buy you some new clothes for when you go back to the university," gushed Momma.

"And we're gonna have a big lunch at Randy's Diner!" added Tommy. Our parents looked at him blankly for a moment before dragging the grinning cheer back out.

"Well, maybe we'll bring along some peaches, sandwiches and drinks in a cooler," Momma amended.

"Boy oh boy, y'all've got it all figured out, aincha?"

They ignored my carefully crafted "dubious" tone. "C'mon," urged Momma. "Y'all go get ready. I'll fix up the sandwiches and a breakfast-to-go for Sarah while you get dressed. Then you can load up the cooler and put it in the truck while I throw something on."

"I will clean the table," Daniel offered.

"Oh, thank you, Daniel. That'll be a big help." Momma positively glimmered with appreciation.

I'd already begun heading to the bedrooms like my father and brother were doing, but I stopped and turned to tell Daniel that we "clear" a table of dishes and silverware and only "clean" it when we find dirt and spills. I opened my mouth to clarify all this when it struck me that Daniel was being allowed to clear the table for the first time since he'd arrived weeks ago. "Wait," I said, believing I'd begun to grasp the shape of things. "Aren't you coming?"

Tommy and Daddy were already gone to their bedrooms, and Momma ducked into the pantry for the "fixins." Daniel faced me alone, and said, "No, I have to order my room. I have turned it into a pig stall."

"Pig sty."

"Yes. Thank you. Pig's. Tie."

"No, not…never mind. Look, why don't you come along with us? You can clean your room up later."

"No. I am sorry, Sarah. I am sure I would like very much going with you, but I must make my room clear. I must be ready to go soon."

"What? No. Look, let's just all go out and have a good time. Just 'cause…I mean…you don't have to go so soon."

"I came here to meet your father, and to learn some things. I believe that I have learned very much." He smiled at me with a warmth I didn't deserve. "I will still be here when you return. We can all talk more then. Perhaps, if you still wish for me to stay longer, I will stay. With an orderly room!" He laughed shortly at his joke. I chuckled along with him, only slightly relieved.

"Well, okay. But promise me that you'll be here when we come back!" *Things've only just started.* "And we'll talk more about you stayin' a piece longer. Promise?"

"Where would I go?" he shrugged, "How would I get there?" Then he smiled a weak smile; the corners of his thick mouth only just barely turned up. "I will be here." Was he sad to be stuck here? Had he lost interest in me just as mine was finally getting a chance to breathe, like Tommy had predicted?

Momma was still hiding out in the pantry, and I knew she wouldn't come out until I'd gone. So I went. I was looking forward to a day in town with my family anyway.

When I came out dressed for a tour through our great metropolis the kitchen was cleared, Daddy and Tommy were arguing over the best way to pack the cooler and Daniel was gone; the door to his room closed.

"Hope you like squished tuna and cheese sandwiches, Sarah," called Tommy.

"No, Tommy, if you put them in the side like *this* they'll be fine, and you can reach the fruits and drinks more easily at the top."

"Sarah, will you come tell this old soldier that these ain't army rations."

Laughing, I went to help.

I ended up out in the wind, while the other three Hanovers talked in the cab; too quietly for me to hear over the engine and the air battering my hair and ears. Tommy wanted to drive his own truck (there's only enough room for two or – if you squeeze – three in the cab.) I thought it was a bit weird, being put out in the back when this little trip to town was supposed to be about me. But I found myself crunching a peach from one hand and a fried egg, cheese and bacon sandwich from the other. Under the rolling reaching shadows of the trees lining the twisting road I stretched my legs across the flatbed. The sun kept me warm and the wind kept me cool. All things considered, it wasn't such a bad deal.

My old partner-in-gossip, Theresa, and her little sister Abigail stopped by Mrs. Paul's dress shop while Momma and I were there. Tommy, as if by magic, had excused himself "to ask somebody something," just in the nick of time before her arrival.

"A little bird" had apparently told Theresa that we might be there that morning. All eyes were on Momma, who looked guilty as sin and proud of it. Daddy excused himself next, saying that he'd track Tommy down, and see if Mr. Barker (the local grocer) or Denny Green (who ran the bait & tackle shop at the south-west edge of town) could keep our cooler cold while we "ladies" went about our business.

To my surprise it was good to see Theresa and her sister

again. We laughed a lot, and the gossiping was minimized by Momma's presence. Daddy and Tommy had taken the truck, but it didn't matter. The dime store was next; only across the street and a few doors down. Between the clothes, the school supplies and much conversation and laughter about nothing at all, the morning sneaked off unnoticed.

Daddy and Tommy showed up with the truck (and a few fresh bottles of beer in the cooler.) Tommy and Theresa barely looked at one another, though they greeted each other in a friendly enough way. Theresa and Abigail suddenly remembered something that their parents wanted them to do that afternoon (much to Tommy's relief,) so we decided to eat our sandwiches and drinks picnic style.

"It ain't summer without at least one picnic," Daddy observed.

"And at least one ice cream!" added Momma.

So, we stopped by Mr. Barker's grocery and repaid his generosity with his cooler, by emptying it of a cardboard container of strawberry ice cream ("Aw yuck!" cried Tommy) which we swapped back for a cardboard container of chocolate ("I can handle it just this once." allowed Momma.)

We emptied the cooler of everything but the ice, and reloaded it with the ice cream, more ice, and some paper bowls and plastic spoons. We picnicked at the P. Rogers Elementary School yard on a blanket from the flatbed (it would've been cleaner just to sit on the grass,) and tried not to rush through our tuna and cheese sandwiches in anticipation of desert. The ice cream softened enough to be declared "scoopable," and the afternoon passed under our plastic spoons in the playground.

Tommy recognized right away that he was too big to fit into the swings of the playground, but when he realized that he had outgrown the slide he looked sorely betrayed. Who would be so cruel as to switch that big slide we once knew, back when we finger painted the walls here, for this narrow trick slide? And then replicate our graffiti onto the new one? "I'll bet half the kids who go to this school can't slide down this thing!" grumbled Tommy.

"Hey Tommy!" I shouted in mock excitement.

"What?"

"Ice cream!" I held up a bowl, hamming it up like I had with the water for Daddy by the stream.

"Oh boy!" he cried in equally fake joy.

We went to the park that borders the school grounds. The trees were denser there, and the earth harder; less gentle and civilized than the school's. It made the park ideal for summer strolls and terrible for picnics. So, after our picnic on P. Rogers' grassy back lawn, we toured the park grounds, and enjoyed how the late afternoons and early evenings of summer refuse to darken.

After strolling in the park for a while, my parents

confessed that they were trying to stall because they'd hoped to have a nice dinner at Randy's Diner. This also explained why they'd insisted on sandwiches for lunch and then the park, and had given Tommy the stink-eye all the way down into town for suggesting we go to Randy's for lunch.

The sandwiches weren't so filling, but the ice cream made us thirsty. We decided to leave the remaining bottled drinks unopened, and to get glasses of water at Randy's. None of us had appetite enough for a grand meal, so we settled for three platters of buffalo wings. We even had a few extras to bring home to Daniel.

I was full of good will for Daniel, and repeatedly thought it was a pity he hadn't come with us. I even said it aloud once as we headed to the truck in the beginning twilight, and got looks of nervous confusion from the others. "What? We get on well enough at a dinner table. It wasn't him I had a problem with anyway." They looked at each other, like I'd started screaming out obscenities. In Swahili. With two tongues hanging out of my mouth. Forked purple tongues.

Chapter 31

Some measure of that strange disconnect seemed to hover among us all the way to the driveway; a nervous quiet in my brother and parents that spurted up more and more as we approached the house. Daddy had driven, and Momma had sat between us while Tommy had volunteered to sit out on the flatbed.

I was smiling and cheerful, trying to keep my parents buoyant until the last driveway stone popped from under our tires. The engine cut, and I heard it. Hammering.

My smile fell, and I felt blood drop out of my face and rushing up my spine to the base of my skull at the same time. I popped the door open, and the sound of steel (or iron or whatever metal they make hammer heads out of) impacting stone was clearer. "What the Hell." I didn't care who heard me say it.

"Shoot, I thought he'd be long done by now." I heard my father say to my mother from the cab.

"What the HELL!" I shouted louder, and started running toward The Hill.

"Sarah!" Tommy shouted after me, "We just wanted it done and finished already."

I stomped my foot and pivoted on it. "Don't you worry Thomas Jefferson. I'm gonna finish it, alright!" Then I pivoted back towards where the hammering sound had been, and started marching faster than wild children run.

Daniel was tossing the sledge onto the ground, away from the tarp. There were a few chunks of stone lying beside him. There was no boulder. There was no Boulder. He was bent slightly, left hand on left knee. He was gasping for breath, and he was holding his right hand out to his side like it was dirty or wet. He watched me approach, and he shook his head slightly before I exploded all over him.

"Have. *You*! *LOST*! **YOUR!** ***DAY'M MAHND!?!?***"

He straightened, but refused to step back.

I continued. "Are you DEAF?! Are you STUPID, maybe? I don't know. Maybe I'M *CRAZY*. You *were* there last night, weren't you? Didn't you hear what my father said? Did you not understand!?" He stood silent, and let me caw. "You understand me! Yes you do! And you understood every word of our talk last night. *What are you doing out here!?* You don't have to do this!"

"Yes, Sarah," Daniel said hard voiced. With his strange accent and tone, it barely sounded like my name at all. "I do have to do this. I have heard your father's stories. Did *you* listen? I *must* do this."

It was easy to keep exploding. All I had to do was look down at those miserable last few scraps, and I was off like a roman candle. "Must!? You *must*!? You *must* be delirious! Aw crap, you don't even know what that means, do you. CRAZY, Daniel! You're talkin' crazy, and…" I stomped a foot and pounded my fists in the air as a few more dots connected within the inferno that counted for my mind. "…and you hoodwinked my own family into helping you! ***How could you!***" I couldn't scream that last sentence at Daniel in front of me and the house behind me at the same time, so I screamed it at the sky with such force that my head seemed to vibrate and my throat burned from the effort.

"Sarah," he said, suddenly calm as I slumped.

"No!" I answered with the low growl of my roughened throat.

"If you let me explain, then you can see why I believe I must…"

"NO!" I coughed for a moment from the outburst, but a few swallows gave me my voice. "You will not explain and lawyer your way out of what you have done. I don't want to hear your tricks."

"But it is just like…"

"I said no! No more stories. No more of that." Now I put my hands on my knees and shook my head. He was silent, and I tried to cool myself down enough to tell him the truth.

"I'm going to say it plain, Daniel. I liked you. Heck, I like you still." Saying it out loud stirred that familiar energy down in my stomach, but there was no chance it would overtake me now. I didn't try to beat it down, or question its presence. I'd already said it aloud, so I just left it there. And it actually seemed to give me strength without confusing my thoughts. "I like you just fine, but…but you've got to leave those rocks where they are. You've got to stop clouding things up with this…this nonsense. Leave them. We can still say that meeting was destiny. We can still say *buh-shert*. We can…we can have some chocolate ice-cream tonight, and laugh about all of this tomorrow. But you've got to leave those rocks there. And you've got to face that I will not marry y…"

"I have already married you." He said. He let his head drop, and the fading light prevented me from seeing his eyes, but there was something twisting in his voice; something akin to anger.

"Wha?"

"I have already married you in your heart, with these hands." He turned his hands palm up, and looked at them. I couldn't see them myself.

"What do you…?"

"I have married you in your heart with these hands!" He lifted his hands before me, and faced his palms forward. There was blood smeared across both palms. Three blisters had broken on his right hand. Four on his left. There were small scrapes on each of his fingers and thumbs, no doubt from handling rough edged rocks. My eyes flicked over to the handle of the sledge. It looked muddy in the increasing dusk, but I was sure it was blood from his hands.

I was at once heartbroken and repulsed by the open hands in front of me. It was a little bit frightening. But he made no effort to approach me, so I held my ground; ready to run if he tried anything.

Maybe he intuited my feelings, or read it on my face. Maybe he knew that his pose was like a movie monster, and that the blood would only put me off. Maybe his arms were just tired. Whatever the reason, he dropped his hands to his sides, and said, "You do not have to come with me Sarah. I cannot make you wear a ring. But I must finish this, and I hope you will come to understand that in time.

"But even if you never understand it and never try – if you remain here for all of your days – you will have to see that," he pointed to the pile atop The Hill. "And every time you see it, you will remember that there was a man who could have, would have, and – in his way – did move mountains for you."

I looked up to the rocks above, and they seemed to gleam in the rising moonlight. It was probably my imagination, but it struck me as all too real. I felt confusion and fear taking over me.

"Every day," Daniel pressed, "you will have to see and ask

and answer yourself about those stones. You will have to ask and answer yourself about the man who put them there. You will have to answer your heart.

"But I will have peace. I must finish. I will put these last stones up so I can go, knowing that I did what I must."

I didn't have the word at that moment for what he was doing to me with his declarations, but everything seemed to grow, reaching upwards, over and around me. Surrounding me.

Terrified, I backpedaled away from him.

He slumped, and said the final damning words, "I will do what I must. The rest I leave to you."

And I tore like lightning down to the house, through the kitchen in a blur and dove into my room, slamming the door behind me. I wept into my pillow, and ignored the concerned calls of my family. With a full stomach and an exhausted mind I wouldn't last long before my whole system shut down, putting me to sleep.

The word still wouldn't come to me. It was a…bad thing. He had made some kind of bad thing in and over me with his words, and I knew it would've been true even if I hadn't heard them.

A final moan slipped out of me with the realization that it would still be there the next morning. And then I slept.

I haven't seen Daniel since that day.

End of

The Parable of the Hill and the Boulder

EPILOGUE

Four Years One Month Later
Vienna

"I haven't seen Daniel since that day." Sarah cleared her throat. Sophia stared across the small table, scattered with coffee cups, water glasses and plates of crumbled remains of a dish she'd called *Topfenstrudel.*

Every window and door of *Tirolerhof Café* was open to no effect. Sunlight poured in, it seemed, from every direction, but no breeze could find its way into the coffee house. Ducts had not yet been invented one hundred or so years ago, when the building had been constructed, and the Viennese had either not yet heard of the innovation, were unable to install them in such old buildings or were uninterested in trying. The stuffy air did not punch you in the face when you entered, but rather smothered you over the hours.

When they'd first crossed the cobbled *Albertinaplatz* to the *Tirolerhof Café* Sophie had recommended that they take a table outside, but Sarah – embarrassed by her own rumpled appearance and curious to see the interior of such an old building – had insisted they go inside. The woodwork was dark and finely carved as were the chairs. The waiters lounged casually in black pants and white shirts, but the lack of activity in the place gave it a sparse and quiet feel. It was like a catering hall in the last lazy breaths of a wedding reception that had gone gracefully all night long; as if the tables had been cleared and the staff was waiting for the last stragglers to leave so they could lock up. At 10:30 in the morning. Maybe this was just how Vienna coffee houses stretched through summer days.

"Boah!" Sophia finally barked, and looked down at her cigarette; more ash than butt. "It is unbelievable! *Unpossible*!"

"But," Sarah began, stopped and started again, "Daniel must've told you at least some this when he came back." She winced as Sophia continued to stare back in amazement. "He did return to Vienna that same summer, didn't he?" Sophia nodded without blinking, tapped the ash from her cigarette, lifted it to her painted lips and pulled. "He didn't say *anything*?"

Sophia shook her head, exhaling smoke. "Before he left he was saying that he would find his bride in America. When he returned alone, I looked over his shoulder and asked if his wife was out somewhere getting her bags. I was making a joke! I did not mean to be cruel! I mean I really had no idea. He just shook his head.

"I didn't mention it again for some time, but he stayed sad for many days after. I did ask what happened, but he said only that he made his usual biggest mistake. Then he looked into my eyes. I thought he was going to say something more about what happened back there, but he changed his mind. I asked him again what happened. I asked what his 'usual biggest mistake' is. He said that it was 'saying too much too soon.' I didn't ask what he meant, but I did ask what he would do. He shook his head, and told me he isn't saying too much again." She tilted the cigarette hand to her right and her head to her left, like petals spreading apart as the next thought opened to her. "I suppose that is why you and I are sitting and talking here now." She smiled at the idea.

Six months prior Sarah had sent a letter to Daniel at the return address from which her father had received Daniel's letters. Her letter cautiously wondered if he would be willing and interested in reestablishing contact.

A letter from Sophia came back seven weeks later, informing her that Daniel had moved to his own apartment, leaving their old place to his little sister. Sophia – who, "of course, would never have opened Daniel's mail had I noticed his name on it" – could not resist the opportunity to get more information about a mysterious woman from America. She insisted that Sarah come for a visit, and assured her that she would be more than welcome.

"Come!" She'd written, "He wishes to see you, but cannot decide how to tell you. I have never seen him so mixed up in writing! I fear he will never complete a letter and send it! Do not be worried by my getting in the middle. I have told him what I am writing to you. He threw his ink pen on his writing table, and said, 'Yes, okay!' He surrenders. So, come! Come this summer, and we will show you our city!"

Sarah made the arrangements, and was unsurprised (though still disappointed) to find this coal haired sprite, only a year or two younger than herself, bouncing up and down at the arrival area holding a brown card with thick black letters saying **Hanover, Sarah!!!**

Sophia had assured her that Daniel was working, so was not available to pick her up. "But he will be meeting us later!" On the train to Vienna from the airport, Sophia assured Sarah that she could stay at her apartment as long as she liked. "Unless, of course, you decide you wish to stay with Daniel." She'd said it with an over dramatic wink, and watched for Sarah's response.

Deciding that this was more of a dig for information than a hint at Daniel's disposition, Sarah only smiled and said "Thank you." Her baggage was dropped off, and Sophia decided that the best cure for such a long trip was an "authentic Viennese coffee house." And here they were with their questions and their stories.

"Hmph," said Sarah through her nose, "Well, I guess I should be glad he learned to hold his tongue. I just wish he'd been a little bit quicker with his pen."

"Yes," said Sophia with impatience, "but, your family! They tricked you, or?"

"Yes," Sarah murmured into her coffee cup.

"Did they explain?"

"Eventually."

"What do you mean?"

"Well," Sarah took a sip from the small glass of water that had come with her cappuccino. "The next morning I came barreling out of my bedroom, ready to tell Daniel that he'd done his damage and could just shove off."

Sophia's head tilted.

"I was going to tell him to go away," Sarah clarified. "But, like I said, he was already gone. I stormed out of the house (and back in to change out of my pajamas.) I threw together a basket with bread, cheese, peaches and a thermos of lemonade, and stormed off to my stream for the day.

"No one bothered me. I didn't find much peace or many revelations by the water, but I did manage to figure out one thing. I realized the word for that 'bad thing' Daniel had made. It was a 'curse.' Do you have this word?"

"Yes," answered Sophia.

"I realized that day that I had been cursed, and that I had to find a way to break it. But I'm getting ahead of myself. It was enough that I knew I was cursed, and that I needed more information to figure out where to go from there. Eventually the thermos ran dry, the cheese and breadcrumbs went to my stomach or else the stream itself, and the light began to fade. I headed back to the house for warmth and answers.

"When I came in it was dark, so it must've been around eight thirty or nine o'clock."

"You are talking about nine o'clock T.M.?"

Sarah took a breath. "I came home just at the end of twilight. When I came in, I came looking for answers."

"Yes!" cried Sophia, indignant through the sunlit smoke. "Why did they trick you?!"

"'Why'd y'all trick me?!" I asked all three at once.

Like they'd heard a starter pistol, Tommy slapped his book shut to rise from the couch, Momma stood up from her chair as she scooped up some darning she'd been working on. The two of them headed to their rooms as Daddy beckoned me sit by him.

"Momma pointed out a plate of warm leftovers waiting for me at my place at the table, and was gone. When it was just the two of us alone in the quiet of the living room, my father explained at least *some* things to me."

Sophia waited silently refusing to interrupt or even move.

"Well, The very first thing: It was important to Daddy that I know that they had sincerely wanted to take me into town. Originally they'd planned to hold off until Daniel left, but were glad to do it when they did." More silent waiting on the other side of the tiny circular table. Sarah inhaled, and said, "Simply put, he wanted Daniel to finish the boulder job."

"Echt!?" – a sound that resembled trying to say the first letter of the alphabet and hock up a loogie at the same time, which Sophia managed to create with the facial expression and tonal hints of incredulity. Sarah offered her a glass of water, thinking that she was choking on a flake of *Topfenstrudel.* "No. Thank you. I mean to say, '*really?*'"

"Oh. Yes. Really. I was pretty angry to hear him say it, but when I heard his reasoning I had to admit it made sense."

"*Wieso*?"

Sarah was able to guess what this meant. "Well, first he asked me to tell him what Daniel had said the previous night to make me run to my room and cry myself to sleep. I told him all about the marrying-my-heart-with-his-bloody-hands business, and how I'd realized that I'd been cursed. A real and true curse.

"'Y'reckon it's true then?' he asked. I had to admit that it felt right; that my soul 'agreed' with it. 'Well,' he told me, 'just imagine what it would feel like to see it *unfinished* every day; to look out at that thing sticking out of the ground and know that – to play with Daniel's words, seeing as how he played with mine the day before yesterday – there was a man here who could, would but never bothered to finish moving a mountain for you.'"

"Oh!" Sophia blinked wide over the rim of her cup; eyes thick with too much eyeliner, framed by the cigarette smoke and the bob of her black hair.

"Yes," nodded Sarah. 'Oh. Also, Daddy said he didn't like how it looked after that contest. Got on his nerves just to look at it, pointing up like a fat, curved, misshaped thumb. My father has never been one to stomach an unfinished job. Funny thing: Daddy figured that if Daniel hadn't finished it, he, Daddy, would've gone out to do it himself just to get rid of that eyesore.

"So, when they found Daniel up that last morning, before anyone else, he told them that Daddy's story about Mr. Bergmann made it clear that he *had* to get the rest of that Boulder to the top of The Hill. After much discussion Daddy decided that if Daniel hadn't won the hammering contest, he certainly hadn't lost either. It seemed 'cleaner' to let Daniel finish.

"'Besides,' he told me, 'with all the meaning that's been loaded into that job, what would *that* mean; your daddy moving the last bits of the boulder. Kind'a weird, right?'

"Daniel was given the day to finish the job without distraction from me. But he was also advised to be ready to leave when he was done. Enough was beyond enough. Daniel was willing to agree to anything, as long as he could finish the job.

"He should've been finished before we arrived, but those blisters opened up, and he had to treat them several times because the handle of the hammer was getting slick with blood. The way he told it to Daddy while I'd locked myself away, he wasn't sure if God was testing him or if the devil was tormenting him. (I sometimes wonder if there's really much difference.) But he knew he had to finish either way."

Cups clinked around them. Forks scratched. German speakers chirped.

Sophia said, "Your father makes it sound like Daniel did

you a favor in the end, clearing the boulder away."

Sarah returned a weak smile, and the conversation lay flat until she looked up and asked, "Did he cheer up? Is he happy now? Four years is a long enough time, don't you think?"

"Is that why you have waited until now to seek him? You thought to give him time to…cheer up?"

"No. It's not like that. I…I wonder what to expect. Will he be annoyed to see me, coming and breaking up his fun-filled life? I mean, I hope that he *is* happy, but…unh! Is he still sad like when he came off the plane?"

Sophia took a final drag before stubbing the cigarette out. She shook her head again. "When we were children, Daniel was a fun boy. We played together very much. But as we got older, he became more religious. I, as you can see, was never very interested in religion." Sophia gestured at her long slim legs in cream stockings, barely capped by a *very* mini skirt. She had short dark hair, and too much makeup (by Kentucky standards) highlighted her crystal blue eyes.

But then, what did Sarah know about Vienna standards? Seeing the *Omas* shuffling by in their fat striped, ankle-length skirts and carrying loaves of dark bread and fresh fruits in woven baskets along cobblestone sidewalks, Sarah realized that Sophia's mini may be just as big a sensation in Vienna as it was in The South and Midwest.

"As we grew older," Sophia continued, brushing a crumb from her leggings, "I became more of a 'party girl,' and he became more and more boring. Before today I have never heard of this Daniel-with-the-big-hammer." Her grin was a sickle moon. Her teeth seemed sharp. "He was a boring lawyer-man when he left to find…well…you, I suppose, and he is a boring lawyer-man today. Is he happy? Who can tell? He is definitely still boring to his little sister, but what should that mean to his…what did your father call it?"

"*B'shert*?"

"Ja! Yes, that is it. *Ba*shet." Sophia seemed satisfied enough by all of this to start on another cigarette. The waiter (a distant memory by now, as he'd only been there a short time to take and deliver their orders and remained otherwise invisible for the following four hours) reappeared only to provide a light. Sophia said "*Danke*." The waiter said "*Bitte*," and disappeared again without mentioning the check. "So, what happened with you after that summer? I am sure there must be at least a few handsome American men in your University in Lexington, Kentucky."

Sarah looked at her hands. There were no cigarettes, and only a modest dabbing of nail polish. But her fingers were still long, and her frame was still slim. She had put on a bit of weight when she'd first returned to college, but had shed it within the following six months. Her skin was smooth and unbroken, despite her hours as a waitress. "Yeah," she finally said "there are men there. Some of them are pretty cute too." Half grinning, she looked up to see Sophia leaning forward with intense focus.

"Oh! I am sure they are all with big shoulders from farm

work, and smile big white smiles, or?" Sophia enthused. But there seemed to be some life missing from her energy as she tried to construct the fantasy.

"Pshhh! The men are there, Sophia. And they can be cute too, when they stop trying to impress."

"So you dated after you returned from the summer holiday?"

"Yeah." Sarah's face fell, and her eyes returned to her hands. "But it didn't…I mean *I* didn't. I couldn't…"

"You couldn't bear to be with another man!? That is *so* romantic!"

"It ain't exactly like that either. Not exactly. I mean I *did* date a few other men."

"But they could not measure up against my big brother. I am loving this!"

"They were…one of them at least, was a very decent man, Sophia. Okay, the first few were shallow nothings. I went back to school with an eye for one part redemption and two parts revenge to break that curse, you follow?"

"I understand you."

"I had spent the rest of that summer in the shadow of that pile of rubble Daniel left at the top of The Hill. Nothing I did seemed good enough to me." Sarah's head dipped towards the coffee cups as she nearly descended into tears. She shook her head fiercely. "Fact is he *did* curse me that evening before dragging the last load. You know the expression 'try to not think of a banana, and all you'll be able to think of is bananas'?"

"We say oranges, but yes."

"I was like a cat chasing my tail after he'd gone. I went back to the university to break that curse with the lips of every prince or frog I could lay my hands on." Sarah looked sheepishly at Sophia, but only a shark's grin was coming back.

"The more I learn about you, Sarah, the more I like you! It is a shame you are here for Daniel. We could have some great fun at a few discotheques around this district." She lit a new cigarette as Sarah laughed a grateful exhalation.

"Well, the frogs were no trouble to find, but dancing with them (I even let one or two kiss me) just made Daniel seem to grow bigger in my mind. The spell wasn't going to be broken that way."

Sophia's eyes sparkled and her smile was crooked. She released smoke through her mouth and nose as she said, "Oh, sometimes the frogs can be quite a lot of fun. So, what about the princes?"

Sarah popped two knuckles, and sighed another breath. "A prince, Sophia, is a prince because he's noble." She couldn't help looking away. "There was one after Daniel. But he looked in my eyes…"

Again and more Sophia waited, detaching her attention only to tap her cigarette ash into the ashtray as Sarah chewed her lower lip. When she returned her gaze grief was twisting Sarah's face. She leaned over her end of the tiny table. "And," she soft-spoke, "in your eyes he saw Daniel?"

Brown eyes pinched shut, and tears leaked. But Sarah shook her head, no. "Fire," she choked out. "He saw...He said that he saw Herr Bergmann's fire."

Sophia's mouth dropped open in concert with her eyes "*Wie bitte*?!?!"

Sarah began to twist and swivel in her chair. "Uh, where's the waiter? Can we get out of here? It's so stuffy in here."

"*Aba...Aber...*What do you mean he saw *Herr Bergmanns* fire?"

"Please. How did we sit in this coffee shop for all these hours, and we still haven't even seen the bill?"

"But..."

"Please Sophia. *Bitte*. We can talk more outside. Ah cain't breathe!" the last word squeaked of mice instead of women.

Sophia spotted the waiter, and beckoned to him. Eventually he came to the table, as if it were only for a little chat. After a blur of German from Sophia, he pouted an if-you-*must*-go face, and took out a tiny pad of plain paper. Sophia listed off what they had consumed as the waiter scratched furiously at his tiny pad. He carefully summed up the values as Sarah struggled not to climb out of her skin.

A little more incomprehensible chit-chat between herself and the waiter, and Sophia finally began to rise. Sarah bit her tongue to keep from sprinting out of the muggy coffee shop.

Sophia let Sarah use her *Tuch*, a small white handkerchief. "You must have left yours in one of your bags," she suggested. *Weird*, thought Sarah, *Why would Sophia assume I brought handkerchiefs with me on a intercontinental flight?* But she was simultaneously too grateful and distressed to ask.

"Come," Sophia urged. Let us go. We will take the *Strassenbahn*." They walked two blocks before reaching the *Ringstrasse*, an intense and (compared to most of the streets she'd seen in Vienna so far) very broad road, which, Sophia explained, circled the *Innere Stadt*; the inner-city, where they'd had their coffees. Sarah looked back at the way they'd come. Cobble stones, quaint quiet centennial buildings and streets. Trees and grass. The occasional horse drawn carriage ("For the tourists," Sophia had insisted as though Sarah was not, herself, a tourist.) *This is their inner-city?* Sarah wondered. *What do their suburbs look like?*

"You must tell me, you know," said Sophia after they had walked past the *Oper*, a grand and opulent opera house, to what seemed to be a bus stop. "You must tell me what this means with this University man…"

"Paul," Sarah stated. "His name was Paul."

"With this *Paul*," continued Sophia, "seeing Herr Bergmann's fire. You cannot…ah! Here she comes!"

She was a streetcar, bottom half red, top half white. She had a single circular headlight below her broad windshield, and the number one in a changeable window mounted above. A car swerved in front of the larger red and white vehicle, a bit too close for the streetcar driver's comfort. Instead of a horn, streetcar number one let loose with a running bell that sounded like a fire alarm. People nearby jumped even though they weren't in the way.

After climbing into the streetcar Sophia began dropping coins into a boxy orange machine mounted to the floor. It was nearly as big as she was, and displayed three modest rectangular buttons, a coin slot and a crevasse from which Sophia removed two small yellow tickets after pressing and then paying.

Only half the seats were taken so the young women were able to sit together.

Sophia handed Sarah a ticket, and said, "Here. Now say what you mean that you have a Bible-burning fire in your eyes."

Sarah closed her eyes for a moment, and smiled. She'd made the same mistake when Paul had used the term "Bergmann's fire," just before the inevitable drama of breaking up was finished.

The streetcar began to shudder and then wobble as it carried the passengers along its track, passing the *Oper* as it went.

"You're thinking of the wrong fire, Sophia. The fire that singed the Bible and heated up that cross was built by my father, not Mr. Bergmann. The one who threw them in was my father. You could say that I inherited Daddy's fire. It certainly helps explain my childish behavior, but that's not Bergmann's fire."

"So then! I do not understand," Sophia said, and paused in thought. Sarah gave her a moment to try to puzzle it out. Just as she was about to begin, Sophia looked up and shook her head. "No. I understand what you are saying, but then I do not know what fire is Bergmann's."

Sarah leaned towards the younger woman, and held a hand up like one of her professors explaining a point. "Bergmann's fire isn't the kind of fire that can burn books. Bergmann was burning on the inside. It burns in me too; in all of us to some degree. It burned so fierce and hot in him that he couldn't resist it. Bergmann's fire is what drove him to save my father's Bible and cross." Sarah blinked and then nodded. "And his faith in the balance."

Sophia's face was turned slightly away, but her eyes were fixed on Sarah. The streetcar passed the Greek-renaissance style *Parlament* house with gold crowned Athena, goddess of wisdom, in front. Thirty yards on, it stopped and opened its doors to the many-pillared Italian-renaissance *Burgtheater*. The theater seemed to bulge forward, as if to challenge the Gothic-renaissance *Rathaus* – the city hall – across the Ring. The administrative mansion was visible through the windows on the other side of the streetcar. Neither woman spoke or looked as passengers boarded, disembarked and changed seats. The doors closed, the streetcar began again and Sarah heaved a sigh. “You don’t understand what I’m saying, do you?”

“I understand your words,” Sophia said carefully. “I was always better than Daniel in English. Did you know that?”

“No. I didn’t, but I can tell.”

“What you say sounds nice, but I am not sure I really…” Sophia looked from sided to side as if the words she sought could be found between the wooden seats.

“…buy it?” Sarah guessed.

Sophia’s face lit up. “Yes! How American!” she said, with childlike delight. She nearly applauded, but her hands never touched. “Yes, I think that is right. What fire burned in him that burns also in you? How does it make him run to…save…your father’s belief? How does it also make this Prince Paul and you break apart when he sees it in your eyes? What is this fire!?”

They had only traveled a short distance, but the streetcar stopped again. Sarah was too deep in thought formulating her answer to notice the double-spires of the French-Gothic *Votivkirche* through the window at her left. It was Vienna’s second most spectacular Gothic church – built to thank God for the failure of an assassination attempt. Instead, she looked over to Sophia.

As the passengers shuffled in, out and around them Sarah said, “Did you ever use candles when you were a kid? Maybe on a special family event?”

Sophia blinked with surprise. “Ahhh…well…yes. I used candles every year for *Laternenfest* as a small child, and of course we lit candles for my Oma and Opa every year at *Allerheiligen*."

"Right," Sarah said, tapping her forehead with her knuckles. "Catholic. Plenty of candles. Okay," she turned in her seat to fully face Sophia. "Did you ever play with the candles on this Alleh-high-lah-whatchacallit?"

"No, Sarah. Even children do not play with candles placed on their grandparents' *Grabstein*…eh…" She snapped her fingers a few times, struggling with vocabulary before saying, "Tombstone."

"Ooh. Okay. Sorry. Bad example. What about that one with the lanterns? Did you ever play with those?"

"Ye-es," Sophia replied starting with her sideways look again, but she warmed to the memory. "Daniel and I would take turns daring each other to run a finger through the flame. It was exciting how it would jump over the finger as it passed."

"Right! Did you ever have that contest to see who could hold her hand over the flame the longest? I did it at a sleepover once."

"I do not remember ever playing this game, but it may be that we played it. I understand what you are speaking about."

"Good enough." Sarah had regained her energy, but it was energy without enthusiasm. "We are free, Sophia. Free to choose what we do and how we do it, right? The whole game with the candle is to test when you will choose to give in to your instincts and take your hand away. The flame hurts, so it's hard to keep your hand there, but you can."

"But it is stupid to keep your hand there," said Sophia in a tone of confusion, "or?"

Sarah's face flushed white then red, like the streetcar in which she rode. She looked down at her lap, and tried to clear her throat. "Yeah," she choked out, like it was her dying breath. "Real stupid." She grimaced. A clear drop fell onto her hand, and the *Tuch* went back into action.

Sophia's mouth hung open again, and she said, "Sarah! What do you do? Why…What have I said? This is not my language. I did not mean to…"

Sarah shook her head again. "No, Sophia. It isn't your fault. It's all my doin'." She shoved the bit of cloth back into her face.

The tram stopped and started again while Sarah pulled herself together. Sophia said nothing, but put an arm over her shoulders. Sarah mumbled into the saturated *Tuch*.

"What did you say?" asked Sophia, now stroking the back of Sarah's head as if they'd been life long friends.

"Four years," Sarah said with a soft croak.

"What do you mean?"

"I've been holdin' my stupid hand over a stupid candle for four stupid years!" she muttered through clenched teeth. She gripped the handkerchief in a fist, and pounded it into her thigh. "Only it ain't my hand and it ain't no candle!"

Sophia was startled by the ferocity of Sarah's scowl,

and held still for a dozen heartbeats before she dared to speak. "It is your heart?" she asked in the gentle beginning of comprehension. Sarah looked at her, mute and wet faced, and nodded twice. "And it is Herr Bergmann's fire?" Two more nods, and Sarah collapsed into tears again in streetcar number one on the *Ring* in Vienna.

They stopped once again, but there were no sights to see. The Viennese shuffled about, and did their best not to notice the two young women holding each other. When the streetcar rumbled back to life, Sophia spoke softly to her guest. "Our stop is next. I still have no idea what all this means, how Bergmann's fire is burning your heart. I do not understand how it scared this man, Paul, away. I hope you will tell me more, but it is better to get out at *Schwedenplatz* than to continue around the *Ring*. That would take us back; it will take us nowhere."

"Then let's get out," Sarah said with iron in her voice. "I'll explain it to you outside. I can't go back yet. I've had enough of goin' nowhere."

Unlike the neighborhood of the *Tirolerhof Café* in the *Innerenstadt*, there was plenty of wind on *Schwedenplatz*. There were also plenty of ice cream shops and more cafés, all on the side of the street where the young women stood. On the other side, beyond the streetcars and the *Ringstrasse*, was a rail, and the mast of a boat could be seen tilting and bobbing beyond that rail. On the other side of the water were the dark blocky buildings of Vienna's second district.

Sophia looked at her watch, then ahead towards the second district and then to her left. She turned to Sarah, and said, "The wind is drying your eyes, and a treat will lift your smile. Come. This place over here has the best ice in the world!

Indeed the line, six or seven people wide, eight or so deep certainly suggested that the ice cream they offered couldn't be too bad. When they reached the counter, Sophia ordered what sounded like a laundry list of flavors before turning to her. "What flavors do you like?"

"Um. I think chocolate will be fine."

Sophia stared at her, waiting for her to continue. One of the six women behind the counter offered Sophia a cone with four tiny scoops, each one a different color. "Two times chocolate? You don't want anything else?" She looked at Sarah like she'd proposed putting on woolly earmuffs at a symphony.

"Uh…" was all Sarah could think to say. She decided to just hold her tongue and see what the natives would do.

"Two chocolate and one milk. Trust me," said the young Austrian, and turned to the woman at the counter without waiting for a response from Sarah. "*Zweimal Schokolade und einmal Fiocco, bitte.*" The woman at the counter scooped out the order, and gave it to Sophia for Austrian shillings. "Try this," said Daniel's little sister. "Best in the world!"

It is not commonly said that ice cream makes the world go 'round. That honor, among many others, is reserved for love. But, the delicacy in Sarah's mouth could easily grease the wheels on which love and the world spin.

"You feel better," Sophia smiled then licked a green scoop and a red one in a single pass of the tongue. "Good. Now you can answer my questions: What do you mean with Bergmann's fire, and what does it have to do with you and Paul the Prince? And with my brother...who must wait for us until you tell me *everything*."

They walked towards a broad concrete bridge that allowed streetcars and other automobiles to cross the strip of water where the boat was moored, and into the second district.

"Bergmann's fire is just a name Paul came up with to describe a fire that burns in everyone. My family and I like it, and we've adopted the term for ourselves.

"While we were dating, I told him about that summer after my freshman year. When I told him my father's and Mr. Bergmann's story he'd just nodded, and said, 'Wow.' I told him about how Daniel thought the story meant that he had to finish moving The Boulder. Paul was a smart guy, and he loved stories; probably even more than Daniel and Tommy. I asked him if he could see how Daniel got that meaning. At the time he said he wasn't sure, and that he'd need to think it over for a while. I left it at that. Each time I told the story to someone, especially Daddy's stories, it all seemed a little bit clearer, but I could never quite grasp that hidden meaning; whatever it was Daniel had seen in the story."

They hustled across the *Ringstrasse* to reach the bridge. There were walkways along both sides. They stopped there to look down at the green and blue water as well as the boat they'd seen from the ice cream shop.

"Well, Paul must've thought about the story more because he explained it as part of his reason for breaking up with me."

Sophia turned her head to look at Sarah's face, but said nothing. Sarah continued to tell her story to the flowing canal.

"He said he could never get close to me; that I never wanted to be serious with him, except for when I told him about that summer. Every time things got calm or serious or comfortable between us I would jump up and insist that we do something fun, that we mess around, or that I had to go. If he didn't go along with me, he said – if he wanted to try to use the calm time to get closer – I'd fly into a rage. At least that's what he said." She stared at the water, and Sophie held her tongue.

Forty nine seconds later Sarah said, "Ah. Who am I kidding? He was right. I was distracting myself. I was using him as a distraction."

"A distraction from what?"

"From the fire. From the pain of being stupid, and holding my heart over Bergmann's fire. You see, it's the burning we feel when we aren't doing what we're supposed to be doing; what we feel called to do. You see, even though we're free, there are still things that each of us is meant to do. When you act against what you were built to do – what your guts or your spirit or heaven or your heart or whatever tells you what it is you should be doing – when you act against it, you're sticking your hand in the fire."

Still staring ahead, she flexed her fingers absently and breathed in the wind that came off the water.

"Life is full of possible distractions. In the last two years I saw lots of students distract themselves with pot and other drugs. Some people play around with mystical crystals and cosmic powers or something like that. I hear tell some folks in California are getting themselves lost in some kind of "Free Love," whatever that is. I wasn't much better. I dallied with kissing frogs and princes.

Sophia took a pull from a cigarette she couldn't remember lighting, and glanced at it for half a beat before tossing it into the canal.

"We all distract ourselves sometimes," Sarah continued, still focused on the water, "because you don't notice the burning so much when you're distracted. For some it can be numbed down to a feeling that things are wrong or unsatisfying. Others only manage to distract themselves to the point that they feel lost. For some of us…" Sarah gazed from the water up to the sky. "Well, some of us feel the burn and it makes us angry. At ourselves. At everyone and everything around us.

"I reckon that was me from the beginning.

"It's no fun, but we are free to do it, Sophia. We can go against our own grain any time we want. For as long as we want. We are free to burn ourselves to bits. Maybe that's its own kind of Hell; a sort of lake of fire: To look back on a life where you only ever burned yourself to a crisp."

Sophia shook her head. "This all sounds horrible to me. God is burning us and whipping us like donkeys to do what He wishes."

Sarah smiled, and thought of her mother – though she couldn't guess why. "God is calling to us, Sophia, not browbeating us into obedience. He's trying to help us understand what we're here for. The fire is our own feelings of failure and frustration when we choose to go against it, even if it's only because we don't know how to hear His call."

The Austrian party girl twisted her mouth, and raised an eyebrow.

"Look," Sarah tried, "Imagine a bicycle. We give it life and the freedom to choose to do as it pleases, and tell it that it is made for rolling forward and backward. But it chooses to do something different altogether. It tries to roll its front wheel forward and its back wheel backward. The wheels are spinning in opposite directions, and the bike is going nowhere. Maybe this frustrates the bike. The tires go so fast that the rubber starts smoking; burning. Are we cruel? Did we really make that fire? Are we cruel because we gave the bike freedom to choose?"

Sophia shrugged, noncommittal.

"It burned Herr Bergmann to see my father throw his faith away, and he thought he could ignore his own nature by waiting for God to tell him to do something; something he already knew, deep in his heart, was the right thing to do. But God didn't tell him what to do; at least not through heavenly voices. It was more useful – better – for Mr. Bergmann to learn how to hear that call from his heart. Better that he learn to heed his personal fire. Better that he become aware of what he was made for, and to take his actions into his own hands. All these things better than if he'd become some sort of puppet, robot…slave to voices. Even God's voice. After all, how better to be sure it even *is* God's voice than to be able to listen to your heart in the first place?"

"What do you mean?" asked Sophia, unreadable face and tone.

"Tommy asked Daniel how he even knew it was God talking to him, and Daniel said that one just knows. But that isn't entirely right. You know when you can hear your spirit agreeing, and can sense Bergmann's fire waiting on the other side of the wrong choice."

Sophia turned away from Sarah to face the waters of the

Donaukanal. Both women waited until Sophia finally spoke. "And you? And Paul? And my brother?"

"I burned, Sophia." Sarah answered without looking at her. She gave a wobbly sigh, and said, "I burned inside like a bonfire to be with your brother. Even now I could light this city up, burn it down and still keep burnin' 'till Armageddon for Daniel." She faced Sophia, and the younger woman felt compelled to return the stare. "I am burning like a forest fire across the Amazon, and Paul saw that in my eyes." Sophia stepped back, as if she might catch fire standing so close. "He saw it," Sarah said, shaking slightly. "He understood what it was, and he saw that it was not for him."

The thick finger of water would have relieved Sarah, if it weren't for the suited man sitting on the grassy bank holding a thin branch. He sat and watched the stick trace patterns in the steady waters. Sophia pointed him out long before Sarah could make out his face or shape. He looked up frequently and scanned the bank, looking for her, but never spotted her until she was about 50 feet away.

He stood to meet her approach, leaving the stick at his feet.

"Hello," was all he said, hands now dead at his sides; their job done four years ago.

"Hello, Daniel."

They stood stiff, painted with uncertainty. Sophia tried to walk away without looking back, but control was nothing she'd ever prided herself on. Only a little bit further uphill she finally stopped pretending, and looked. She was saddened by their stuck pose.

They stood. They stared. They refused to dare, and Sophia – younger than either of them - could not stand another second of such childish cowardice.

"*Sie* brennt, *Daniel,*" she called. "*Sie brennt von Bergmanns Feuer!*"

He seemed to watch her words roll down the bank and into him, but he did not respond.

"*Sie* brennt*!*" Sophia repeated for any passerby to hear.

His eyes locked onto Sarah's. He nodded his head, and spoke with a shivering strength neither Sarah nor his sister had ever heard from him. "*Sie brennt nicht allein.*"

Sophia knew she shouldn't let herself stare in such an obvious way. The last thing she saw before turning was Sarah asking…

"What was that all about?"

Daniel shrugged a shoulder, letting the left corner of his mouth go the same way. "I should be asking you. She says you are burning."

"Oh my," Sarah heard a southern belle coo from behind

her lips. *Oh mah.* Their shoes had never before fascinated her as much as they did at that moment. She could see that his were brown from the office and hers were white tennis shoes worn down from diner work and international travel. All further detail escaped her. There was nothing else she could bear to look at.

Daniel's shoes began to walk along the river bank, and Sarah was content to watch hers as she was carried along beside him.

Note From The Author

This story, the one you have just enjoyed, is not the exact same story I received on my knees in my ratty shared apartment in Columbus, Ohio, less than two days before leaving for my first trip ever to Jerusalem. I was overwhelmed with gratitude that I was going to go to that torn holy city in that torn holy land. And I believed with all my heart that I would find my future wife while I was there.

I was so excited, and I prayed with eagerness. I prayed, "Oh God, it would be so great – so nice and easy – if my future wife was right there when I got off the plane. I mean, I would love to step onto the tarmac at Ben Gurion International Airport, spot a beautiful woman and hear You say 'That's her. She's the one.'"

"Mmm-Hmm," said a calm voice in my mind. "What would you do if that happened?"

"Oh! I would run right up to her and tell her that she's the one, and that I was going to marry her!" I was so fervent in those days (especially at that moment) that I really thought I'd have the nerve to do something like that.

"Mmm-Hmm," the voice responded again with a tone of entertaininment. "And what do you suppose *she* would do if *that* happened?"

I saw myself in my mind, racing up to a tall dark olive skinned (probably Israeli) woman with long flowing black hair, and telling her everything with nearly mad excitement. Even in my imagination, I could not see a woman suited for me doing anything other than looking shocked and slapping me spectacularly across the face for such aggressive and ridiculous behavior.

Mmm-hmm.

And what would I do if that happened? What would she do? How would I deal with having put myself in a mess like that?

And that is how the kernel of this story –the parable at its center – was formed. It had to evolve for many years before the story came back to The States, and before I found that it had to be told from the woman's perspective (not the pursuant man's) in order for it to be told right. It took a long long time to get Sarah Hanover and her Kentucky clan occupying this story.

So this story is not the one I told Eva, the petite light skinned (Austrian, not Israeli) woman with short blond hair who wasn't even in the region – let alone on the tarmac – when I landed at Ben Gurion. It was about twelve or thirteen days after I'd arrived. We were on the Hebrew University campus (I was in beginners classes, and she was in the most advanced class.) She was intriguing and beautiful, to be sure, but I had no clear idea whether Eva and I would marry or have any sort of romance at all.

We told ourselves and each other that it was best not to start anything romantic. There was no future in a relationship carried out from opposite sides of the Atlantic.

On the eighteenth day of August of this year, 2009 – the same month when this story will finally be printed and bound as a book – Eva and I will celebrate our seven year anniversary with our son, Samuel, and our daughter, Olivia. I will Thank God, as I often do these days, for many things. And I pray that this story has enriched your life in some measure as it has enriched mine.

David Firestone
Vienna, Austria
July, 2009

Acknowledgements

Big thanks to We-All-Know-Who for sparking the idea and the many great ideas that followed, and for pointing my nose back to this book when I let it stray. I get choked up thinking of the time and space my wife and children have given me to chase this project out of the shadows and onto the pages. Stephen Blackmon – long time friend, part time cheerleader, full time editor, husband and father down Virginia way – has played a fundamental role in the development of this story into a proper book. My mother must be acknowledged. I awoke to her typewriter many mornings. It was always a good way to rise, and she taught me the love of many things; writing and story telling were just two of those things. My father gave me a kind of bottom line advice that got this book started when I most needed it.

Life Blumberg, wherever you are, Sarah Hanover is not based on you, but without you and the scant visits I was honored to make to your home near Berea neither Sarah nor any of the Hanovers would have come to dwell southeast of where you lived. Helen Chappelle read a rougher version of this book with great sensitivity and care, and I thank her for it. The remarkable and fine individuals who taught me through the New York City University's Masters Program flew to Vienna to teach, and I learned about more than education. I owe them for so much of what I have today, including the will to finish this book and to start the next. Manuela Almarales worked her photographic mastery for my mug shot at the Tirolerhof Cafe, and deserves praise.

www.ingramcontent.com/pod-product-compliance
Lightning Source LLC
Chambersburg PA
CBHW030918260626
47169CB00002B/307

* 9 7 8 0 9 8 0 2 4 6 0 7 0 *